NAKED JUSTICE

DALLAS BARNES

WOLFPACK
PUBLISHING
— EST 2013 —

WOLFPACK
PUBLISHING
— EST 2013 —

Published in the United States by Wolfpack Publishing, Las
Vegas

Wolfpack Publishing
6032 Wheat Penny Avenue
Las Vegas, NV 89122

wolfpackpublishing.com

Paperback ISBN 978-1-64734-160-2
eBook ISBN 978-1-64734-159-6

Library of Congress Control Number: 2020931394

NAKED JUSTICE

LAPD

TO PROTECT AND SERVE

This book is dedicated to the men and women who carry a badge and gun in service to others. Being a Police Officer is a life changing experience, not for the faint of heart. Police Officers are authorized to carry and use deadly weapons. They have the responsibility to protect the lives and properties of others. A decision to use deadly force is irreversible. Few other professions have such demands or responsibilities.

Becoming a cop is a choice…Being a cop is a privilege.

Among the privileged are, my daughter, Lorie Taylor, Detective III, Domestic Violence Coordinator, LAPD, her husband, Miles Taylor, Police Sergeant II, Command Pilot, Assistant Watch Commander, Air Support Division, LAPD, and my son, Sergeant Steven Barnes, Veterans Administration Police, Facilities Security Operations, Small Arms & Tactics Trainer, as well as friend, ally and fellow Novelist, Supervising Senior Detective III, Paul Bishop.

The city still slept as the patrol car rolled east on Hollywood's Melrose Avenue. The black and white's headlamps were on, but the growing half-light of dawn was lifting the shroud of darkness from the skyline. The glitter of colored neon and the shadow-stealing glare of streetlamps were yielding to daylight. Officer Keith Canfield was glad. He was tired. More than tired, he was weary. At thirty-two, Canfield felt old. He longed to stand under a hot shower, to fall into bed and forget another night of being a cop in Los Angeles. Canfield wondered if his desire to shower was a false hope that somehow hot water would wash away the haunting images from the night just past. He glanced at his dark-haired Hispanic partner, Jesse Martinez.

Martinez was staring out the window on the passenger's side. Hell, he didn't even look tired. Together, over the past ten hours, the two policemen had handled twenty-two calls. A typical Saturday night in Hollywood Division. In Canfield's mind the night was little more than a blur of vicious family disputes, stolen autos, burglary reports, foul mouthed drunks, and a chalky, swelled five-year-old girl found drowned in the family hot tub. Canfield was glad he was driving, and Martinez was keeping the log. He didn't want to remember any of it.

"Flip a U," Jesse Martinez said tersely breaking the silence between the two policemen. They had been partners for three years, so Canfield braked and turned the patrol car in a tight U-turn before he questioned Martinez's instruction. "What is it?"

Martinez's head was turning, his dark eyes searching. "Silver Mercedes in the alley near the liquor store."

Canfield swung the patrol car toward the mouth of the alley. "Probably some trash roach going through the dumpster."

Martinez's eyes were searching ahead. "Naw, Mercedes in an alley this hour of the morning, we're talking dope deal."

The patrol car bumped up over a curb cut. Its headlamps illuminated the dim alley. Ahead a polished silver Mercedes coupe sat parked in the center of the alley with both doors standing open.

"There he is," Jesse Martinez pointed at a slender man clinging to the side of a large trash dumpster.

The man was holding the metal lid up. Hearing the approach of the patrol car, he squinted into the headlamps. The man was young, olive and gaunt.

His open-collared shirt, pleated slacks and low-cut leather shoes made him look out of place in the alley. He dropped the lid of the trash bin and jumped down from its side.

"Told you he was a trash roach," Canfield braked the police car to a halt several car lengths from the Mercedes. Martinez picked up the radio mike. "Six-Adam-forty-seven, Code Six, Melrose and Gramercy, in the alley near Century Liquor."

"Roger, Code Six, Melrose and Gramercy," a filtered feminine voice answered promptly from the radio.

The gaunt man didn't seem alarmed. He wiped his hands together, watched, as the two officers climbed out of the car.

"What were you doing up there?" Canfield questioned walking toward the man.

The man stared blankly at the two officers, still wiping his hands. He had dark eyes and skin. An Arab, Canfield guessed.

"You dumping trash in there?" Canfield said, stopping just beyond arm's reach. Jesse Martinez walked to the passenger's side of the Mercedes and glanced into the open car. "This your car?"

Dark eyes swept to Martinez and then back to Canfield, still the man did not answer.

"Either he's an Arab asshole or just deaf?" Canfield said to Martinez, hoping to provoke a reaction. He kept his eyes on the man's face, watching for what the words might bring. He saw nothing.

3

"There's always the chance he's just a deaf asshole," Martinez leaned into the Mercedes, reaching to open the glove box.

"Turn around," Canfield ordered, stepping toward the man. "Let's see if you have any identification?"

As Canfield reached out the man kicked quick and hard. A leather shoe struck Canfield in the center of his groin. Canfield grimaced and doubled over in pain. The gaunt man grabbed at Canfield's gun belt, quickly unholstering his nine-millimeter automatic. Gun in hand, he wheeled.

Jesse Martinez grabbed for his pistol, but the man was fast; he crouched and fired through the open doors of the Mercedes. The first bullet ripped into Martinez just below the belt. He staggered backwards, firing his gun. It was more reflex than intent and the shots went into the pavement. The gaunt man fired again, twice in quick succession. The first shot pierced Martinez's right eye, the second hit two inches higher and ruptured his skull. Martinez was dead as he fell backwards.

Canfield pushed up on a knee. His groin was on fire with pain. His ears buzzed from the concussion of the shots and he was nauseated. His vision was gray with shock. He tried to focus on the man, and then he saw the muzzle of the gun pointing at him. The barrel was black, and pencil sized. "Don't." He reached out with a hand. The gun exploded.

The bullet punctured Canfield's palm, tearing bone and flesh, hitting him in the upper shoulder, knocking him onto his back. The nine-millimeter barked again. Bullets ripped into Canfield's groin and thigh.

Canfield knew the wounds were serious. He lay stunned. The dark eyed tossed the gun and walked to where Canfield lay. He knelt and quickly unbuckled the small video camera strapped to Canfield's chest. He jerked it free and stood. Canfield groaned and fought against pain. The man turned his attention to Martinez. Martinez showed no sign of life as his camera was ripped away.

The Mercedes came to life and roared away. Canfield knew he had to get help. "Jesse!" he screamed taking a halting breath and pushed up on an elbow. There was no answer. He struggled with breath. Shock was sweeping over him, tightening his chest. He was surprised at the blood on the front of his uniform. His blue shirt was matted to his chest. He placed a palm on it. Blood oozed out between his fingers. He knew he had to hurry. He tried to push to his knees and nearly lost consciousness. A wave of nausea washed over him leaving him weak and short of breath. He collapsed slamming his head on the asphalt. He struggled and crawled on elbows toward the police car, dragging his numb legs, leaving a crimson swath of blood to measure his progress. He collapsed near the open door.

The surface of the alley was wet and coarse against Canfield's cheek and the musty wet smell reminded him of falling off his bike as a boy. He knew he was hurt. Afraid to move, he lay still. Soon his dad would be there gathering him up in his arms. Time blurred and spun. The buzzing in his ears grew louder. He hoped his dad would hurry.

A jogger, dressed in a hooded sweatshirt and Addis sneakers, was half a block away when he heard the burst of shots. He stopped to listen, holding his breath. It was difficult to tell direction with the sound reverberating in the concrete corridors of Melrose Avenue. He wasn't even sure it was gunfire. Only the distant sound of early morning traffic and a few sparrows reached his ears. He resumed his run. He had gone only a few hundred feet when three more sharp cracks shattered the stillness a second time. He stopped; now certain it was gunfire.

Seconds later, the Mercedes roared from the mouth of the alley just ahead. The car turned right and raced by him, gaining speed. The olive faced driver gave the jogger an angry look in passing.

At the mouth of the alley the jogger saw the gray automatic pistol lying on the pavement. He picked it up. It was warm and its smooth surface was scratched from being thrown. A hundred yards ahead in the alley a patrol car sat idling. Its headlamps were on. The jogger could hear the muted sound of routine radio traffic. "My God!" he muttered nearing the car and recognizing the two uniformed forms lying near the car. The jogger pushed his hood back and walked slowly toward the police car, pulse pounding in his ears like a drum.

"Hey!" a voice shouted. A jolt of fear shot through the jogger. He froze his movement. "What the hell you doing?"

A barrel-chested black man in an apron from the liquor store was standing in the mouth of the alley beyond the police car. A large black Weimaraner stood at his side, barking. The jogger stared in frightened silence.

"Get 'im, Judge," the clerk ordered the dog, thrusting a finger in the direction of the jogger. The Weimaraner snarled and charged. The jogger turned and ran.

The jogger had gone only a few steps before the big dog was on him. The first bite ripped into his right buttock. Flesh and sweatpants tore away. The man stumbled and fell. The dog, fangs bared, pressed the attack. The jogger kicked and swung the nine-millimeter pistol. The barrel of the gun struck the dog on the muzzle. The Labrador yelped in pain and turned to retreat. Dropping the gun, the jogger pushed to his feet and limped away with blood running down his leg.

Three ominous electronic beeps preceded the masculine sober voice of the Link, from the 911 communications division. Every cop with a radio knew a high priority emergency call was coming. All other police radio traffic was silenced. Stomach muscles tensed in black and whites across the city.

"Units in the vicinity, and Six-Adam-Seventy-six, shots fired, officers down! Fifty-two-oh-four Melrose Avenue. Six-Adam-Seventy-Six, your call is code three! Ambulance en route."

In the sprawling San Fernando Valley, the early morning sun was erasing shadows from windshields and rows of manicured lawns and beige two-story stucco homes as the city stirred awake. On Stonegate Drive, Lee Hollister slipped a hand under his wife's arm and carefully cupped her breast. He half expected an elbow in protest. When it didn't happen, he inched closer molding his near nudity to hers. He paused again, reading her body language, much like a male spider approaching a black widow. She didn't respond, but he wasn't rebuffed. He massaged the breast gently in his palm. He had been eager to make love when they went to bed, but a quick kiss and a turned back were less than a subtle answer to his desires. Then, waiting for sleep, Hollister wondered why he always wanted sex after their social encounters. It didn't seem perverted, but he wasn't sure it was normal. Perhaps some primal pack instinct, he rationalized, but now the warmth of her body and the musky smell of sleep urged him on. He moved his hand from her breast and slid it slowly down over the smooth flat of her stomach. He kissed her gently on the neck through a tangle of blonde hair as he remembered the night before. He noticed other men at the Realtors' cocktail party admiring her long legs and flashing green eyes, but he was the one to take her home and he was the one about to have her.

Kim was a sultry thirty-three-year-old, green-eyed blonde and although they had been married for eight years Hollister still hungered for her sensual plea-sures. At thirty-eight, Lee Hollister was trim and athletic and capable of turning a female head, but in Kim's presence, his sense of male prowess often failed him. He was obsessed with her and the busty blonde was not only his wife, but his iconic prize, his show piece and his ego.

It only seemed natural that the new branch man-ager of one of the largest realty companies in Los Angeles would provide him an open house. He fought an urge to laugh at his early morning wit. Hollister pushed the sheets aside to expose his wife's form. She was naked except for sheer black panties. He reached for them. The electronic chirp of a bedside city cell phone froze his movement as if it were the shutter of a camera.

"Damn," Kim hissed through clenched teeth as she pushed her husband aside.

Hollister drew a breath and reached for the cell phone. An illuminated bedside clock read five-fifty. "Hollister," he said, picking up the department issued cell. He knew it was a call-out.

"Sergeant Hollister, it's Owens from morning watch."

Hollister didn't know the man. "Yeah?" he said, urging him on. He was frustrated and impatient. Behind him his wife pulled the covers over her nudity.

"Lieutenant Stratton asked me to call. We've got two officers down...both dead."

Hollister bolted upright in the bed. "Two! Christ, what happened?"

"We don't know. Witness saw a man in a hooded sweater. Looks like he used one of the officer's guns."

Hollister swung his bare feet to the floor and switched on a bedside light. His wife and his passion were now forgotten as his mind raced ahead. "Who was it?"

"Canfield and Martinez from morning watch."

"Christ," Hollister muttered a second time. He had seen both men just days earlier at the scene of a shooting when a mini-mart clerk had been shot to death. "Where'd it go down?"

"Alley near Century liquor at Gramercy and Hollywood."

"Have you called Baxter?"

"Not yet."

"Tell him I'll meet him at the scene."

"Right."

Hollister laid the cell phone aside and reached for pants on a nearby chair. "We've got two cops down."

"Does that mean dead?" Kim questioned cautiously.

Hollister didn't want to say it. "Yeah, dead." He answered pulling on the pants. He gathered a holster and nine-millimeter from a bedside drawer and moved for the bathroom.

"Lee, this is no way to live," his wife called from the shadows of the bedroom. He paused to look at her. "I'm really tired of it. You've got to find something else." She warned, "Get another assignment." There was a threatening chill in her tone. Hollister chose not to answer, searching for a shoe. Where the hell was it? "I'm serious, Lee."

"Yeah, I got that," he said, pushing on his shoes. "Can't we have this talk later. I got two dead cops to deal with."

Kim sat up pulling the sheet over her breasts. "You're dealing with it by choice. What about me, Lee? I'm telling you I'm sick of it."

Hollister grabbed his holstered gun from the nightstand and headed for the door. "Go back to sleep," he urged.

There was an unmarked detective car in the driveway. The upper middle-class neighborhood with its long row of sprawling beige stucco homes and carefully manicured lawns with an assortment of SUVs, Beamers and occasional Lexus dotting driveways was quiet. A sharp contrast to the world that had reached out to him, Hollister thought as he walked to the car and unlocked it. Kim's tone had chilled him. He climbed in and cranked the car to life. Find something else. He tensed, remembering his wife's words. Christ, this wasn't a matter of who he was, it was what he was. She spoke of it as if it he was deciding what shoes to wear. "Lee, find something else." Fuck you. He pulled the car in gear.

It was Sunday morning and the San Fernando Valley had yet to awaken as Hollister drove the detective car quickly over the twisting streets to the Ventura Freeway. He only half listened to the routine chatter on the radio mounted beneath the center of the dashboard. Much like his neighborhood it seemed unchanged by death. "Fuck," Hollister muttered as he again thought of Canfield and Martinez. The cloudless morning and tall green palms stood in sharp contrast to the azure sky. A picturesque California morning, a morning for beaches, picnics, bike riding and horses. Not a morning to die, Hollister thought, but while the city stirred from sleep, while some tried to seduce their wives, two cops had been killed. Hollister wondered why these deaths in the early morning hours seemed even more tragic. The answer was simple. Murder itself was a heinous crime, but killing a cop was a contemptuous attempt at killing law and order itself.

Hollister swung the car onto the freeway and gunned it. The Sunday morning traffic was light. He drove fast across the face of the valley and up through the Cahuenga Pass into the sprawl and distant towers of Los Angeles. The alabaster iconic "Hollywood" sign stood high on its perch on the edge of lumpy green Hollywood hills overlooking high-rises and splashes of concrete and glass. The city looked alluring, peaceful. It was stirring from its night of rest much like his wife, Hollister thought, beautiful, sexy, and desirable. But, beyond the palms and glitter of Hollywood Boulevard two dead cops were waiting. Somewhere their murderer was hiding. All Hollister had to do was find him. Find him in the sprawling metropolis that was home for millions. As a member of the homicide "Stand-By Team" from the L.A.P.D.'s Hollywood Area, Hollister and his partner, Max Baxter, were responsible for the investigation of human death occurring within the sixteen square miles of urban sprawl commonly known as Hollywood.

Through the world's eyes Hollywood was the fabled glamour capital of the world. "Moths to a flame," Hollister mouthed as he thought of it. The lights of Hollywood drew the young and the restless, the beautiful and the not so beautiful, as well as the rich and the destitute. The eclectic mix of humanity, hungry for fame and ripe with passion, fueled primal instincts. Thus, murder in Hollywood wasn't the exception, it was more the rule. The approach of the Melrose off-ramp brought Hollister back to reality. He pushed on a turn signal.

A police helicopter made the crime scene easy to

find. It orbited low overhead in a tight rotor-slapping circle like an angry hornet. The mouth of the alley near the liquor store was now hidden by a cluster of police cars parked at hard angles to one another. Their red light bars flashed out warning pulses and the air was alive with the stereo sound of police radios.

Hollister spotted a familiar green detective car among the others as he approached. It meant his partner was already at the scene. He parked across the street from the tangle of official cars. As he climbed out, a mini-cam van with a bold "Eyewitness News" logo pulled in behind him. A news crew with cameras scrambled out. The sidewalk was crowded with a growing knot of curious. A uniformed officer in the center of the street waved slowing curious traffic by. "Come on, move it, goddamn it!"

Hollister reached for his I.D. card and pinned it on as he crossed the street. A young uniformed officer was leaning on the side of a patrol car with his head low. He gagged as his stomach convulsed. Hollister shot a look at him in passing. "Go around the corner, kid. Don't throw up in front of the cameras."

The alley was full of sober uniformed cops. Hollister pushed his way through them. He spotted a sergeant standing near the lifeless form of a man laying covered with a wrinkled bloody sheet near the open door of a police car. The form's exposed blue pants and high black polished boots announced a cop was hidden there.

The uniformed sergeant was surrounded by a

ring of solemn cops. "Sergeant," Hollister said with authority, "get the ally cleared, this is a crime scene, and get a log started."

The sergeant's eyes were rimmed with tears. His face was an angry mask. He looked to Hollister, then to the other cops. "All right," he barked, "you heard the man, move it."

The crush of cops, uniformed, helmeted motor officers, plain-clothed metro officers, began moving away, silently, each taking a final look at the bloodied bodies.

Hollister walked to the fallen man near the police car and knelt to lift the sheet. Canfield's body lay on its back, eyes partially open and glazing as they dried with the fixed stare of death. His uniform shirt and trouser legs lay open after being cut away by paramedics. Evidence of their efforts dotted the ground around the body. Bloody gauze squares, sterile paper wrappings, a discarded syringe. A pool of coagulated sticky blood beneath the body told why the effort failed. Hollister stared at the body. He fought an urge to reach out and touch, as if it might stir life where there was none. He had seen many dead men, women and even dead children. Death was his business, but the man lying in front of him was a policeman. He was wearing a bloodied badge on his shirt. The same badge Hollister was wearing on his belt. He had never seen a dead cop, and seeing this man, a man he had recently seen alive, walking, talking, and, taking care of business, going home at the end of his day, waking up in the morning with his wife! All of it was now gone. Some son-of-a-bitch had taken if from him. It shook Hollister deeply. He lowered the sheet as Detective Max Baxter reached Hollister's side. "Fucking shame," Max breathed.

Hollister stood, nodded agreement and inhaled in an effort to recapture a professional persona. He looked to his partner. Max was a big man. Six-two, two-hundred and sixty pounds. His short-cropped hair and thick neck always reminded Hollister of a Marine Corps drill instructor, but forty-two years of age and a seemingly endless optimistic spirit made Max a gentle, patient man. Hollister wondered how Max felt, but he knew he would never ask. "Been here long?" Hollister questioned, deliberately turning away from the fallen Canfield.

"Couple minutes," Max answered. "Long enough to walk the scene. It looks like Canfield's gun is laying back there in the alley. Martinez still has his in hand. Nothing but nine-millimeter casings on the ground. I'm betting the shooter used Canfield's gun."

A uniformed lieutenant Hollister recognized as the watch commander stood thirty feet away leaning against a weathered brick wall, weeping. Hollister disliked dealing with emotional men. "What's the story on him?"

Max glanced at the lieutenant. "Jesse Martinez is his son-in-law. He said Jesse has three kids."

"Christ."

"Yeah," Max agreed, glancing at a small notebook

he carried. "The first unit on the scene, Six-Adam-Seventy-Six, found an eyeball wit. Same guy that dialed nine-one-one. They took him to the station. He's a black man, early sixties, clerk at the liquor store... told them he heard shots; he's not sure how many. He came out with his dog. Weimaraner, I think. He sees the shooter and the two cops down."

"We're lucky we don't have a dead witness."

"Man doesn't lack balls," Max agreed. "He put his dog on him. Dog bit him and knocked him down."

"Suppose he's injured?" Hollister questioned.

"Hope so. The old man wasn't sure. He said the shooter was average height, average weight, wearing a hooded sweater or jacket."

"White, black?"

"He's not sure."

"Hell, it could be anyone."

Max nodded. "This one's going to be tough. Shooter is savvy. He took body cams off both men."

"Let's get an alert out to the local hospitals," Hollister suggested with a final look at Canfield's body. "Maybe this prick got hurt."

On Bonita Terrace in East Los Angeles, Angela Martinez was sitting at a kitchen counter in her three-bedroom home. She was reading the travel section of the Los Angeles Times while breast feeding her five-month-old daughter. The chatter of two other children drifted from the hallway. Angela was hoping for a weekend cruise to the Mexican Riviera. Three-day cruises were affordable if Jesse continued working overtime. Angela glanced at the dark-haired child at her breast. The baby sucked rhythmically. The occasional nip of budding teeth warned Angela that breast feeding would soon have to end. A month, Angela told herself, and then she could pick a date for the weekend cruise. She was sure Jesse would like the idea. She would ask her mother about watching the children, after mass. Every Sunday her mother invited them to lunch after church. When Jesse wasn't too tired, they would accept. She hoped his night patrolling Hollywood had gone well.

Angela heard the car pull into the driveway. She was sure it was Jesse. The thought of him walking in and finding her breast feeding the baby stirred a mild excitement. She smiled as the thought took her back to the morning they sat at the counter, sharing doughnuts and the Sunday paper. She couldn't remember what sparked it. They simply looked at each other, smiled, and then Jesse was in her arms, unbuttoning her blouse, kissing her breasts. The bedroom was too far away. They made love on the kitchen floor. Later, passion spent, lying in his arms Angela asked, "What if I'm pregnant again?"

"If it's a girl we'll call her 'Morning'." Jesse smiled. "A morning to remember."

The chime of the doorbell startled Angela. Why was he ringing the bell?

"I'll get it, Mamma," five-year-old Jesse Junior shouted from the hallway.

"Me too!" his three-year-old sister added.

The two children ran through the kitchen and into the living room. Angela pulled the child from her breast, a moist nipple popped from its lips. Angela slipped her breast into a bra cup and lifted her dress up over an exposed shoulder.

In the living room, Angela heard the door open. "Momma," Jesse Junior called, "it's the cops!"

"My daddy's a cop too," she heard her three-year-old say, and then an icy stab of fear jolted through Angela, stealing her breath.

"Is mommy here?" a strange masculine voice questioned.

"My dad's got a gun like yours," five-year-old Jesse Junior answered.

In the kitchen time stood frozen in a blinding terror that kept Angela from moving. The child in her arms began to cry, but its voice seemed distant, unreal. She heard the door close, the footfalls on the carpet and then the uniformed men were in the kitchen. Angela's lungs screamed for relief, but she wouldn't breathe. She refused to look up. She could see their polished black shoes, the creases in their dark blue uniform pants. A tear spilled and ran down Angela's cheek. She didn't wipe it away. One of the officers reached and took the crying child from her arms. Angela lowered her face to her hands as the torrent of emotion broke in a soul deep sob.

"Momma, what's wrong?"

One of the officers laid a hand on Angela's back. Her shoulders jerked with wrenching sobs.

"Where's my dad?" five-year-old Jesse questioned, looking up at the two officers. He held onto his mother's skirt with a fist of material.

Seven miles across the face of the city, which was now basking in the growing warmth of mid-morning sun, a gray Los Angeles County Coroner's station wagon held the answer. Covered in a zipped rubber body bag, Jesse Martinez and his partner were taking their last "on-duty" ride. Cameras flashed, fingers in the crowd pointed as numbed cops watched in silence, cursing, hungry for revenge but silently thanking God it wasn't them. The gray Coroner's wagon pulled from the mouth of the alley and rolled away equally as silent.

Hollister drew in a breath and let it out slowly. He was glad the two bodies were gone. He had felt inhibited with the bodies of two cops at the scene. Bodies and death were the reality of a homicide assignment and Hollister's two years in the role had prepared his senses to ward away the shocking reality of what one human could do to another but this time it was different. It was rare a homicide cop had ever seen his victim alive. This time was different. Not only did he know them, but they were fellow cops.

As Max worked on the patrol car with a technician from Latent Prints, Hollister busied himself drawing a sketch of the scene. He walked to where each of the officers laid, then drew an intersecting line from each to the cluster of expended shell casings dotting the surface of the alley to approximate the position where the shooter stood. He tried to imagine what provoked this. Motive was always key to identifying the suspect. Anger, greed, fear? The killing of two cops had to have a compelling motive. He hoped they could find something. There would be pressure to solve this. You hurt a cop...you paid with a pound of flesh. Justice had to be quick and sure. Cops would hunt you down and fucking hurt you. It was the unwritten blue creed that protected the poor bastards working uniform. The ones that had to walk into harm's way ten times every day. Hurt a cop? You had no place to hide. No matter how long it took, the cops would track you down. No matter what, you would be found. Hollister hoped it would be true this time as he noted the location of the swath of blood from Canfield's body on his sketch. A pungent foul odor teased at his nostrils. He turned to its source. A large metal dumpster sat less than six feet behind him.

Hollister studied the big metal dumpster. It stood nearly ten feet high and was, he guessed, at least thirty feet long. Hollister pushed his sketch into a pocket and moved to the dumpster.

Climbing up on the rim of the large trash bin, Hollister pushed the hinged metal door up and open. A pungent syrupy odor of decaying garbage reached up to greet him. Hollister turned his face away to let the air trapped in the bin dissipate. A swarm of flies buzzed around him. When he turned back, he saw the reason the two cops had been shot.

"Christ!" he said as his breath left him. Several feet below, lying in the midst of an assortment of bulging trash bags, bottles, glass, crumpled newspapers and raw garbage was the body of a young shapely woman dressed in shorts and a sleeveless top. The flesh on the girl's legs and arms was ashen gray with the color of death. Her body was in a fetal position as if she were cold although the exposed buttocks and legs were unmistakably those of an attractive female. The body's face was hidden in a tangle of long blonde hair.

"Max!" Hollister called as he pushed the lid higher.

Max came quickly and climbed up on the dumpster to Hollister's side. "What is it?" But he saw the body before Hollister answered. "Oh, shit," Max groaned. "It's the 'Man from Glad'."

Hollister knew what Max meant. How long had it been since the last one, five days? He tried to remember the girl's name and couldn't. He did remember she was fifteen and a ninth-grader from the Valley. Her body had been found in a trash bin behind a supermarket on Western Avenue. Her head and shoulders were covered with a large, double strength, green trash bag. She'd been sexually abused and suffocated. She was the third in what had become known city wide as 'The Man from Glad Murders'. Now it seemed they might have a fourth.

"Hold the lid," Hollister said, "I'll take a look."

Max held the big metal lid high as Hollister climbed over the lip of the rigid metal bin and stepped down into the trash. "Shit!" Hollister complained as his weight pushed him almost knee deep in the wet pungent garbage around the girl's body. He tried breathing through his nose as the flies swarmed around his face. He swung at them.

"She looks older than the other girls," Max suggested from above him.

"Wearing Adidas, maybe a workout outfit," Hollister suggested, bracing a hand on a slimy interior wall of the bin to balance himself. Reaching, he grasped a clear trash bag partially covering the girl's head and shoulder by a corner and pulled. The plastic sack stretched and slid away. Long blonde hair fell from around the girl's head and face. There was a thin nylon cord wrapped tight and deep around the girl's bruised neck. Hollister stared. Her eyes were open as if she were looking at him. The tip of a tongue showed between ivory white teeth.

"She's beautiful!" he heard Max say from above.

Hollister saw a green bracelet on the girl's left wrist. It had lettering on it. Hollister reached, grabbed the wrist and lifted it. He read aloud so Max could hear. "Shannon Roberts. Warner Brothers Studio Stage Ten." Hollister's breath left him as the name brought recognition to the figure. His memory of seeing the girl was vivid. He had watched as she walked into a clearing in the woods wearing a thin cotton dress. She was barefoot. The straw blonde hair played around her face in the light breeze. She was carrying a basket of wildflowers and her eyes were searching for more. It was then her eyes spotted the pool of water. She had moved to it, smiled, and tested the water with a toe. He could see the thought forming in the sultry eyes as they searched the clearing. Only the sound of a distant Meadowlark disturbed the stillness. Confident she was alone; the girl reached and pushed the straps of the cotton dress over her tanned shoulders. The dress slipped to the ground, revealing the perfection of her nudity. She was the most beautiful woman Hollister had ever seen. She stepped to the clear water and waded in. A shiver made her jelled breasts dance as the water crept up over the flat of her stomach.

It was the opening scene from the motion picture "The Nude in the Woods" and it had cemented sensual young actress Shannon Roberts' growing worldwide stardom. Somehow, she had blended sensuality and innocence into a combination of charm and beauty. Her face had adorned every popular magazine cover, she had been crowned the most beautiful woman in the world, and countless millions had seen her films. Hollister didn't like being a fan, and he had never spoken of it, but to him Shannon Roberts was, as it was with most, the epitome of femininity. Hollister took unspoken pride in the fact there was a subtle resemblance between Shannon Roberts and his blonde wife, but now all he could do was stare in mute silence.

"You sure it's really her?" Max questioned softly from above. It was as if others might hear him.

"Yeah," Hollister answered, looking at the familiar face and blonde hair. He reached and carefully laid a hand on the flesh of a cheek to reassure himself she was in fact dead. The flesh was cool to the touch. He pushed on it with a forefinger. The dimple made in her flesh did not change color. It was near gray. There was no circulation. He pushed on a bare shoulder with the palm of his hand. The body moved in its cushion of trash. She hadn't died in the dumpster, he concluded. Hollister wished he could cover her. Her body was having a strange unnerving effect on him. It was an embarrassment and uneasiness he couldn't comprehend. Perhaps it was that he had watched her alive and seductive on television recently, where was it? Kimmel? ...Now she lay dead in a trash bin. The sex goddess of the century at his feet, but there was no pleasure in seeing her. The fantasy had become flesh. Fragile flesh that suffered death like any mortal. A dream had died. It didn't seem right for her to be laying in the trash.

"Is that ligature around her neck?" Max asked, pushing the lid even higher until it fell over backwards to clang loudly against the bin. Flies swarmed in shock.

"Yeah," Hollister answered, chasing the flies off the girl's face. He grimaced, pushed trash aside and turned to climb out. His mind rushed with thoughts. Two dead cops and now maybe the sex goddess of the century. Was it really her? Maybe she was just a look alike? Hollywood was full of them. A trio of murders was staggering. Add the possibility one of them was a dead star and you had a challenge few cops had ever faced.

"Company coming," Max said as Hollister dropped down off the trash bin. The odor of the garbage clung to him like a wet curtain. A sticky piece of paper stuck to the bottom of his right shoe. He pawed at the asphalt like a horse and glanced at the two men approaching. He recognized Captain Harris, the Commander of Hollywood Detectives and the Homicide OIC, Lieutenant Stratton. Hollister thought Captain Harris looked more like a stockbroker than a police captain. He was a handsome man in his early fifties, graying at the temples.

Hollister was glad Stratton was with the captain. There would be fewer questions. The call out for two dead cops had both men looking sober. "What have we got?" Stratton asked as they reached Hollister and Max. He had friendly eyes and a gentle manner, but this was not a time for small talk.

"More than we thought," Max said.

"What do mean?" the lieutenant questioned.

"There's a dead girl in the trash bin," Hollister gestured with a glance behind them.

"What!" Captain Harris blurted.

"It gets worse. Bracelet on her wrist says Shannon Roberts," Hollister added. "And the description fits."

"Shannon Roberts...the movie star?!" Captain Harris questioned incredulously.

Hollister raised a foot and pulled away the piece of paper stuck to his shoe. "Have a look," he suggested soberly. There was much to be done and he was finding the intrusion by the two men an annoying distraction. He knew their motive was to find something to offer the growing horde of press gathered on the sidelines as well as the area commander certain to be sitting near a phone somewhere waiting on their call.

Captain Harris moved to the trash bin and climbed up. Lieutenant Stratton followed. The horde of officers drawn to the scene with the news of two officers down stared from the sidelines in bewilderment.

"This is not good," Captain Harris muttered as he

and the lieutenant climbed down from the bin, brushing at their hands. The captain looked to the crowd of waiting press and spectators behind a yellow police line tape across the mouth of the alley. Then looking to Hollister and Max, he said, "You can't say for sure that's her."

"She's got one of the most recognizable faces in the world," Hollister challenged, "as well as a studio bracelet on her wrist."

"We deal in facts, not speculation," Captain Harris cautioned. "You may suspect that's Shannon Roberts, but until you have positive identification, she's just another victim."

"Just another victim?" Hollister countered sarcastically.

"I didn't know we had a point system for homicide victims, Captain."

Harris's jaw tightened. "My point is, Sergeant," he said in a tone emphasizing his rank. "The death of two officers is enough to generate heat. Add the murder of a major Hollywood star and the heat gets a hell a lot worse."

"You know what they say, Captain?" Hollister answered as his irritation with the captain grew. "If you can't stand the heat?"

"There isn't going to be another Michael Jackson fiasco, Sergeant," Harris warned, "Not while I'm Commander of Hollywood Division."

"You take care of the press, skipper," Max interjected with a smile in an attempt at easing the tension, "and we'll take care of the investigation."

A young technician from SID, Scientific Investigation Division, was finishing his work on the patrol car and gathering his equipment when he heard the arguing detectives mention the name Shannon Roberts. He paused and listened. One of them said she was dead, in the dumpster! Jesus, he was going to be a part of something really fucking big!

As the detectives continued their exchange the technician, hardly able to contain his excitement, walked to a uniformed officer near the police tape strung across the mouth of the alley. The technician offered a smile to the officer. "You know who they found in that trash bin?"

"What trash bin?"

"That one." He pointed. "Shannon Roberts, the actress and she's fucking dead."

"You're full of shit."

In minutes every uniformed cop at the scene had heard Shannon Roberts' body was in the trash bin. The tsunami traveled quickly and soon emails and texts were finding their ways into every fiber of the Internet. The growing agitated army of paparazzi, press and news cameras made it obvious they had heard too.

The passport on the dresser in the room on the third floor of the LeParc Hotel in West Hollywood identified its owner as Phillip DePaul, a French citizen, but the man's real name was Abu Assad, an Iranian by birth. Assad had been in the United States for six days, spending four days in New York, visiting friends before flying on to Los Angeles. Now with work complete he would call an associate in Washington, perhaps visit with him and be out of the country by Tuesday.

The shirtless, lean, Assad was in the bathroom, shaving with the radio tuned to an all-news station. Finally, the bulletin he had been expecting came.

"This just in," the radio announced as the copy was handed to the reporter. "The body of famed actress Shannon Roberts, star of both motion picture and television, was reportedly found early this morning in an alley in Hollywood. Police at the scene are refusing comment, but an informed source reports the actress was found in a dumpster. The circumstances surrounding her death are under investigation and KFWB's Mike Warren is en route to the scene. We are expecting his report soon. Shannon Roberts' rise to fame started..."

Assad switched off the radio, wiped the traces of shaving cream from his face and picked up the bedside telephone. He dialed the number on a notepad and listened as it rang.

"Beverly Hills Hotel," a female voice answered.

"Suite two-twelve," Assad said with a French accent.

The extension rang four times before a groggy male voice answered. "Hello." It was obvious the man had been sleeping.

"You sleep late for a man with many problems," Assad said into the receiver.

The sleepy man recognized the caller's accent and was now wide awake. "It's the lag you know. I just got in yesterday afternoon. Bloody flight over the pole."

"Well, go back to sleep. Your business difficulty has been resolved."

There was a pause and then the man in the Beverly Hills Hotel said, "We will forward the remaining payment as promised," he stammered.

"That would be appreciated," Assad hung up abruptly.

It was one thing to talk about murder. It was another to announce it had been done. The Englishman was obviously shaken. No wonder their island nation was run by a queen. Englishmen had no balls. He had killed several throughout his career. All had died without resistance, hardly a challenge. Americans were different. They were always a risk. It was an American Army colonel in Paris that nearly turned the tables on him when his pistol misfired. The colonel, knowing he was facing an assassin, had fought violently after the misfire gave him the opportunity. Had the man not been near sixty and dressed in a heavy overcoat, the outcome may have been different... As it was, Assad came away with a broken finger and a bloodied nose. The colonel had not died easily.

The injuries made it more difficult to get out of the country, but the Palestinians that hired him helped and he was smuggled into neighboring Spain without incident.

Assad found great irony in his struggle with the American colonel for it was the Americans who had trained him. An American marine assigned to the Shah's secret police had befriended Assad at a riding stable where he worked and recruited him as an informant. His loyalties were rewarded with covert trips to the hills of Northern Virginia. There in the quiet, secluded, woods he learned the science and art of killing.

When the Shah fell and fled Iran in disgrace, Assad's American friends flew him to Paris where he was provided with an apartment and a substantial expense account. Two years of the good life passed before they asked anything in return.

Assad seldom knew anything more about his targets than their names. It was better that way. More impersonal and business like.

During his third year in Paris he was contacted by the English. They had a job for him in Argentina. It paid well, went without problems and he enjoyed the trip west. Shortly after Assad's return, his American contact warned him about freelancing.

"We cannot protect you unless you work only for us," the man warned. "We will not tolerate any American targets."

Later that same day Assad watched television as the then American President denied the dethroned and dying Shah entrance or medical treatment in the United States. So much for American loyalties, Assad thought. Two days later, he took the job on the American colonel. If the Americans knew, they never said anything and they continued to use his services, along with a growing list of others. He worked for corporations as well as countries. He cared nothing about the motive or the morality of it. His country and his family were dead. There no longer was any morality. Morality was also dead.

The early psychological training he received in America taught him that killing was simply a defense. When viewed in that context it then became an avocation, a business, but as the years passed and the numbers increased, his perception blurred, and he began to enjoy it. He had particularly enjoyed the blonde girl. Blonde women always seemed repulsed by him. They had a superior attitude, especially American blondes. Well, this blonde and her fame had paid the price for all of them. She had fought, begged for life. But the rope around her neck quickly had her limp. The bag near her head would have the police blaming it on the Man from Glad, a serial killer he had read about in a local paper. His visit to the States had been an enjoyable one. Although he had shot and killed two police officers, he was not worried. He didn't think the police were very smart.

FIVE | FADE OUT

The news of Shannon Roberts' death brought not only additional press, and stunned fans, but an army of police department brass as well. Captain Harris was soon overshadowed by the area commander, then a deputy chief, and finally the chief-of-police himself. In the eye of the hurricane were Detectives Hollister and Baxter who continued their investigation, trying to ignore the constant clatter of rotors overhead, as a variety of airborne telecopters recorded their every move. They videotaped the girl's body in the trash bin, took digital stills and tolerated a continued string of commanders and deputy chiefs, that just wanted a quick look.

Hollister watched as two black windowless station wagons backed to the mouth of the alley from the street. Several patrol officers ushered the crowd aside, lifted the police line tape and the cars backed in. A small black man got out of the first vehicle to join two men climbing out of the second station wagon. They spoke with the officers who pointed to Hollister. The man nodded, walked to the rear of his station wagon, opened the rear door and pulled out a wheeled stretcher. It had a long strap and the man used it as he pulled the stretcher down the alley. The other two men also pulled stretchers from their wagon. Hollister watched in silence. There was irony in seeing coroner's deputies pulling wheeled gurneys into an alley on a bright Sunday morning. Hollister wondered if anyone else would see it that way. He supposed not. Two of the deputies went to work at the recovery of the officers' waiting bodies. They worked in a near silent reverence as the army of sober officers watched. The small, thin, black deputy pulled his stretcher to where Hollister waited.

"Hey, Leon," Hollister said as the man reached him.

"Hey, Hollister," Leon answered. He was a short, frail, man with a lined weathered face and an unlit, chewed cigar in the corner of his mouth. He had once explained the cigar. It wasn't that he liked to smoke them, but the taste of soggy tobacco in his mouth and the aroma in his nostrils helped combat the smell of death. Leon took the cigar from his mouth, spit and looked to Hollister. "Hear you got a celebrity in there?"

Hollister nodded. "Shannon Roberts."

"Shannon Roberts," Leon puffed. "I'll be god-damned. Who'd want to kill a fine-looking woman like that?"

"That's why we're here," Hollister answered.

"Hey, the Ice Man's here," Max called as he returned from the far end of the alley with an SID photographer.

"Hello, Max."

They made small talk for a minute allowing Leon to slip on latex gloves. He offered similar gloves to Hollister and Max. Gloves on, they climbed up on the rim of the dumpster.

"Good Lord," Leon said as he stared inside. "I've never seen a woman that pretty."

With help from the two detectives, Leon climbed over the rim and down into the dumpster beside the body. They watched as Leon knelt beside the nude and felt along the rib cage. There was no hint of reluctance at his touching the flesh. "Her temperature doesn't feel that low. How long she been here?"

"We're not sure," Hollister said as they watched Leon pull a small oval thermometer with a long stainless-steel shank from beneath his jacket. Its end was needle sharp. Leon laid the thermometer in the trash beside the body and pulled out a notebook.

"Looks like strangulation killed her?" Leon said as his pen scribbled. "Also see an abrasion right upper pelvic area."

Finishing, Leon pocketed his pen and notebook and took out a small digital camera and began shooting a variety of pictures from various angles.

"Bag her hands for us, Leon, and ask the lab for vaginal slides," Hollister instructed.

"You figure rape?" Leon said, squinting through

the lens of the camera. A flash blinked and washed away the shadows for an instant.

"Probable," Max answered.

"Yeah," Leon agreed. "She's a candidate for it." He pocketed his camera and reached to another pocket to pull out a packet of clear vinyl. He unfolded the vinyl into two clear bags. Reaching to the body, Leon picked up the right hand, slipped the bag over the hand, secured it with a rubber band and let it fall. The limb was limp. Rigor mortis was yet to set in. Leon picked up her left hand and bagged it. Hollister noted there was no jewelry on either hand, and that the long-colored nails were intact. That was a good sign although there were no signs of a struggle, bits of flesh, blood, hair or fiber beneath fingernails may indicate otherwise.

Done with the hands Leon picked up the thermometer. He studied the reading. "Fifty-nine degrees environmental at..." he glanced at his wristwatch, "nine-fifty-one."

Hollister made a note.

Leon pushed the sleeveless workout sweater aside and ran a hand along the girl's rib cage, searching for the feel of her liver. His bony experienced fingers kneaded the pale flesh. Finding the spot, Leon readied the long-shanked thermometer and forced its sharp end through the flesh. Hollister winced involuntarily as Leon pushed the shank deep into the girl's side.

Leon straightened, leaving the thermometer looking awkward and foreign, protruding from the body. Max and Leon made small talk about fishing, the weather and the Dodgers. Hollister envied their detachment. He didn't want to look at the girl, but his eyes kept going to her. Jesus, she resembled his wife, or was it just his fantasy.

"Well," Leon puffed, "let's see what we got for a liver temp." He reached down and unceremoniously pulled the temperature shank from the girl's flesh. It was blood free and left a small dimple on the side of the body. Leon studied the dial on the thermometer. "Eighty-nine degrees," Leon said, raising an eyebrow. "If she was any warmer, I'd have to take her to a hospital instead of the morgue."

Hollister made a note of the reading. "Close only counts in horseshoes, Leon."

"Well, let's get her up outta here," Leon said, chewing on his cigar and brushing away flies swarming around him.

Leon wrapped the body in a white wrinkled sheet he unfolded from a jacket pocket. He lifted one of the girl's bare arms and held it up to the detectives. Hollister grabbed it by the wrist. The other arm was lifted to Max. The two men pulled and as the body raised up out of the trash, Leon grasped arms around the shapely long legs to add to the lift.

As the dead star was lifted over the rim of the dumpster by the three struggling men the paper sheet tangled and tore away. Shannon Roberts was making her final scene. Arms flailing, legs dangling, chin down, face covered in a tangle of blonde hair, and a three-day old copy of the L.A. Times, sticking to her buttocks. The crowd sighed audibly as iPhones and cameras flashed, shutters clicked, and video lamps winked on behind the police line, while overhead, telescopic lenses reached down from three orbiting news telecopters.

Four uniformed officers tried to offer a makeshift wall of privacy as Hollister, Max and Leon laid the body carefully on the ground near the dumpster. Leon knelt and wrapped what was left of the paper sheet over her nudity. Her face was uncovered. Hollister noticed the capped white teeth were biting into her tongue. Death had not come easy.

Hollister and Max stepped aside as Leon worked the wheeled, padded gurney into position beside the girl's body. Then digging beneath the pad on the stainless stretcher, Leon unbuckled the straps on the gurney and laid them open. Folding a blanket open he looked to Hollister. "I'll get the feet. You get the head."

Hollister had hoped he wouldn't have to touch the body a second time, but he nodded and knelt at the tangle of straw blonde hair. As Leon grasped ankles, Hollister slipped his hands behind the girl's head. Even through the latex gloves her hair was smooth and silky to his touch. He remembered the touch and smell of his wife's hair earlier, just before the call out, as he held her warm, tight and naked, and then he remembered her words. This is no way to live, find something else! Great fucking send-off. Have a great day at work, Hon! Managing a realty company, she worked with bigger fucking crooks than he did. His wife was pretty, smart, successful, but unhappy with what he was. Fucking deal with it. The rush of thoughts angered him. Maybe he'd take her to Vegas, maybe a weekend on Catalina would help?

The body sagged awkwardly, arms dragging, as Strom and Leon picked it up and onto the stretcher. Leon dropped the ankles on the gurney. Hollister set the blonde head down carefully slipping his hands out of the hair. Leon pulled a rubber sheet from the gurney and folded it over Shannon's body. "Damned shame to be so pretty and so dead," he said, chewing on his unlit cigar as he worked feet and head into the body bag before he zipped it up. Then working straps into position, he cinched each tight.

"Leon," Hollister offered, "we think it's Shannon Roberts, but?"

"You want positive ID?" Leon said, taking the chewed cigar from his mouth. It was soggy and wet. "I'll take prints as soon as I get her there."

Hollister nodded appreciation.

"Well, good luck finding the motherfucker. Two cops and her. I'm glad I'm me instead of you," Leon said with sincerity. "See you next time." He gathered the lead on the wheeled gurney and pulled it toward his waiting van. The two policemen were already being loaded into the second van.

Hollister stood with Max and watched. Sometimes when a body was taken away from the scene, Hollister would have a feeling about the case. How the investigation would go. Was it going to be tough, easy, routine? This case was different. Two cops and a dead star. It had a dark foreboding ominous side that both frightened and excited him. Was it being close to Shannon Roberts even in death? Was it that he knew the two dead officers? Whatever it was, it had already taken its toll. Hollister momentarily wished another team had been called, but then quickly decided that was a lie. The coroner's wagons pulled away. News cameras panned to follow their departure. It was as if they were watching the end of a film. It was surreal and unnerving.

Lieutenant Stratton approached from the midst of uniforms along the police line. After the tense exchange, Captain Harris Stratton had deliberately stayed away as the detectives worked with the coroner. "Maybe this will whine down now," Lieutenant Stratton said.

"Not for us," Max intoned.

"What's next?" Stratton questioned.

"We find who killed Shannon Roberts, we'll find who killed our two policemen," Hollister said, beginning to frame the investigation in his mind.

"Try to stay out of the captain's way," Lieutenant Stratton cautioned.

"Is that what you were trying to do?" Hollister said with an accusing look.

"You bet your ass," Stratton answered without hesitation. "I'm ten days from my captain's oral and I got a kid starting USC in the fall. You think I'm looking for problems, you're crazy."

"We're not here because of a fondness for dead cops or a fallen star in a trash bin," Max defended.

"You're right," Stratton agreed. "But you're going to have the whole world looking over your shoulders. The skipper is already talking about having Homicide downtown take this."

"We've got two good teams in our squad to back us up. We don't need downtown," Hollister answered firmly, exchanging a look with Max.

"You mean you don't want help. This is going to be big shit, Hollister."

"We treat every homicide as big shit, John."

"What I'm saying," Stratton answered soberly with a look at both men, "is if you fuck up, I'll be the one sending it downtown."

The momentum of the investigation was growing. Lieutenant Stratton, taking Max's unmarked car, was on his way to the station to interview the eyewitness. Captain Harris and the area commander had retreated to conference and develop an action plan. There were the families of the fallen men to visit, and if the identity of the dead girl was Shannon Roberts, they needed build a shield to protect the investigation. The chief of police would call a press conference. He had already spoken briefly to the press at the scene, and although he was aware of the finding of the body in the dumpster, and her probable identity, he wisely avoided confirming identities. "Confirmation on identity will be made by the coroner's office."

A second team of homicide detectives had been called in and were checking hospital ERs and Immediate Care Centers in search of anyone with what could be a dog bite. Detectives were also going door to door, shop to shop, on Hollywood Boulevard searching for locations with security cameras. There were hundreds. Both dead officers had been stripped of their personal video body cams. The killer obviously knew the cameras held his identity. Hollister and Max wanted images from any security in the area that may show passing traffic, cars or pedestrians, views of the alley, or intersecting Gramercy Place. And yet another team of detectives were knocking on doors, looking for yet-to-be-identified witnesses. Experience had taught, not everyone stepped forward, not everyone raised their hands, and not everyone cared.

Max made two calls on his cell from the scene. The first brought a department tow truck to remove the patrol car manned by the two fallen officers. It was a solemn task that brought a silent pause as the black and white police car was winched onto the bed of the tow truck. Uniformed officers offered a reverent hand salute as the truck pulled away with the patrol car, looking awkwardly foreign and lonely on its back.

Max's second call brought an even larger truck. This time a city refuse truck and with Max's direction it backed into the alley, electronic alarm barking, to connect with a loud clang to the big blue metal dumpster. Bumping to a halt, the big truck's engine labored as it pulled the dumpster's squeaking wheeled metal hulk aboard. The dumpster, lid down and locked, was wrapped with crime scene tape and evidence stickers. After delivery to the Police impound lot it would be emptied and its contents closely examined, piece by piece, by SID.

Before the yellow crime scene tape came down, Hollister made yet another call. This one to the LAFD, the Los Angeles Fire Department. They were determined the waiting horde of reporters, cameramen and morbidly curious would not walk in the spilled blood of the two fallen officers. Evidential samples had already been taken. Two massive hook and ladder fire trucks, emergency lights flashing, arrived within minutes. Six helmeted firemen working with high pressure hoses washed down the short alley beside the liquor store where the officers fell and then the intersecting longer alley that connected beyond the dumpster. Again, shutters clicked, iPhones were aimed, and above, the telecopters circled like waiting vultures. It was true Hollywood.

Hollister and Max walked shoulder to shoulder around the scene after the wash down and departure of the fire trucks. The asphalt was wet and gray with grime and an oily petroleum smell crept up into the air. Evidence of the violence occurring in the early hours of dawn was gone. The two detectives exchanged a glance as they turned to look at the waiting cops, the yellow police line stretched across the mouth of the alley and the crowd beyond. Max knew the question and asked it, "We done here?"

Hollister nodded agreement and then added, "I wonder what they're waiting for." He was studying the crowd. "What is it they want?"

Max joined him in looking at the distant waiting

faces. "Maybe the same thing we do," Max speculated. "Answers." Then with a wave to the uniformed officers, he shouted, "Take it down."

Several reporters and cameras followed Hollister and Max to their waiting unmarked detective car, but they were tactfully ignored. Hollister silently hoped some of the images would find their way to his waiting wife, as he remembered her urging, find something else. The car was a welcome refuge after the long hours at the scene. Hollister cranked it to life, pulled it in gear and gunned away from the crowd.

In the trunk of the detective car, in sterile sealed bags were blood samples, empty shell casings and Keith Canfield's nine-millimeter automatic pistol. Believing it was used by the killer, Hollister was not entrusting it to others. There was also the plastic trash sack removed from Shannon Roberts' head, the newspaper once stuck to her buttocks, seventy-eight DNA swabs taken from the patrol car, the dumpster, inside and out, and from blood on the asphalt pavement. Additionally, there was crime scene video and three hundred and ninety-four digital photos, along with a handwritten log identifying every officer, at, or visiting the scene. As well as their serial numbers, time of visit, purpose, vehicle license number, and assignment. Along with the log were extensive notes and drawings made by both Max and Hollister. Murder in Los Angeles, as it was in major urban centers across the nation, was a labor-intensive business. Successful investigations were always team efforts.

Murder, ironically, had become an economic stimulus.

The evidence in the trunk of the detective car was reinforced by the work of the three SID investigators called to the scene. SID had taken latent prints, DNA samples, collected hairs, human and animal, took independent photos, videos, blood samples, environmental air and ground samples and readings as well as collecting, tagging and bagging a variety of cigarette butts, empty beer bottles and cans, three used condoms, gum wrappers and two bullets recovered from the asphalt surface of the alley. They had also recovered a bullet from the brick on the side of the liquor store wall fronting the alley. They also took as evidence, Officer Martinez's pistol, three bloody splintered fragments of human skull with hair, an assortment of trash from the dumpster, detailed scaled crime scene drawings and made environmental audio recordings.

"We've got a lot more evidence than ideas," Max said as they drove west on Melrose Avenue. "Where are we going?"

"Shannon Roberts didn't put a bag over her head and go dumpster diving," Hollister answered. "And not likely she often went out dressed in work out gear."

"So, we're going to?" Max questioned.

"Her house," Hollister said with a glance as he drove. "If she was killed in her home. It's a crime scene, and the place where we start."

Max nodded. "And she lives, where?"

"I have no idea," Hollister granted with a shrug. "Maybe we could call intelligence Division. They must have it?"

"I'm sure they have, but it's Sunday," Max defended, shaking his head. "We'll have to wait for someone to come in. Plus, odds are Shannon Roberts' address and utilities are in some accountant's name. Hell, rich people don't pay their own bills. They hire people to do that."

"I wouldn't know," Hollister answered as they passed a lone jogger. Max twisted in his seat to look at him. The man was tall and balding and wearing sweats. He was dismissed as a suspect.

"Alright," Hollister said with another glance at Max. "You got a better idea?"

"Maybe so." Max smiled. "When you get down to Fairfax turn north."

Several miles away the siege of Hollywood Station had begun. Five mini-cam vans, microwave dishes extended, along with a collection of press cars jammed the street in front of the building. The gathering camera crews and technicians crowded the street, swapping stories, complaining about overtime and the lousy coffee from the station's coffee room.

Inside the crowded lobby two desk officers who had expected a quiet, lazy Sunday on which to work crossword puzzles and play video games on their iPhone, found themselves facing a demanding horde of impatient reporters. Captain Harris and Lieutenant

Stratton had made a brief appearance to promise an update by the network's one-thirty deadline. Anything later missed the all-important prime news for the eastern United States.

Captain Harris, when pressured for information and not wanting to look uninformed in front of the cameras, admitted they were talking with a witness. "We have a witness who saw a suspect. We're working on several leads." There was a clamor for more, but Harris refused. He'd whet their appetites, but the fact was, there was nothing else to give.

Retreating down the station hallway after facing the glare from the camera lights, Captain Harris looked to Lieutenant Stratton. "You heard what I told them. Nothing! Make sure Hollister and Baxter get us something, damn it!"

Harris secluded himself in his office at the head of the detective squad room. It was his job to brief the area commander, the operation's duty officer, the commander of public affairs, and the assistant chief of police. They all had more questions than the captain had answers. It made him feel defensive. Commander Paulson, the operations duty officer, was annoyed with the lack of information. "You don't know much, Captain," he told Harris over the telephone. "Are you sure you were at the scene?"

"I work for the LAPD," Harris defended, "not the National Enquirer."

"Obviously," the commander retorted, "the Enquirer wouldn't want you."

The detective car was west of La Brea on Sunset when Max spotted what he was looking for. "There, pull over."

"Where?" Hollister questioned. All he saw was a black youth with a hand-painted cardboard sign that read, "Maps to the Stars' Homes."

"Pull over," Max demanded, "next to the kid."

The fifteen-year-old, wearing large dark sunglasses and a Michael Jackson glove, had one foot on the curb and the other in the street. His sign was taped to a pool stick he had stuck in a crack in the cement. The eyes behind the sunglasses spotted the unmarked car's approach. He knew the two men weren't tourists. Hollister brought the car to a halt beside the youth. Max had an elbow out the window.

"Hey, police," the sunglasses said with a wide smile. "How you doin'? You may notice I'm not soliciting, blocking traffic, or creating a public mucous."

"Nuisance," Max corrected.

"No, no bother at all." The sunglasses grinned.

"Max," Hollister said from behind the wheel, "you're not going to do what I think you're going to do?"

Max glanced at Hollister. "The Detective Operations Manual urges field investigators to take the initiative in being innovative and imaginative in exploring new investigative techniques." Max returned his attention to the big sunglasses. "Those maps really good?"

"Is Rand proud of McNally?" The sunglasses

smiled.

"You ever heard of Shannon Roberts?" Max continued.

The Michael Jackson glove adjusted the sunglasses confidently. "Heard of her? Shannon Roberts sells more of my maps than all the other tits in them there hills, Partner."

"I can't believe this," Hollister groaned.

"How much for a map?" Max said, reaching for his wallet.

"I got a Sunday special today," the sunglasses assured, leaning an arm on the car. "And today only..." He pulled a folded map from a rear pocket. "...only twenty-one-ninety-five."

"Twenty-one-ninety-five!" Max complained. "That's not a map, that's a felony."

"Hurry up, damn it," Hollister complained, checking the rearview mirror. "Someone's going to see us."

"I got expenses," the sunglasses defended. "These little gems got to be updated on a daily basis. You know how often rich folks move?"

"Is Shannon Roberts' address good?" Max pressed.

"Do ducks fly south?"

"I'll give you ten bucks."

"Nineteen."

"Eleven."

"Give him the money, Max."

"Eighteen-fifty."

"Eleven-fifty."

"Shit! Seventeen and that's it."

"Max, just take the damn map?" Hollister urged.

"Twelve dollars."

"Okay, 'cause I like you, sixteen-fifty."

"Twelve-ninety-five."

"I'm insulted," the sunglasses defended.

"Twelve-ninety-five," Max repeated. "Take it or lose it." He dug in his pocket for the money.

The sunglasses watched him, and then stuck the map through the open window. "Okay, you got a deal."

Max took the map, stuck the money in the waiting palm.

"Thank you, mister secret agent man," the sunglasses smiled.

Hollister tramped hard on the accelerator and the detective car roared away. Max began to unfold the map.

Max's finger traced over the grids of the map as his eyes searched.

"Is she on there?"

Max's attention was on the map. "Let me see, Reese Witherspoon, Vin Diesel, David Rose."

"Who the hell's David Rose?" Hollister questioned as they crossed Fairfax Avenue.

"I think he's a conductor," Max said, looking to another fold of the map. "Mel Gibson."

"He moved to Australia?"

"I don't know. Here we go. Shannon Roberts."

"What's the address?"

Max studied the map. "Twelve-eighteen Laurel Way, Beverly Hills."

"Give me the nearest major intersection," Hollister said as they continued west on Sunset Boulevard.

"Beverly Drive and Sunset," Max answered. "Turn north on Beverly, second intersection on the left."

West Hollywood melted into the strip and grew in stature as Sunset laced toward the eastern boundary of Beverly Hills. The magical transition from Los Angeles to fabled Beverly Hills never failed to amaze Hollister. Upon crossing the line, the high rise, commercial clutter of West Sunset immediately yielded to the quiet, tranquil, green parkways of Beverly Hills. Trees, flowers, shrubs, and grass, the color of money, covered everything but the street. It reeked of affluence and wealth.

It never entered Hollister's mind that he might someday visit Shannon Roberts' home. Nor had he ever thought he'd see her...nude, or dead. Although he suspected a couple of million others, daydreamed of it. Death, the great equalizer, had brought him the opportunity. He had to admit he was mildly excited about seeing her home. He was going to see the bedroom where she slept. What man wouldn't want to see that? How many men had? He had to remind himself he was a cop, not a fan, or at least, not a fan first. He wondered how Max felt. Max seemed to be enjoying the sights of Beverly Hills.

"Hey, Max," Hollister questioned, "have you seen any of her pictures?"

"Doris and I watched 'The Nude in the Woods' on cable a couple months ago. Doris liked it. Looked to me like the director had a nipple fetish. You know the picture she made with Ryan what's-his-name?"

"Summer's Shadow?"

"Yeah, now I liked that one. Good story. She was a pretty good actress. Even looked good with her clothes on."

Two blocks later Hollister swung the car onto tree lined Laurel Way. They had no problem spotting Shannon Roberts' home. It was an English Tudor with high steeples secluded behind a stand of pines and a five-foot used-brick wall. But it wasn't the house that identified it. A television crew in a mini-cam van told them they had the right address.

"Shit," Hollister complained.

"Looks like the kid sold more than one map," Max quipped.

Hollister drove by without slowing. They drew curious looks from the television crew, but the interest quickly faded and returned to the house.

"You think they know she's dead?" Max asked as Hollister reached the end of the block.

"Probably knew before we did, Hollister answered. He made another turn, this time into an alley behind the twelve hundred block of Laurel Way.

"Damn," Max said. "Their alleys look better than the streets in my neighborhood."

"It was the Tudor with the tall pines," Hollister rolled the car down the alley.

"You going to try the back?" Max questioned.

"No," Hollister answered. "We're going try the

back."

A dog barked in a nearby yard when they climbed out of the car, but the fences and gates were too high to see where. After several yaps, it fell silent. The only sound was a gentle breeze and the chirp of birds.

"Lot of birds here," Max said, moving around the detective car to join Hollister in the middle of the alley.

"They probably plant them," Hollister suggested, studying the gates and garage doors that lined the alley.

"Why have an alley in a neighborhood like this?" Max questioned, looking up and down the long alley.

"Deliveries, trash, servants," Hollister answered, "all the things the wealthy don't want coming to the front door."

"Oh," Max agreed. "Guess now we're in that club."

"I think that's the gate," Hollister said, gesturing across the alley. They could see the gables of the Tudor and the tall pines beyond a high block wall.

Hollister pulled a cord that hung through a hole near the top of the wooden gate and heard a latch click inside. The tall gate swung inward to reveal a lush green yard and a glistening pool that danced light patterns off the back of the house. The two detectives stepped in and closed the gate quietly. Their eyes searched the yard. It was quiet and inviting. The scent of honeysuckle filled the air.

"Nice," Max whispered, "must have a great gardener."

"Let's hope she doesn't have a Great Dane," Hollister answered.

They stood quietly looking for movement behind the curtained windows.

"Well," Max said, breaking the silence.

"Yeah," Hollister agreed and they moved up the walk that led to the pool and the house.

A gas barbeque and a countered window hidden behind wooden shutters told Hollister where the kitchen was and he headed for the door. Max followed.

Hollister paused at the door and knocked lightly. As big as the house was, he expected at least one servant, maybe two. Along with the servant there was a chance of a live-in-lover, a mother; rich women did not like living alone.

There was no response to Hollister's knock. He knocked again. Heavier this time. There was no going to the front where the press would see them. After a moment he looked to Max and shook his head.

Max shrugged. "Is it locked?"

Hollister took the doorknob in hand and turned. It twisted freely. The door opened without resistance.

On the second floor of the Wesco security office on Beverly Drive an electronic alarm sounded on a computer console and a soft green light flashed, "Intruder," on the video screen. The monitor on duty, thirty-two-year-old Delbert Homes, laid a dog-eared copy of Penthouse aside and punched several keys on the keyboard.

The computer beeped and printed its answer on the video screen.

> *residence: ROBERTS, SHANNON*
> *1218 laurel way, Beverly hills*
> *4700 sq ft 11 rms*
> *servants: 1 out of residence-d.o.*
> *owner/occ out of residence*
> *6 ext doors 5 doors secure*
> *1 ext door - open w/wall, s/w corner, resid.*
> *intruder: silent alarm only - notify B. H.*
> *police 274-7171*
> *11:57 AM END.*

Hollister and Max stayed together as they searched the first floor. The telephone rang twice. Three rings on both occasions. Hollister bet on finding an answering machine somewhere. The house was big, yet there was warmth about it. It was obvious the owner had wealth, but the furnishings spoke of reality and livable comfort. Hollister had been in the homes of the wealthy in the hills high above Hollywood. Most, he thought, looked like the lobby of a Holiday Inn or something cold and sterile out of Architectural Digest. This house was different. It looked and felt like a home. They found a friendly Himalayan cat in the family room. It was curled and asleep on the top of a pool table. "Hey, kitty," Max said as the cat jumped down and began rubbing against his leg. Hollister studied the room. It was neat and clean as the others had been. Nothing aroused suspicion or told them anything about the woman who lived there. "Strange she left the place unlocked," Max suggested.

Hollister was thinking. "Maybe she didn't," he said, picking up a polished white cue ball from the pool table. "She may have been taken from the house."

"By someone that knew her," Max said, eyeing the comfortable room, "no evidence of a struggle." Then glancing at the cat. "And the cat's in the house."

"Or she left of her own will, expecting to be back," Hollister added, placing the cue ball back on the table. We have to find what she has for a car."

"You figure the servants are on a day off?" Max questioned.

Hollister nodded agreement. "You can bet she doesn't take care of this place herself."

"Maybe the butler did it?" Max suggested with a smile.

"There's a light on in the kitchen," Hollister said, thinking about it. "Two in the living room. One in here. Looks like she left last night."

"Wonder where she spent the night?"

"I don't know," Hollister agreed. "Let's look upstairs." He heard the distant muffled chop of rotors and the whine of a turbine engine high above the house. Another airborne news crew, he told himself.

The stairs were near the wide front entry way. The cat followed the two detectives up the carpeted stairs.

The telephone rang again. After three rings it again fell silent. Hollister noted there was a light on in the entry way as well as at the top of the stairs.

A wide hallway led to the double door entry of the master bedroom. Hollister and Max paused in the open doorway to look at the room. "Wow," Max breathed as he stood at Hollister's shoulder.

A king-sized canopy bed draped with lace and covered with a billowy silk spread highlighted the spacious room. The wall at the headboard was mirrored and made the room look even bigger. There were soft lights glowing on the dark walnut night tables that flanked the bed. Sunlight filtering through the layers of sheer curtains covering the windows added to the room's glow. A fireplace, its mantle covered with a flowing fern, stood at the far end of the room. A comfortable loveseat and chair faced the fireplace and a clear glass cocktail table where a glass decanter of amber liquor sat waiting with crystal glasses and a bouquet of colorful fresh flowers.

"Doesn't look like Goldilocks slept in that bed last night?" Max said with a look to Hollister.

The silk spread on the wide bed was smooth and undisturbed. There was a hint of perfume teasing the air. Hollister was enjoying the scent when the sharp command shattered the stillness.

"Hands in the air...or you're dead!"

SEVEN | LIVE AT FIVE

Neither Hollister nor Max had heard the two Beverly Hills police officers move quietly up the carpeted stairs behind them to the mouth of the bedroom. The helicopter over the house should have warned them but Hollister had concluded it was the press. A mistake. Not a serious one, but an embarrassing one. Hollister didn't like making mistakes.

Arms above his head Hollister glanced carefully over his shoulder at the two uniformed officers. They were dressed in tan, smartly creased uniforms. Their leather gear was dark brown and highly polished. They were years his junior. It made Hollister conscious of his thirty-eight years. Hands stretched into the air he said, "We're cops. LAPD."

The taller of the two uniformed officers was listening to a walkie-talkie. "Looks like an unmarked LAPD car out here in the alley."

"Roger," the officer said into a microphone. They could see the handcuffs on the back of both Hollister and Max's belts as they stood arms stretched into the air. "Code Four, friendlies on the scene. No four-five-nine. Code four at this location. Okay, put them down," the officer added as guns were lowered.

Max dropped his hands and headed for an open bathroom off the master bedroom. "I gotta go." The surprise arrival of the officers and hours at the crime scene brought on his sudden urge. Hollister turned to the two officers. "Sorry, guys, we should have reached out. Did we set off a silent alarm?"

"Yeah."

"Hollywood Homicide," Hollister explained. "I'm Sergeant Hollister. My partner is Max Baxter. We're here from the crime scene. You've heard about Shannon Roberts' death?"

"Yeah, we heard."

Hollister was being as user friendly as he could. The fact was, and he knew it, he and Max were in a foreign jurisdiction without notice and in a victim's residence without a search warrant. It was a stretch. "Circumstances at the crime scene suggest the victim may not have left here voluntarily." Hollister was being informative but still vague hoping the two Beverly Hills cops would accept them under the brotherhood of the badge.

A toilet flushed and Max, zipping up, retuned from the bathroom. "You guys really wear Gucci shoes?"

"You bet," the shorter, dark-haired, officer answered, "and we drove over here in a Porsche."

Hollister was glad Max was joking with the two cops. It would help cover their mistake. Policy, as well as common sense, dictated when in a different jurisdiction the first thing done was notification they were there, and why. Failure to do so could prove deadly. Hollister promised himself greater concentration. It was time to forget whose murder they were investigating and concentrate on solving it. He had to shake the distraction that was screwing up his focus. It wasn't big mistakes that got cops killed. It was the little ones.

"You ever get any calls here?" Hollister questioned.

"An overzealous fan climbed over the fence a month ago," the taller officer answered. "We booked him for trespass. It was the maid that called."

"Then she does have servants?" Hollister added.

The officer nodded. "Black woman. In her fifties."

"How did she die?" the second officer questioned.

"We're not sure," Hollister answered, again being deliberately vague. Needlessly telling how a victim died, the position of the body, what they were wearing, many times resulted in convincing false confessions. Hollister had little doubt there was an army of nuts waiting a chance to confess to the murder of Shannon Roberts. It was guaranteed instant fame, and the city was full of mindless migrants searching for it.

"Could you give us a hand searching?" Hollister asked, knowing drawing the two officers into it would eliminate criticism.

"Sure," came the quick reply. "What is it we're looking for?"

"Anything suspicious," Hollister answered. "Max and I will take the master bedroom. You split up and take the rest of the upstairs."

"You find something," Max warned, "come to us. Don't touch it."

"And if you turn a light on," Hollister added, "turn it off. If it's already on. Leave it on."

"Got it," the taller officer assured. The two men left the room.

"I'll take the closets," Max said.

Hollister found the small digital answering machine in the cabinet of a nightstand on the right side of the bed. He pushed a button. The sultry recorded voice of Shannon Roberts spoke. "For your convenience please leave your name, number, and a brief message. I'll call you back as soon as possible." A tone sounded. Hollister pushed the play button. "Good morning, Miss Roberts. This is Bruce, your friendly AD. It's five-thirty and make-up beckons. The limo will be waiting. Thank you." ...Beep! "Shannon, it's Lucy at the Agency. People Magazine wants to do an interview by the sixth. Only gives us five days, Dear. See, that proves agents can count. Give me a call, Ciao." ...Beep! Hollister now had a date reference. The message was three days old. Beep! "Shannon," an irritated male voice complained, "you know how I hate talking to this fuckin' machine. Why can't you hire some poor unemployed bastard to answer your calls or answer your cell. We're getting close to agreement on the credits on this piece of shit Paul DeSilva film...I got you top billing. I just read the script. 'Memories in Blue!' Sounds like Perry Como wrote it, but DeSilva's money's green and we're gettin' most of it. Give me a call, babe. Let's talk." Hollister was making quick notes of calls. Beep...Miss Roberts this is Eric Flowers' office at Universal, calling. Would you please give Mister Flowers a call at nine-eight-seven-five-four-three-two? He said to mention - you met at Sid Bolman's party. Thank you." Beep..."Hello, Shannon you doll. This is Paul DeSilva. Enjoyed lunch with you and Monty, but next time let's send Monty to Tel Aviv. I'm really excited about the picture. You're keeping us right on schedule. Give me a call, beautiful. We got things to celebrate." Beep!...

Max walked to Hollister's shoulder listened for a moment and glanced at his notes and then walked away. The messages were turning out to be like most of Hollywood. Less than glamorous. Beep! "Shannon," the digital voices continued. Hollister had had enough to recognize the voice. It was Monty Golden, Shannon's agent. "What is this shit? Paul DeSilva tells me you told him to stuff his picture up his ass. Come on, Baby, don't do this to me. This is a big flick, Baby cakes. I know DeSilva is a sleaze. He grabs everybody's ass. I told him he had to keep his hands off of you. He said he would. Come on, Sweet cheeks; let's put Humpty Dumpty back together again. Call me."

Beep! "Ah, Shannon, this is Paul DeSilva. Did you

get the roses? Hope you like 'em. Listen, I'm sorry about our little misunderstanding. I'd like to get together with the director Saturday night, talk over the revisions you want. Give me a call on my cell. I'll set it up."

Hollister noted the mention of Saturday. Now the tape was nearing messages left on the eve of Shannon's death. Hollister listened carefully.

Beep! "Hello, Miss Roberts, this is Kim from Mister DeSilva's office at Stonegate Studios. We've arranged for an interview with Entertainment Tonight. Mister DeSilva would like to do it on the primary set of 'Memories in Blue'. Would you please give us a call to coordinate the dates? Thank you."

Beep! "Shannon my love." It was Monty Golden again. "Paul told me about Saturday night. I'm so glad you crazy kids have made up. Bring me lots of money. Hey, has anyone ever told you you've got a great set of tits?"

Beep! "Hello, Shannon, it's Lucy. Entertainment Tonight has some questions they'd like you to preview. Give me a call. Please. Love you!"

Beep! "Shannon, it's Paul DeSilva. Come on, it's Saturday. If you're trying to worry me it's working. Give me a call!"

Beep! "Hello, Thelma, it's me, Shannon." Hollister straightened, looked toward the answer phone. "Leave the back door unlocked. I forgot my keys. Enjoy your day off. Love you, bye!"

Beep! "Shannon, it's Monty. Call me, goddamn

it! Paul says you didn't show up last night. What the fuck's going on?"

The tape went on with several more hang-ups but there were no more voice messages. Hollister had learned two things. Shannon Roberts had a Saturday night meeting with Paul DeSilva she didn't keep, and she left the house of her own free will. He had two people to talk to. Paul DeSilva and the maid. He re-set the machine and pocketed his notes. He found a red leather address book atop the cabinet. Hollister thumbed through the pages. Every page of the book was full.

"She must have fifty pair of shoes in here," Max called from one of the walk-in closets.

"Some people hoard food, others hoard shoes," Hollister answered.

"Got enough clothes to remake Gone with the Wind," Max added.

"Sergeant Hollister," the taller uniformed officer said from the open door of the bedroom.

"Yeah."

"Found something."

"Max," Hollister called.

They followed the officer down the hallway and into a room to the left of the stairs. The room was bright, mirrored, and equipped with an exercycle, a rowing machine, parallel bars, and a variety of other chromed and padded work-out equipment. The second officer was waiting near a big screen T.V. and a DVR. "The T.V. and the DVR are on," he explained.

"Looks like the CD just stopped."

"What is it?"

"Zumba Work-Out," the officer answered. "And, here's a towel and what looks like a drink."

"Lights were on?" Max questioned.

"Just like they are now."

Hollister walked to the padded bench and looked at the towel. He could picture it sliding off of Shannon Roberts' shoulders. Max moved to his side. "The drink tells us it's been here since the maid hasn't."

"And that someone expected to come back," Hollister suggested.

Hollister turned to the two cops. "You did good. We're going to put evidence seals on the doors and close the place up. Have Prints and SID come out and go over it. We'll make sure your guys are alerted."

"You think she was taken from the house?" the officer questioned.

"Looks that way doesn't it?" Max answered.

Hollister left a business card sticking in the frame of the stained-glass window of the back door after he taped the evidence strip near the doorknob—

Warning. this property is sealed by the Los Angeles Police Department.

it is unlawful to tamper or trespass. violators will be prosecuted.

information and questions—485-2121.

The press had found their way to the alley and they were waiting when the four cops pushed open the gate. Several flashes and the lenses of video cameras followed them. The two Beverly Hills cops moved them back as Hollister and Max crossed to the detective car. "Can you believe all those cameras?" Max said as they pulled away. "I should have dressed better."

They were eastbound on Sunset Boulevard when the radio between them called, "Six-William-thirty to Six-William-twenty-two."

It was Lieutenant Stratton's voice. Max picked up the microphone and keyed it. "This is twenty-two, go."

"Twenty-two, meet me on Wilton just north of Hollywood Boulevard, Code-Two."

"Roger," Max answered, "we're on the way."

Stratton's detective car was parked facing north on Wilton Place just off Hollywood Boulevard. Hollister pulled to the curb behind the car. Stratton climbed out and met the two detectives. He had a confident grin.

"You were right." Stratton smiled. "Your jogger went to the hospital to have his ass sewed back on."

"What hospital?" Max questioned.

"Fairfax General."

"Who is he?" Hollister pressed.

Stratton was already digging out a small notebook. He flipped it open. "His name's Garth Mead, age thirty-four, five-ten, one-sixty-two, brown and brown. Lives at seventeen-fourteen-three Gramercy Place, apartment two-oh-seven. Drives a two thousand and six red Toyota Corolla, California license,

Ocean-Charles-Sam-nine-nine-three."

"Is he home?" Hollister questioned.

"I did a drive-by," Stratton answered. "Didn't wanna push too hard and spook him. It's a three-story building with subterranean parking. Couldn't see if the Corolla was in there. I let my fingers do the walking. Got his number from the hospital."

"You called him?" Max asked.

"Yeah, the old, 'is Suzie there,' routine, but he didn't answer."

"How long ago was that?" Hollister questioned.

"Fifteen, twenty minutes," Stratton said with a glance at his watch. "I ran him for a record check, wants and warrants."

"And?" Max questioned.

Stratton looked at his notebook again. "He's a sex offender from Texas. Arrested six times for indecent exposure and prowling. One arrest in California, eight months ago. Indecent exposure."

"Proves things improve with age," Max suggested. "He's moved up from weenie waving to murder one."

"Here's the plan," Hollister had it laid out in his mind. "Max and I will move onto Gramercy, find a place where we can see the garage, and sit on it until he comes home." He looked to Stratton. "You stay on Wilton until we notify you that he's home. You'll be our back-up. We'll stay on Tac Two."

It took Hollister three attempts before he succeeded in backing into a narrow parking space on Gramercy Place. There was a station wagon close behind and a Ford Pinto in front.

"Any tighter and you'd get the virgin of the month award." Max smiled.

"I'm going to have a look in the basement, make sure the car didn't get out while it wasn't covered."

The early afternoon temperature was warm and comfortable. The apartment building was on the left. They had a view of the garage as well as the walk-in entrance. Hollister climbed out and headed across the street. A young couple in shorts was washing a Volvo with a hose and a bucket of soapy water. They were playing and splashing one another. In the street three men played Frisbee. It was a typical lazy Sunday afternoon and as Hollister neared the apartment building, he envied them. They were living. His business was death. He wondered why he was becoming so conscious of that. Get ahead of the case, he warned himself, or find something else as his wife suggested.

"Shit," Hollister muttered when he reached the driveway sloping down into the shadowed basement garage. It was covered with a steel security gate. He was about to turn away when a car swung into the driveway. It stopped near the key operated switch where the driver inserted a key. The wheeled security gate rattled and rolled aside. The sedan rolled down the driveway and into the garage, ignoring Hollister. The gate began closing automatically. Hollister casually walked through the narrow space that remained as the gate clinked shut behind him.

The subterranean garage was cool and shaded. Its

smooth cement floor was stained with tire marks and oil stains. Hollister stood in the shadows of a corner while the couple from the sedan gathered groceries from the trunk of their car and disappeared through a door he guessed led to stairs or an elevator.

Stepping from the shadows, Hollister walked the garage. There were four rows of parking spaces and all were dotted with cars. He checked them all. The red Corolla wasn't among them. He headed for the stairs.

He could smell chlorine and hear the laughter. At the top of the stairs he saw a wide oval pool shimmering in the inner courtyard. Hollister paused and studied the blue water and the collection of bathing suits around it. The bodies were glistening with oil, sprawled on lounges and towels spread on the decking. There were fewer men than women. The bathing suits were cut high and some were no more than strings.

Hollister followed a walkway to the lobby where he found a bank of mailboxes. He searched until he found a name strip that read, "G. Mead."

Hollister took his time walking back to the detective car. "Anything happening?" He said to Max who sat slumped on the passenger's side.

"Poodle pissed on our tire," Max answered without moving. "That's about it."

Hollister still standing on the passenger's side of the car glanced over his shoulder at the sound of an approaching car. His heart jumped. "Shit," he hissed.

It was a red Corolla. Hollister was looking directly into the eyes of Garth Mead. He quickly averted his eyes trying for a casual look but knew it was futile. He'd seen the wide-eyed look on Mead's face. Two men, an unmarked car. Mead had connected the dots. Hollister heard the Corolla's engine roar as Mead punched it and flashed by. "Sonofabitch!" Hollister yelled, scrambling around the car. "It's him!"

"Oh, shit!" Max bolted up in the seat, staring after the Corolla as it roared down Gramercy place toward Hollywood Boulevard.

Hollister twisted the ignition. The detective car growled to life. He jammed the selector into reverse. The car jumped backwards slamming into the station wagon behind it. Glass fell onto the street. Max grabbed the microphone. "Six-William-thirty, suspect is fleeing southbound on Gramercy in the red Corolla!"

Hollister wrenched the steering wheel to the left and floored the accelerator. The detective car surged forward with a roar, its tires screaming, sending out billows of blue smoke.

Lieutenant Stratton had his car started and racing toward Hollywood Boulevard before he picked up the microphone. "William-Twenty-two, give me a direction!"

At Hollywood, Detectives Captain Harris, a commander and a deputy chief crowded around the radio at the head of the squad room. Max's filtered voice boomed from the speaker. "West on Hollywood!"

"Go to frequency three," Stratton's voice barked in an urgent tone. He reached the intersection of Wilton and Hollywood Boulevard and braked the detective car. He was a block ahead of the Corolla. "Come on, you mother," Stratton flexed his fingers on the plastic steering wheel. The Corolla burst into view, closed quickly and flashed by him. Stratton gunned the car after the Corolla. He held the microphone close to his mouth as the speed climbed toward seventy miles an hour. "Six-William-thirty is in pursuit."

A moment later the Emergency Command Control Communications male radio voice answered, cutting across all police frequencies. "All units, all frequencies, stand-by! Six-William-thirty is in pursuit. Six-William-thirty, your location?"

Hollister braked hard as they neared Hollywood Boulevard. The detective car had no red light or siren. He laid on the horn and drove through a stop sign, turning west on Hollywood Boulevard. Horns blared; tires screamed as brakes were slammed on. The detective car narrowly missed a city bus as it swung wide in the intersection. "Shit!" Max cried, hanging onto the frame of his open window.

The Sunday afternoon traffic was building as the Corolla flashed west along the curb crossing over the Hollywood freeway. The pursuing detective cars were only a half block behind.

"Air Six," the link in communications broadcast, "Six-William-thirty is westbound on Hollywood at Van Ness in pursuit of a red Corolla."

"Roger, Air-Six has a visual on the suspect," the voice from a police helicopter answered.

Garth Mead was begging the Corolla to go faster as he flashed by a Winnebago motor home with a Wisconsin license plate. He weaved by another car. Traffic looked even thicker ahead. His mind was in a panic. He needed time to think, time to prepare a story. He checked his rear-view mirror again. The detective car was gaining. He glanced at his speed. Almost eighty. God! Traffic ahead was stopped at a traffic light. He down shifted and swung into the clear on-coming lanes.

"Units in pursuit, the suspect is turning south on Bronson from Hollywood," the calm voice of the observer in the police helicopter said. They were following overhead at nine hundred feet.

The two detective cars weren't far behind. Max had his eyes closed as they flashed through the intersection against a red light.

The Corolla raced three blocks south and turned west on wide and busy Sunset Boulevard. Black and white police cars were converging from all over the north end of the city. The air was thick with the sound of sirens. They were closing off the grids around it. The helicopter overhead ensured it wasn't if they caught him, it was when. "Units in pursuit, the suspect is now westbound on Sunset approaching Gower."

The western regions of the Daughters of the American Revolution were concluding a three-day convention at the Hollywood Palladium after a stirring address by Beverly Winston on the urban crisis in America. A crush of dignified women was pouring onto the sidewalk when the Corolla screamed by at seventy-six miles an hour. A horde of six police cars and two detective cars followed in a noisy train filling the air with an ear-shattering crescendo of electronic sirens.

"I've had enough of this prick!" John Stratton said and gunned the front bumper of his detective car up against the rear of the fleeing Corolla.

Garth Mead swerved to get away from the maniac chasing him. His right front tire hit the curb and burst the side wall. The car jumped the curb, hit a cement bus bench, spun wildly several times and came to a screaming stop at the curb. The frightened Mead knew he was about to die. The flight instinct took over and he had the door of the Corolla open before the police cars slid to a noisy stop.

The building had a towering white facade facing Sunset Boulevard. Garth Mead did not glance up at the bold block letters KCBS standing on the roof beside the infamous eye of CBS.

The Live at Five, newscast was just underway in studio three. A security guard had a fresh cup of coffee and was settling into his chair behind the reception counter in the front lobby looking forward to sports report on his laptop when the front doors crashed open. The startled guard jumped, spilling coffee down the front of his uniform pants and desk.

A fuzzy-haired man bolted by him and down the hall toward the studio. He was still staring after the man when the first of the eighteen policemen ran by, guns in hand. Lee Hollister was leading them.

Garth could almost feel the hot lead of the police bullet ripping into the middle of his back. He had to get away. He spotted a set of double doors to the left.

In Studio Three, Pamela Norton, the perky blonde, Sunday anchor, looked to Gordy Trent, the black weatherman. "Gordy, how do you explain the thundershowers that kept me awake last night?"

"Well," Gordy smiled, gesturing to a large blue weather map, "in Southern California it's difficult to predict anything."

A second later Garth Mead burst through the big weather map, ripping California and the three-day forecast to shreds. Pamela Norton proved female anchors were real people by filling the news set with an ear-piercing scream. Gordy Trent, convinced it was a terrorist, ran. Hollister was only two steps behind Garth Mead as he dove directly in front of camera three. "Gotcha, you sonofabitch!" Hollister growled.

Approximately one-million-four-hundred and twelve thousand Californians stared at their television sets in shock. Chief-of-police James Peck was among them. "Fuck!" he said in shock.

Paul DeSilva was on the patio of his Beverly Hills estate with Raymond Mathews, Vice President of Production at Stonegate Studios, Ted Pell, a senior vice
president from Wilshire Bank, and George Franklin,
a financial consultant from London, who special-
ized in foreign rights. There were a number of girls,
shapely would-be starlets, provided by a producer
who owed Paul DeSilva a favor. The girls were tinsel.
It was T&A to keep the mood festive. After all, this
was Hollywood. The "Eagles", as Paul DeSilva called
them, because they shit money, had gathered for a
briefing after the first week of production on "Memories in Blue", DeSilva's eleventh picture and his big-
gest budget ever at seventy-four million dollars.

The four men had spent the morning on the greens
at the Bel Air Country Club. Now they were relaxing
before lunch was served. The drinks were flowing,
and the air was thick with bullshit and cigar smoke.
The first week's dailies were to be screened early in

the evening.

An English butler approached the glass topped table where DeSilva sat with Raymond Mathews and two smiling girls. Mathews was asking a petite brunette at his side what it would take to convince her to do a nude scene. "Oh, I wouldn't do it unless the script was good," the girl answered with glossed lips.

"Well," Mathews winked at DeSilva, "that's certainly a sound moral standard."

"Pardon my interruption, Mister DeSilva," the butler said.

"Yeah?" DeSilva took the cigar from his mouth. His other hand was on a thigh beneath the table.

"Mister Altice is on the line."

"Oh, he is, huh? Probably wants to run the dailies early," DeSilva smiled. "Bring me a phone."

The butler moved away.

"Hey, guys," DeSilva called, "our esteemed director's on the phone. Probably wants to show us the dailies now. What do you say?"

"Tell him to come over," Ted Pell answered, lifting a drink. "We've got an extra girl."

The butler returned and offered a cordless telephone to DeSilva. "Hey, Walt, my man, how are you doing? The dailies are looking real good, right?"

"Wrong. Hold onto your ass, Paul," the director's voice warned.

DeSilva straightened in his chair. "What the hell are you talking about?"

"You stupid wop, don't you listen to the news?" It

was an accusing tone. There was no love lost between the two men.

"Listen, you two-bit little porn peddler," DeSilva answered, squeezing the telephone as if it were the director's neck. "You demean the Italian people again and I'll kick your red neck ass off the picture."

"You don't have a picture, grease ball."

"What!?"

"You heard me. The twenty-eight million you've spent is in the toilet. Shannon Roberts is dead."

"Dead!?" DeSilva bolted to his feet. The others fell silent and looked to him. "What the fuck are you saying?"

"She was found in an alley in Hollywood this morning. They've got her killer in jail."

A jolt of fear shot through DeSilva like a bolt of electricity. His knees shook and felt weak. A lump rose in his throat. He thought he was going to be ill.

"Enjoyed working with you, asshole. You owe me three-hundred and fifty thousand, pal. Pay or Play." The line clicked in DeSilva's ear and a dial tone sang. He laid the phone down on the glass tabletop. The shocked look on his swarthy face told the others the news was bad. "He said Shannon Roberts is dead. They've got her killer in jail."

DeSilva walked from the patio toward the house. His shoulders were slumped, and he looked broken. George Franklin followed him.

The two men entered through a set of French doors, moved around a pool table and sat down on padded stools at a well-stocked bar. DeSilva reached over the bar for a bottle of scotch. His hand shook as he poured. "You want some?"

"No," Franklin said with an English accent. "It's important we have clear heads."

"Clear heads!" DeSilva barked, after taking a heavy swallow from his glass. "It was your clear Limey head that got us into this fuckin' mess."

Franklin lit a cigarette and exhaled. "I don't re-member having to twist your arm, ol' chap."

DeSilva shook his head and looked to Franklin. "I thought he was a pro. How in the fuck did this guy get himself arrested?"

"He came highly recommended by people who know about these things," Franklin defended. "He sounded very confident this morning when I talked to him."

"That fuckin' Arab's gonna cough up our names as soon as they swing the cell door shut. Those sand niggers don't know what loyalty is."

"Let's not overreact," Franklin cautioned.

"I think we already have," DeSilva answered sar-castically.

"Don't say 'we'," Franklin warned, "when you're talking about problems you've created. Don't do something stupid and make a bad situation worse."

The waiting press got the tag they needed for the evening newscasts when Hollister and Max arrived at Hollywood Division with the handcuffed Garth Mead. Hollister, after his news cast intervention, was now a celebrity. He wisely declined comment as they took Garth Mead from the car and headed for the station's rear entrance. Shutters clicked and the bright lamps for video followed them. Garth Mead hid his face. The questions came in a rush. "Why did you kill Shannon Roberts?...Are you her lover?" Mead bent his face even lower. "...How long have you known Shannon Roberts?"

Garth Mead waited in a windowless interrogation room for nearly thirty minutes. A uniformed officer was standing guard outside the door. Hollister's instructions were simple. No one in. No one out. The brass had drunk all the coffee in the homicide office. Hollister walked to the coffee room to buy a cup while Max telephoned Doris to tell her he wouldn't be home for dinner. He was still on the telephone when Hollister returned. Hollister considered calling Kim but decided against it. He was already late; calling wasn't going to make her any happier.

The isolated Garth Mead was experiencing what Hollister and Max called "worry time". The law dictated how the police could talk to a suspect. Combining that with what most suspects saw on television convinced them that as soon as the police got them alone, they would be bombarded with relentless questioning. So, Hollister and Max began the warm-up by refusing to talk to the suspect. It was a psych game, but it usually worked. The suspects, full of anxiety after arrest, were eager to talk, argue, and duel. It was a vent, an escape valve for a welling flood of emotions.

Even in denials and lies there was relief. While in isolation and silence, fear and worry reigned supreme. The conclusion had to be if the police weren't talking, it was because they didn't have to.

Garth Mead, overwhelmed with fear, was close to throwing up on the small wooden table in front of him. What were they doing? My God, why weren't they talking to him? He dared to get up once and knock on the door. A brooding black officer opened the door. "Sit down and stay away from the door," he ordered before Garth Mead gathered enough courage to speak. It was part of the humiliation process and it worked. Alone, with no idea what time it was, and frightened, Garth Mead was desperate to talk to someone, anyone.

Finally, the door to the interrogation room opened and Garth Mead bolted straight. He dared a look at the two men. The thinner one was graying at the temples and he had green eyes that seemed to look right into his brain. The detective's face was tanned against the collar of his shirt. He was a handsome man and Garth was almost certain he'd seen him on television. He was wearing a holster, but it was empty. It was as if he didn't need the gun. The other detective was a big, broad-shouldered, round-faced man. His cheeks were rosy, and he had a perpetual smile on his face that was accented by a single dimple. His hair was short. He reminded Garth Mead of an army sergeant. The two detectives sat down across from him. The thinner man turned his chair around and sat in it backwards with his arms crossed on the chair back. Garth glanced at the detective's watch. It was six-forty-five.

"Garth," the big man said, looking at him, "I'm Max Baxter. This is my partner, Hollister. We're the detectives investigating the murder of Shannon Roberts."

"My God," Garth blurted as a wave of fear washed over him.

"I didn't kill her; I swear to God I didn't kill her. I've never even seen her!"

"We're professionals," Max warned. "You can make our job difficult by lying, but you can't keep us from finding the truth, and you can't take away the evidence we already have."

"I'll tell you everything," Garth plead, looking from one man to the other.

Neither seemed impressed with his willingness.

"Before you say anything," Max cautioned, "we want you to understand your rights."

"I know what they are. I don't want an attorney," Garth said. He was eager to tell his story.

"I still want you to hear them, and I want to make sure you understand them."

Garth wiped at his face with a damp palm. He nodded agreement and shifted his weight in the wooden chair. The sutures in his buttock were stinging.

"All right," Max said, pulling a small notebook from an inside jacket pocket. He read from the cover of the notebook. "You have the right to remain silent. If you give up the right to remain silent, anything you say can and will be used against you in a court of law."

In the monitor room Lieutenant Stratton and Captain Harris sat at a desk, watching video from the interrogation room, Stratton made an adjustment on the volume. "You have the right to speak with an attorney and to have the attorney present during questioning," Max's voice said.

"If you so desire and cannot afford one, an attorney will be appointed for you without charge before questioning. Do you understand each of these rights I've explained to you?"

Garth nodded. "I understand. I don't need an attorney to tell you the truth."

Max slipped his notebook back into a pocket. "Okay, then in your own words, tell us what you know about Shannon Roberts' death."

Garth glanced at the thinner detective. He still hadn't spoken. He was staring and it was making Garth even more nervous. "Well," Garth said, clearing his throat. The room felt cold and he was damp with perspiration. "I was jogging. I got bored sitting in my apartment, so I went running - just to get out."

Max nodded. "Go on."

"I was jogging on the street below Melrose."

"What time did you go out?"

"Six-thirty or so."

"What direction were you running?"

Garth thought carefully before he answered. "I'm not sure but I could see the sign."

"The sign?"

"The Hollywood sign. Up on the hill."

"Okay."

"So, I was jogging, and I heard shots, or backfires I wasn't sure."

"Then what?" Max pressed.

"I started running again and I heard more shots."

"How many?"

"I don't know. Three, four...but I was sure it was shots. Then this car comes racing out of the alley."

"What kind of car?"

"A Mercedes, hardtop. It was silver. I see a lot of them over at Universal."

"Did you see who was driving it?"

"You're not going to put my picture on TV, are you?"

"We don't put anyone on TV."

"This guy killed two cops. I don't want him knowing who I am."

"What guy?"

"The guy in the Mercedes."

"Tell us what he looked like?"

"Dark, Italian or Mexican. I'm not sure."

"How old?"

"Thirty maybe. I'm not sure."

Max didn't believe him. "Then what did you do?" Garth wiped sweat off his chin. "I went and looked in the alley."

"And?"

"I found a gun on the ground."

"What kind of gun?"

"An automatic. I picked it up. Then I saw the two cops. I couldn't believe it. I walked up the alley."

"Did you touch anything?" Max questioned. A denial would be important if fingerprints were found on the patrol car or the plastic covering the nude Shannon Roberts.

"No," Garth answered. "Just as I got there this black guy yelled at me."

"What did he say?"

"I don't know. I was scared."

"What did you do?"

"The guy had a dog. A big one. He put the dog on me. I heard him say 'Get 'im' so I ran."

"And?"

The dog bit me. I swung at it and got away?"

"Why didn't you call the police?"

Garth was trembling and pale. "I was scared. The guy in the Mercedes he saw me ...I was afraid."

"Okay," Hollister said standing up. His chair scraped on the tile floor. It startled Garth. "I've heard enough of this bullshit, book him."

"I'm telling you the truth," Garth pleaded convincingly.

"How close to the girl did you come?" Hollister demanded.

"Girl? I didn't even see a girl!"

"Where did you meet Shannon Roberts?" Hollister added, glaring at Mead.

"Shannon Roberts! ...I, I've never met her."

"Bullshit." Max said soberly, "Where did you meet

her?"

"You've got to believe me," he answered emotion-ally. The pressure was building.

"You know what?" Hollister said, leaning on the table to speak directly into Garth Mead's worried face. "We don't have to believe shit."

"My God!" Garth said, lowering his face to his hands. "I can't believe this."

"Tell us about what you do?" Max suggested, sensing they were getting nowhere.

Garth wiped at his eyes. "I'm an actor," the broken Garth answered, rubbing the tense muscles along the back of his neck. "But I haven't worked in fucking seven months."

"So, an unemployed actor just happens to stumble onto the murder of a Hollywood superstar?" Hollister mocked.

"It's the truth. I swear to God it is. I'll take a lie detector test."

"Have you ever been to Shannon Roberts' home?" Max questioned. He was hoping they'd find Mead's fingerprints there which would tighten the noose.

"No, never." He answered quickly. "I don't even know where she lives. I swear."

"Okay," Hollister said, "I want you to start with the moment you left your apartment this morning, and go step by step, minute by minute right up until the time you were arrested this afternoon."

It went on for two hours. The story never changed. Each time they ran through it the details grew. The unchanging growing details he provided convinced Hollister he was telling the truth.

They were past the two-hour mark when Garth Mead said, "I have to go to the bathroom...please?"

Max pushed out of his chair. He took Garth Mead by the arm. "Come on, let's go potty."

As they moved through the door into the squad room Lieutenant Stratton appeared in the doorway. He gave Garth Mead a curious look in passing. "What do you think?" he asked Hollister.

"I think maybe he's telling the truth."

"Shit," the lieutenant looked worried, "I sent Captain Harris home an hour ago because I told him it was all over."

"It's not over until the fat lady sings," Hollister suggested sarcastically.

"Shit," Stratton complained again. Then he added, "What's next?"

"We've gotta print Shannon Roberts' house and Garth Mead's apartment," Hollister answered. "Maybe we'll find his prints in her house and maybe, if we're real lucky, he had her in his apartment."

"You gonna do that tonight?" Stratton questioned.

"If we don't and the maid comes in and cleans Roberts' place, we're in trouble," Hollister warned.

"Okay," the disappointed Stratton said. "Whatever happened to nice simple homicides," Stratton complained.

"They died out," Hollister answered.

It was nearly one a.m. when Hollister pulled into his driveway on Porta Loma Drive. A sprinkler was hissing on a neighboring lawn. He climbed from the detective car and followed the curved walk to his front door. The night air was cool and ripe with a musty smell of earth. The years melted away for a brief moment. It was like Ohio after a night of rain.

Hollister paused for a moment where the walk turned toward his front door. The street fell away quickly beyond the walkway to reveal a panorama of a sea of lights on black velvet. Hollister's eyes drifted over the lights as he wondered where the killer was. It was hard to believe seventeen hours had passed since the call-out. Now he was only seven hours from starting a new day. He was glad this one was over. The day hung heavy on his shoulders. He reached for the door.

Hollister walked to the kitchen before switching on a light. He saw the note on the counter. It was in

Kim's precise handwriting.

Lee,

I'm lonely. I didn't marry you for this. Gone 16 hours and not even a call. I deserve

Better. I can't take it anymore. Please don't bother me at work. I don't want any trouble. It just doesn't work anymore. This is Goodbye—Kim.

He walked to the bedroom and flipped on a light. A sliding closet door stood open. A collection of empty hangers hung on the closet pole. Kim's complete wardrobe was gone. He checked several other closets. They were all empty. The bathroom was the same. The shelves were stark and empty, only masculine toiletries remained. A single dark hairpin was the only remaining evidence of feminine habitation, that and the scent of Kim's Chanel. Hollister felt close to being ill. His stomach was in a tight knot as if he'd been struck. "Sonofabitch," he muttered and walked to the living room. He felt powerless and impotent.

He sat at the kitchen counter and pushed off his shoes. He felt old and tired. At thirty-eight he knew it was likely he was beyond the middle of his life. It wasn't that he considered himself old. It was more a realization that he was no longer young. He was sure being assigned to Hollywood Division made him more conscious of age. Hollywood, the land of Illusions, the land of make believe, the land of loneliness. He took off his holstered gun and tossed it on the counter. Jesus, Shannon Roberts was dead, and Kim was gone. The thoughts and images of the two women blurred and ran together like wet paint.

There were two killers roaming the streets. One killed Shannon Roberts. The other killed his marriage. Was he responsible for investigating both? Were they related? They weren't, but they were. The ache in his gut couldn't separate the shock. "Sonofabitch," Hollister muttered a second time as if the declaration would help clear his mind. His marriage and his fantasy had both died on the same day. What went wrong? He believed in marriage. He tried to make it work. What was it her note said? "It just doesn't work anymore. What the hell did she expect? A rerun of Happy Days? What happened to commitment? What about the promise, "For better or for worse, forsaking all others, until death do us part?" It was as if it were written on a napkin from McDonald's. The Mcmarriage is over because the Mcfun is gone. It was a pop marriage. Instant fun, instant gratification, and instant honeymoon. Now the instant was over and so was the marriage.

Pushing off the stool, Hollister walked to the refrigerator. At least she hadn't emptied that. He gathered a piece of chicken and a Diet Coke and moved to the living room. Sitting on a couch, he bit into the cold chicken. The quiet was haunting. he turned on the T.V. A reporter on CNN was summarizing the career of Shannon Roberts. Hollister watched as a succession of stills followed the famed actress from childhood to stardom. He swallowed to clear a tightening throat. When they switched to a video tape of the crime scene in the alley Hollister switched to a different channel. He ran through the 700 club, a late-night talk show, Irion Man, a telethon for the hungry by World Vision, and finally settled on a rerun of the Andy Griffith Show. It was twenty minutes after three and Hollister already dreaded morning. Morning meant going to work and confessing Kim had left him. He pushed the thought aside and concentrated on the television. He didn't want to think. Barney and Otis had found a huge footprint out by the lake while Andy was having dinner with Helen. Helen had class in addition to a great shape. Hollister sipped the coke as he settled on the couch and put his feet up on the cocktail table. He wondered what it would be like to be Sheriff of Mayberry. They didn't have dead stars or runaway wives in Mayberry. Hey, Andy, want to try Homicide in Hollywood? Bring Barney, you're gonna need all the fucking help you can get. Sundays in Hollywood were different than they were in Mayberry. In Hollywood you got up early and drove to an alley and looked at two dead cops and a dead star.

Mayberry was like Shannon Roberts, Hollister decided. A fantasy. A place you could dream about, but a place you could never really go. Dream! Then the television yielded to sleep, and Hollister slept with a piece of half-eaten chicken in his lap.

The woman's voice was irritating. It was high-pitched and breathless. Hollister listened to it for a long time before he realized she was counting. Counting what? He opened his eyes. Jesus! It was the television. A group of three shapely women in leotards were doing exercises. He looked at his watch. Damn, his neck and legs were stiff. It was six-forty in the morning. Light was beginning to gather outside. Reality came crushing down. He was alone. How in the hell had Kim done it? Loaded everything she owned and moved out in what did she say seventeen hours. Hell, maybe she'd been planning this? He felt foolish. He hadn't seen it coming. When was the last time he ever looked in her closet? Where in the hell had she gone? She had to have a plan. A realtor could easily find a furnished place and not only was she one, but she managed sixteen of them. Most assholes he concluded thinking of them.

"Shit," he said as he thought about driving to the alley. There was no reason to call and tell Max and, unless he found something. He considered calling Kim's cell but then decided against. Sometimes there weren't words.

Max had a wife to share a morning coffee with. Hollister didn't and he was eager to get out of the house and away from the reality of it.

A cup of coffee did little to erase the curtain of fatigue that hung-over Hollister's intellect, but once in the detective car and on the southbound Hollywood Freeway, he was finally awake. There was a ghostly overcast hanging low near the tops of the tall buildings in downtown Hollywood. The detective car slowed as it approached the liquor store on Melrose Avenue. Hollister pulled to the curb and stopped.

He climbed out and stood across the street from the mouth of the alley. Hollister wasn't sure what it was he was looking for, but experience had taught him that it paid to return to the scene of the crime at the same hour of day it occurred. If nothing else, it gave him a feel for the case and to Hollister that was important. Two men went by on ten-speeds, puffing and sweating as they pedaled. The early morning traffic on Melrose gave Hollister an idea. Humans were creatures of habit. They did the same things at the same time every day. An early morning roadblock just might net them a witness they didn't have. He made a mental note to discuss it with Max.

Hollister was about to turn for the driver's side of the car when the figure emerged from the alley. He was tall and gaunt and dressed in a tattered gray jacket and baggy pants. His matted hair was long and filthy, and his face was covered with a gray, streaked beard. He carried a burlap sack. He moved to a trash can near the liquor store and began picking through the rubbish. Hollister headed for the alley.

"Keep away from me," the hollow, blood-shot eyes warned from deep sockets as Hollister neared the man. "I've got a knife."

Hollister stopped a few feet short of the man and pulled back his jacket to reveal the oval silver and gold police badge on his belt. "And I've got a gun."

The blood-shot eyes studied Hollister as if trying to bring him into clear focus. Then the man spoke. His voice was tired and raspy. "You get off robbing bums?"

"You have a name?" Hollister questioned.

"Of course, I've got a name. It's the one thing that wasn't repossessed."

"What is it?" Hollister said.

"David Rollins."

"Do you come here every morning?"

"No," Rollins answered sarcastically. He was swaying slightly as he spoke. "I'm a neurosurgeon. This is my day off. I drove over here in my Rolls Royce to get some fresh air."

Hollister was tiring of the attitude. "I don't know why you're pissed off at life, and I really don't care."

"You'd care if your life was shattered by a senseless war in a hell-hole called fucking Iraq."

"What were you in?" Hollister questioned.

"The Seabees."

Hollister nodded. "Yeah, I'll bet it was real hell building officer's clubs and tennis courts, but let's put away the soap box, GI Joe and talk about yesterday."

"Fuck you, draft dodger," the man said with as much defiance as he could muster.

Hollister reached for his rear pocket. Rollins thought he was about to be shot. It didn't really bother him. He'd been dead for three years. He steadied himself.

Hollister pulled out his wallet and opened it to pull out two twenty-dollar bills. He held the bills up, smoothed wrinkles from them. "You know how much wine this will buy?"

The tattered figure wet his lips. "You're a real prick, aren't you?"

Hollister nodded agreement. "Were you here yesterday morning?"

"I owned the place 'till dawn."

"Then what?"

"I saw what happened to the girl. This is what this is all about?"

"Tell me what you saw."

A grubby hand with mud-caked fingernails pointed. "I was sleeping by the trash cans that was over there when this car pulls up."

"What kind?"

"Mercedes."

"What year?"

"You want the fuckin' mileage on it too? I don't know what year. I haven't owned too many Mercedes. It looked new. Shiny. You know?"

"Go on."

"This guy gets out. He's kind of dark, skinny. Bushy hair."

"Black?"

"No. Fuckin Arab, I'd bet. Anyway, he walks around the car and gets the girl outta the other side."

"He helped her out?"

"Lifted her out. She was drunk or drugged."

"What makes you say that?"

"'Cause her arm was just hanging and swinging, you know." He gestured with his own arm. "I know a drunk when I see one."

"Then what?"

"Could see she was naked. He carried her to the big trash bin that used to be right there. Arms swinging and shit." I got the fuck outta here. Went over the fence into a backyard." He pointed.

"Did you see what happened?"

"No, but she was dead right, huh?" It seemed important to the man.

"Why didn't you call the police?"

"Oh, pardon me, I had forgotten my fucking cell phone."

"Do you read newspapers?" Hollister questioned.

"Oh, of course," Rollins mocked with a hand to his chest. "I like to keep up on current events..., so I can wipe my ass with them, like they did me."

"Do you think you would recognize this man?"

"If it paid enough."

"You got any ID. Maybe an address?" Hollister said, already knowing the answer.

"Yeah, in fucking New Jersey. You want my zip code, too?"

"Either you come up with an address or you go for a ride with me," Hollister warned.

"You already got my name. When there's a bed available I sleep at New Hope on Saint Andrews. I get my disability checks there. Salvation Army runs it. They're pretty good about messages and shit."

Hollister stepped closer to the man and stuffed the two twenty-dollar bills in his jacket pocket. "They're having a sale at Target. Why don't you drop in and update your wardrobe?"

"Fuck you, and your gay shirt," the man said, flipping Hollister the finger. "And don't think this makes me your fucking informant or nothing."

Hollister studied the man. "I can't make you anything you don't want to be."

"Oh." Rollins smiled sarcastically pulling the money from his pocket to glance at it. Then his glare returned to Hollister. "Where did you hear that? Latest fucking episode of Doctor Phil? You know the difference between me and you?"

Hollister waited for the man to answer.

"Money," Rollins said. "Just fucking money. That Arab came here in the Mercedes had money. You came here with money. Bet your ass the girl's dead 'cause of money." He snarled crumpling the bills in a tight fist.

Hollister turned and walked away.

George Franklin checked in at the British Airways counter before walking to the coffee shop in the International Lounge. It had been a long, sleepless, night. Every sound he heard in the hallway made him tense and expect a platoon of burly policemen to come crashing through the door. He was surprised when dawn finally came, and the police hadn't. He left for the airport three hours early, eager to get out of the country. He dreaded another cup of American tea but sitting idle was worse. There was a newsstand beside the entrance to the coffee shop. The headline on a morning newspaper read, "Arrest Made in Star's Death." Franklin paused, studied it for a moment and then picked it up. "Police have identified the man accused of Shannon Robert's death as Garth Mead."

Franklin read on. "Mead, a part-time actor from Texas was arrested yesterday after a high-speed pursuit." A sense of relief settled over Franklin as he realized the man with the French accent was indeed clever. He lowered the paper and reached for his cell phone. He had to call Paul DeSilva before the ignorant Italian did something stupid.

On South Wilcox three television mini-cam vans and a SUV from an All-News radio station crowded the sidewalk in front of Hollywood Division. The news and camera crews stood talking, drinking coffee and fighting boredom. Hollister glanced at them as he slowed and swung the detective car into the police parking lot. He was climbing out when a graying detective approached. The man was in his fifties. Hollister wasn't sure where he worked but he'd seen him around. His suit jacket looked baggy. "You're Hollister, aren't you?" the man questioned when he reached Hollister.

"Yeah?"

"You're working the Shannon Roberts case?"

"Do I know you?"

"Hummel, Rampart Robbery," the man answered.

"Listen I got a cousin that's a stringer for the Enquirer. Word's out they're offering a cool hundred thousand for any after death photos of Shannon Roberts."

Hollister bristled. "Fuck off," Hollister said with disgust.

"We could split sixty-forty, your favor," the man called.

"Go to hell," Hollister didn't look back.

"Seventy-thirty?"

Hollister refused an answer.

"You're throwing money away," Hummel warned. "They'll get the pictures from someone."

Max sat at his desk studying an array of pictures taken at the crime scene. His desk was surrounded by other curious detectives.

"Look at those tits," Drum, a detective with bulging arms, said. "Last time I saw them I had to pay for a ticket."

"You've paid for every tit you've ever seen," his partner, answered.

"Did you cop a quick feel after the photo, Max?" a sergeant asked as he peered over Max's shoulder at the collection of digital prints.

"Come on," another detective offered, "you know a Mormon's not allowed to touch an un-Mormon tit."

"Is that true, Max?"

"Of course, it's true," the sergeant defended, picking up one of the photos for a closer look. "If a Mormon touches an un-Mormon tit, legend has it he'll turn into a Jehovah's Witness."

"All right, perverts," Hollister said, reaching the desk, "show's over." He was annoyed. He wasn't sure why. Again, thoughts of Shannon and Kim were blurring.

Max gathered the photos into a neat stack and offered them to Hollister as the detectives moved away. "Autopsy is set for nine-fifteen," Max said.

Hollister nodded and declined the photos to thumb through a stack of telephone messages. KFWB, the Times, Sixty Minutes, NBC, The Star, ABC, People Magazine, A Current Affair."

"Pretty popular guys, aren't we?" Max smiled.

Hollister had hoped to find a message from Kim. Where the hell was she? When he didn't find one, he pushed them all aside.

"I've done the crime report, the five-ten, and the death report. Admin is typing up Garth Mead's statement." Max had a brown case folder and the collection of reports in front of him."

"Anything from Prints on the trash sack?" Hollister questioned.

"Nothing. Shannon Roberts doesn't have any prints in file so they're getting the ones rolled at the coroner's office for comparison. And yeah, Leon called to confirm her ID. Prints from her Canadian driver's license matched. Guess Shannon Roberts was born there?"

Hollister shrugged. None of it was surprising.

"You had any breakfast?" Max questioned.

"Yeah," Hollister answered, flushing with guilt as

if somehow Max knew Kim was gone. He covered it with a question of his own. "How about you?"

Max smiled. "Doris made me French toast and Canadian bacon. It's my favorite. Really gives you a boost too."

"It's called a sugar rush, Max," Hollister warned, "and it'll kill your big Mormon ass as quick as nicotine."

"Bullshit," Max defended, "you ever see a warning from the surgeon general on French toast?"

"We've got to talk to Justin what's-his-name," Hollister said, shifting the subject.

"Justin Conley, our witness?"

"Right. Get a complete statement."

"Why don't we get a video tape of his news conference yesterday," Max suggested sarcastically. "Doris watched it. She said the guy's great. Turns out he's a writer. We've got a dead movie star, the killer's an actor, and our only witness is a writer who works in a liquor store. Steven Spielberg should be investigating in this fuckin' mess."

Hollister leaned into the desk toward Max. "We got another wit."

"Where?" Max questioned.

"The alley. I found a wino that saw someone dumping Shannon in the trash bin."

"Was it Garth Mead?"

"Not unless his skin turned dark and he's hiding a Mercedes somewhere."

"Shit," Max hissed, "I just knew after visiting that

dump he lived in it wasn't him. Now that's two people saying it was a Mercedes."

"Let's reach out to DMV. Get every Mercedes registered in Beverly Hills and LA."

"Holy sauerkraut, Bat Man, there's more Mercedes here than in Germany."

"All we have to find is a silver one," Hollister smiled.

"Shit, my neighbor owns one," Max answered.

"Where was he Sunday morning?"

Hollister picked up a copy of the Times in a hallway as they left the station. The headlines read, "SUPERSTAR FOUND DEAD IN ALLEY." There was a picture of the smiling, vibrant, sexy Shannon Roberts. Hollister scanned the article as Max drove.

"Shannon Roberts, the reigning sex goddess of Hollywood was found dead early Sunday morning in Hollywood."

Hollister skipped a few lines. "An informed source at the Burbank Studios, where Shannon Roberts had just completed the first week on her latest motion picture, reported the actress in excellent form throughout the week. Monty Golden, agent to the actress for the past six years, was shocked by the news of her death. Paul DeSilva, the Executive Producer of 'Memories in Blue,' the motion picture which was to star Ms. Roberts had just begun its' sixteen-week production schedule, immediately suspended filming and announced that the entire cast and crew were stunned and saddened by the tragic news. This was to be Shannon Roberts' ninth feature with a budget of nearly a hundred million dollars. Walter Altice, the Director of the film, refused to speculate..."

"Anything interesting?" Max questioned as he headed the detective car southbound on the Hollywood freeway.

Hollister folded the paper closed. "The Dodgers lost."

The L.A. County Coroner was an elected official, thus, like most politicians, he never let an opportunity for publicity pass and the death of Shannon Roberts was focusing national attention on the nondescript coroner's building that stood in the shadow of the County General Hospital in East Los Angeles. The three major networks, as well as an army of independents, all had news crews waiting for the announcement. What killed Shannon Roberts? Hollister and Max walked through the crush of reporters and cameramen without notice to the automatic doors that led to the reception counter.

The smell, even at the reception counter, warned that death was nearby. It was a unique odor. A teasing aroma that blended the natural scent of human flesh with chemicals and decaying meat. Sensitive filters and a special circulation system helped minimize the smell, yet it hung heavy in the air.

"Hollister and Baxter," Max said to a clerk behind the counter. "Hollywood Homicide." He glanced at a notebook he pulled from his inside jacket pocket.

"Coroner's case number Two-two-one-three-zero-six-zero."

The clerk, dressed in a green surgical gown, searched a computer screen. "Zero six zero," he said, finding it. He looked at Hollister and Max. "You've got the Shannon Roberts case?"

"Want my autograph?" Max smiled.

"You get the celebrity suite. Examination Two-C." He gestured with a ballpoint pen. "Through the double doors. Fifth door on the right. Doctor Schulman will be your tour guide."

The wide polished corridor was lined with offices and harsh lighting, shadow-less lighting. Follow-up investigations unit, identifications, coffee room. Hollister was relieved the examination wasn't taking place in the main examination room where six examination tables were always busy and the corridor outside was lined with the waiting dead. Death in Los Angeles was big business. Shannon Roberts' death had lacked dignity and he was glad it wasn't going to be amplified by a more-or-less public autopsy. Those who never had a chance to see her in life were already elbowing one another to stare at her in death. Hollister resented them. He wasn't sure why. He wasn't even sure he was any different than they were. But this was his case and he was going to protect her... even in death. That was his job.

"E-Two-C," Max said and led the way through the door.

A technician had already made the "Y" cut to lay

wide the upper chest cavity of Shannon Roberts' body. The lower portion of the "Y" opened the lower abdomen. A bone saw had cut away the skull cap and it sat on the stainless rim of the examination table. The straw blonde hair and scalp had been pulled forward and hung in gray, fleshy, inside out folds over the body's sagging, unrecognizable face. The once prized breasts hung like over-ripe chalky melons from the filleted chest. The star had fallen to earth, Hollister thought as he looked at the filleted body.

There was a cameraman, an Asian technician, and a gray haired, barrel-chested man in spectacles and surgical gloves. All three of the men were dressed in green gowns. The gray-haired man was writing on an iPad. Max noticed the tip of his gloved finger was stained with blood.

"Doctor Schulman?" Max said as he and Hollister stepped into the room.

"Morning, you the detectives?" the gray-haired man queried, glancing over his spectacles.

"Baxter and Hollister," Max answered as he looked at the corpse on the stainless examination table and then the doctor.

"Hope you don't mind," Doctor Schulman said, "Figured I'd get the preliminary stuff out of the way."

"We don't feel cheated," Hollister assured. Hollister was always amazed by the fact one human could cut up another. He knew and appreciated the scientific reasons for it but couldn't comprehend the detachment it took to be the one to dismember a body like the once beautiful one laying before them. There was something sacred about the human body, alive or dead, and the thought of, as the saying went, turning them into a "canoe", was unthinkable, but a reality. It required a hands-on courage pathologists displayed on a routine basis.

"Find anything helpful for us, Doc?" Hollister questioned.

"Let me show you," the doctor said. Hollister and Max moved around the table to his side. The photographer and the short Oriental stepped aside. "Here," the doctor probed with his latex covered fingers, "along the back of the jawline. See the slight discoloration? That's a bruise. Hemorrhage beneath the skin. Same on the right side and the inside of her lower lip and lower gum also show signs of bruising."

"Which tells us?" Hollister questioned.

"We see this type of bruising in manual strangulations. I would speculate before the ligature was wrapped around her neck someone was forcing something down her throat."

"Any idea what it was?" Max asked.

The doctor picked up his iPad. "We've done some preliminaries on her blood and stomach contents."

"And?" Hollister pressed.

"She's full of alcohol and meth. I can't give you a quotative breakdown yet, but it was enough to kill. More than a girl like this would ever take by herself."

"And they were taken orally?" Hollister questioned.

"I'll swear to it," the doctor nodded.

The door to the examination room was pushed open by a dark-skinned Latin with a thin mustache. He was dressed in a tailored blue shirt and tie. With a look at the two detectives, he questioned, "Hollister and Baxter?"

"Yeah," Hollister answered.

"Ortiz, from Follow-up. Stop and see me on your way out? I'm down the hall on the right."

Hollister returned his attention to the doctor. "So, we can label this a forced overdose before the strangulation?"

"There's no doubt the combination of drugs and alcohol would have killed her, but there's also evidence that the primary cause of her death was asphyxiation."

"Asphyxiation?" Max questioned.

The doctor nodded agreement. "There's evidence of slight hemorrhaging in both lungs. A final desperate gasp for oxygen."

Garth Mead sat in the corner of his cell with his knees drawn up against his chest. The two burly black men that shared the cell with him had been taken away for a court appearance. Their sweaty stench still hung in the stale air.

Shannon Roberts was dead. They were saying he was her killer. A steady stream of jailers paraded by his cell during the night, pointing fingers, offering threats and obscenities. Garth knew it was only a matter of time before he would die at the hands of the jailors or his cellmates. My God, by now even his mother would know. He could see her on the six o'clock news. She'd be wearing her glasses and apron. "I knew something like this would happen. Ever since the police caught him exposing himself over in Tyler." His acting career was over. His family had turned against him. He had no friends. There was no hope. Sitting hunched in the corner, nervously fingering the cuff of his jail pants, the thought came to him, and even his mother would weep at his death. The insults and threats would be over. There would be no trial. There would always be the question. Was Garth Mead innocent? He slipped out of the trousers and quietly ripped the frayed cuff up the leg.

It was twenty minutes before a jailor making a routine cell check spotted Garth Mead hanging from the metal shield over the ceiling light. The striped trouser leg was knotted securely around his neck and laced through the light's metal shield. Garth Mead's tongue was sticking out through clenched teeth. There was a puddle of urine below his feet.

The autopsy of Shannon Roberts was to last over three hours. Hollister and Max, as every homicide cop did with every homicide victim, stood witness to it all. Fingernails were carefully clipped and taken away for analysis. Major organs were removed. Carefully examined, weighted and bagged. Samples of DNA, hair, urine, and stomach contents were taken. The body was measured and weighed. Dirt was scraped from both heels of her feet and bagged. Every move and every sound were recorded. It was methodical and thorough.

Declaring a finish, the pathologist raised his gloved hands to one of six cameras and then peeled away his latex gloves. His assistant began covering the body.

Hollister was glad it was over. "Her clothing is being examined?"

The doctor nodded agreement. "And when we're done, we'll send it all over to your lab."

"Thanks, Doc." Hollister took a final look at the

open cavity of the woman on the table and then nodded Max toward the door.

"Good luck with this, Gentlemen," the doctor as Max and Hollister moved for the door.

In the hallway Max offered, "So now we know she was likely force-fed alcohol and drugs, strangled and dumped in the alley. Why?"

"Maybe somebody that hates women?" Hollister suggested as they moved down the polished hallway to the examination room where the two dead police officers were being autopsied. Reaching the door Hollister took a deep breath and pushed through.

Fate was kind. The bodies of the two officers were covered. Their autopsies were over. "Got anything?" a sober Lieutenant Stratton questioned.

Detectives Parker and Torres, a second Hollywood team assisting with the shooting of the two officers were looking at a collection of bullets removed from the two bodies, now laying in two stainless bowls. A technician was collecting bloodied instruments and stained gauzes.

Hollister nodded appreciation to the two men and then turned his attention to the lieutenant. "Preliminary on Roberts looks like a probable forced combination of alcohol and drugs followed by strangulation."

"Someone she knew?" the lieutenant suggested.

"And trusted," Max added.

"And next?" Stratton questioned

"We connect the dots on those close to her."

Stratton nodded. "We recovered six rounds in here. Ballistics will have to confirm it, but they all look like nine-millimeter. We're betting all from Canfield's gun. Three in Jesse. Three in Canfield. This prick didn't miss once. He knew how to shoot."

"And he knew how to get Canfield's gun," Max added.

"Find this son-of-a-bitch," Stratton urged.

Coroner's Investigator Raymond Ortiz was behind a cluttered desk when Hollister and Max knocked and stepped into his open office. He gestured for the two detectives to sit down.

Ortiz pushed back in his chair. "I need some help with Shannon Roberts," he said looking puzzled. "Not one call. No one's come into ID the body. No calls from family. No calls from a mortuary. It's as if she's a fuckin' Jane Doe."

"No one wants a fallen star," Max said soberly.

"I thought maybe you guys might know some family, friends, somebody. Something to keep her out of the furnace. We don't need another Jane Doe. I got thirty-one of them on ice now."

"We'll see what we can do," Hollister promised, pushing out of his chair.

Max followed Hollister's lead.

"Appreciate it," Ortiz said as the two detectives

moved out the door.

Lieutenant John Stratton didn't have a good morning. Captain Harris, as Stratton expected, did not take the news of Garth Mead's suicide well.

"Fuck! How did this happen?"

The lieutenant tried to explain, but rationale wasn't of interest to the angry captain. "Either you solve this fuckin' mess or I turn it over to Robbery-Homicide downtown."

Stratton left the captain's office with his stomach in a knot. Retreating to his own office brought him little relief. Three people, one of whom claimed to be a warlock, were waiting with full confessions to Shannon Roberts' murder. The lieutenant told each of the three that confessions were accepted at the District Attorney's office between one and three. The warlock borrowed bus fare.

Calls from the press continued to pour in, jamming the lines as reporters tried for an inside story. The National Enquirer, the London Times, the Washington Post, and a myriad of others all asked for Stratton by name. He referred call after call to Media Relations.

It was noon when the day watch commander came into Stratton's office with word that a body had been found on Santa Monica Boulevard.

"Is it a murder?" Stratton questioned.

"Who knows?" the watch commander answered.

115

"Maybe the guy just slipped and fell on the knife, backwards."

"Shit," Stratton complained. He had no one to send. Parker and Torres were now in court. Cox and Zadie were forty-thousand feet over Kansas City headed for a fugitive in Akron, Ohio, and Hollister and Baxter were tied up on the Roberts' murder. "Okay, I'll roll on it," Stratton told the sergeant.

Thelma Washington always worried when something good came along. She was afraid of happiness because her black heritage had taught her happiness could be a fleeting, fragile thing. Miss Shannon, as Thelma called her, was as beautiful on the inside as she was on the outside and fourteen years at the Burbank Studios cafeteria had taught Thelma Washington that could be dangerous. "It was a place for tough sonsabitches," she once heard David Gerber say. It was there she meet Shannon while serving her lunch. They talked and then the young star offered her a job in her home. She often prayed for Shannon. "Lord, don't let those bastards hurt her." But Sunday night brought the news. News that she expected one day would come. She was visiting her sister Sarah in Leimert Park when the telephone rang, and a friend of Sarah's said to turn on the T.V. The two sisters watched in mute silence. Shannon Roberts was dead.

On Monday morning the grieving Thelma took the number fourteen bus to Beverly Hills. Shannon wouldn't be picking her up anymore. She didn't know what to expect. When she found the evidence seal on the back door, she read its warning, ignored it and went inside. Would it matter what the police did? Miss Shannon was dead, and nothing mattered. She fed the cat, poured herself a drink, and sat down to wait. She knew they'd come. And, soon they did.

After finding the broken evidence seal at the back door, Hollister tried the knob. The door was unlocked. Max followed him as they moved cautiously into the kitchen. The woman was sitting in a chair in the living room. She was holding the cat. The big wing-backed chair nearly hid her silhouette and with the curtains drawn, she saw the two men before they saw her. "Are you the police?"

Max jumped. "Holy, shit!"

"We're police," Hollister answered, as they holstered their weapons. "Who are you?"

"I'm Thelma. Miss Shannon's maid."

The two men sat down on a couch facing her.

"You gonna arrest me for breaking that tape of yours?"

"It's for those that don't belong here. I'm Sergeant Hollister. This is my partner, Detective Baxter. We're investigating Shannon's death."

"Do you know who killed her?"

"We're working on it."

"I know what killed her."

"What's that?"

"Trust," Thelma answered, stroking the purring

cat. "That's what killed her. She just trusted too much."

"When's the last time you saw Shannon?" Max questioned.

"Saturday," Thelma said, pausing to reflect. "About six. I was getting ready to go see my sister. Usually I stay here, but I hadn't seen Sarah in months, and she hasn't been well. Miss Shannon came into my room and said she had to run out. Something or someone about the picture she was making. I'm not sure. She said she'd be back in a couple. I told her I was leaving soon, and she said have a good time."

"You don't know who she went to see?" Hollister pressed.

Thelma shook her head. "I'm sorry."

"How about what door she went out?"

"I was in my room upstairs. I don't know."

"Did you lock up when you left?" Max asked.

Thelma shook her head. "No, I saw Miss Shannon's keys on the kitchen table, so I left the back door unlocked. We got an alarm."

Hollister remembered seeing the keys. "What time did you leave?" Hollister continued his questioning.

"Before six, 'cause I caught the five-fifteen bus at Sunset and Beverly."

Hollister now knew that Shannon Roberts had been lured away from the estate by someone she trusted.

The questions went on. They explored Shannon's daily life. Her routine, her personal habits, knowing

Shannon Roberts would help them know her killer. How many hours a day did she work? What time did she leave? Did she drive? What time did she return? Who called her? Who came to the house? Did she have a male companion? Did men spend the night? Did Shannon spend nights away? Had she ever seen Shannon drunk, drugged? Was Shannon happy? Did she have any family?

"Do you mind if I smoke?" Thelma asked, putting the cat down.

"Go ahead." Hollister smiled. Thelma shook a cigarette from a wrinkled pack she pulled from a pocket of her dress.

Hollister noticed her bony fingers were trembling.

"I don't know any family. Miss Shannon said she lived with her grandmother before. The woman's dead now. Said her parents were killed in a car crash when she was in high school. No family ever called or came by."

"Have you had any phone calls today?" Hollister questioned.

"Nothing. It's been dead quiet," Thelma exhaled.

"No calls, no flowers, nothing?" Max said in disbelief.

"Why would they call? The Golden Goose is dead," Thelma said sarcastically.

"Did she have a cell phone?" Hollister questioned.
"Yes."

"Do you know the number?"

Thelma provided the seven-digit number without hesitation. Max made a note of it. No cell phone had been recovered. If found it would be key.

"If anybody calls or if you think of anything else that might help, we'd like you to call us," Hollister said, offering a business card to Thelma.

Thelma looked at the card. "What should I do with the place?"

Hollister stood. "Continue to take care of it. I'm sure you'll be paid for your services."

"What's gonna happen to it?" she asked with worried eyes.

"I don't know," Hollister answered.

Max stood.

"You can take the seals off the doors," Max said. "We don't need them anymore."

Thelma nodded. There were tears in her bloodshot eyes. "I want you to find the sonofabitch that did this to Miss Shannon," she said, pointing her cigarette at the two men.

"Can you believe no one's called?" Max said as he steered the detective car south on Beverly Boulevard.

"Welcome to the real Hollywood," Hollister answered from the passenger's side. Secretly he was relieved to learn Shannon Roberts was different. She was good. Just as he thought. He was sorry he had never met her. He was certain they would have been attracted to one another. The roots of his withered fantasy were finding new life.

"You want to get some lunch?" Max said with a glance at his watch.

"Let's take a couple burgers back to the station. I want to call the Burbank Studios. Paul DeSilva was the last to call before Shannon left the house."

"You think he's it?"

"I think we've gotta find out. She called home to say she'd forgotten her keys, but Thelma had already left. It's on the answer phone. That doesn't sound much like a kidnapping does it? She knew whoever picked her up, and she called home from wherever she went."

"Any messages on the tape after Shannon's call?" Max questioned as he slowed for a red light.

"One," Hollister answered. "From her agent. Monty Golden. We're gonna have to talk to him too. He wanted to know why Shannon didn't show up at something DeSilva had planned. He sounded pissed."

"Then she didn't see DeSilva?" Max said as he watched a shapely young woman walk a snow-white poodle across the crosswalk.

"Maybe she did," Hollister cautioned, "and DeSilva was just covering his ass."

"DeSilva," Max said, "you think that's Italian?"

Hollister nodded. "Yeah, maybe an Italian that owns a silver Mercedes."

Sitting at Stratton's desk in the homicide office, Hollister picked up the telephone and dialed information to get the number for the studio. After punching in the number his eyes drifted to a photograph on the desk. It was a three by five color photograph of John Stratton, his wife and teenage son in front of a fishing boat. The woman, who looked a bit heavy in her two-piece bathing suit, was holding a fish. Hollister silently wondered what it was like to have a family, a fishing boat, maybe even a son. The vast number of unhappy cops he knew told him it wasn't all smiles and fish. He'd listened to many stories about unfaithful wives, uncontrollable kids and crushing debt to know it wasn't the answer to all his problems. It was the green grass syndrome. He was on one side of the fence; Stratton was on the other. Hollister knew the fence was getting higher every year. Maybe he'd never know what it was like on the other side. He had hoped his cell phone would ring all day. Kim hadn't called. Christ maybe she never would.

"Good afternoon," a female voice said in his ear. "Mister DeSilva's office."

Hollister's attention returned to the phone. "This is Sergeant Hollister LAPD, Homicide, Hollywood Division. I'd like to talk to Paul DeSilva." "I'm sorry," the sensual voice answered. "He's off the lot for lunch."

"When will he be back?"

"I'm afraid he's busy with appointments all afternoon. We do have a three o'clock available on Wednesday."

"Tell Mister DeSilva either he's in his office this

afternoon," Hollister warned, "or we'll talk here, at the station."

"I'll see he gets the message," the voice said with a chill.

"Thank you," Hollister hung up. "Bitch."

Hollister and Max were headed for their car in the station parking lot when Lieutenant Stratton pulled in. He had a tall, gaunt man with him and the way the man was sitting in the seat beside Stratton, it was obvious his hands were shackled behind his back. The lieutenant stopped the car beside them and climbed out the driver's side. "You heard about Garth Mead?"

"What about him?" Hollister questioned.

"Hung himself in his cell. He's dead."

Hollister wasn't sure how he felt about the news. Suicide seemed to fit Mead's character.

"Shit, too bad," Max said.

"Anything more from the autopsy?' Stratton asked, leaning on the roof of the car.

"Like we told you, forced OD—meth, alcohol, and strangulation," Hollister answered.

"So, you think you still got a killer out there?" the lieutenant pressed.

"Don't you?" Hollister countered.

"The captain doesn't think much of your wino witness," Stratton shrugged. "He'd like to wrap this thing up."

"So, would we," Hollister agreed, "but we'd like to

solve it first."

"Isn't it possible Mead was the killer?"

"Possible but not probable," Hollister cautioned.

"You're gonna have to keep on this," Stratton explored, massaging the back of his neck.

"Who's inside?" Max said with a glance at the dejected looking man inside the car.

"Randy Townsend," Stratton nodded, "stabbed his lover with a six-inch knife."

"Appropriate length," Max quipped.

"You got anything solid, something to tell Harris? Commander's pressing him, the deputy chief is pressing the commander. It goes to the top. This may get passed downtown."

"We're on our way to the Burbank Studios," Hollister said, being deliberately vague, "And we're looking at Mercedes owners."

"Fuck," Stratton muttered. "Keep me posted."

"Get Harris off our ass," Hollister cautioned.

"This mess may cost us all our asses," Stratton warned.

A directory in the carpeted lobby of the Ladd building at the studio told Hollister and Max Paul DeSilva's office was on the second floor. The wide second-story corridor was quiet and lined with bigger than life posters of the studio's stars. Max was awed by the pictures. "Boy, if Doris could see this."

A polished brass plaque on the wall beside a glossy

wooden door read "Paul DeSilva". Hollister lead the way into the reception office.

The woman behind the desk had raven hair and green eyes. Contacts, Hollister guessed. Her skin and makeup were flawless, accenting the fine features of her model-like face. Another aging actress become secretary; Hollister concluded. A pair of glasses hung on a gold chain around her neck. They rested on the top of her bosom which accented how many buttons on the blouse were unbuttoned. The woman paused from reading a computer screen and looked at the two detectives. It was a look of recognition. "One of you is Sergeant Hollister, I presume."

"I'm Hollister. This is my partner, Baxter."

The woman nodded to acknowledge the introduction. Her eyes never left Hollister. "I'm Meg Rogers, Mister DeSilva's Executive Assistant. Please sit down. I'll tell him you're here."

Max led the way to an arrangement of couches and tables. The couch was soft and low and sitting in it made Hollister feel awkward as if he were sitting on the floor. The heavier Max looked funny with his knees in the air, but he said nothing as he picked up a copy of Variety from the glass table and thumbed through it.

"Would either of you like a cool drink. Perhaps a bottle of water?" the woman questioned with a glance as she picked up the telephone.

Hollister thought it sounded like a line from a film. In Hollywood, drinks weren't served cold. They were cool. He wondered why it irritated him. Maybe it was because Paul DeSilva was living the fantasy all men dreamed of. Big-titted secretary, big office. Naw, it wasn't jealousy Hollister assured himself. This stuff wasn't real. Behind the secretary's acting lessons were as many fears as any woman carried. Take the movie posters off the wall and the room would look like any other corporate office. Maybe that was it. Maybe it was knowing that it was an illusion. All smoke and mirrors. All pretend. Not so unlike the lie he was living, Hollister thought. He was a frightened middle-aged man whose wife had just left him. Illusions and lies. Life was full of them. Little was as it really seemed. Except Shannon Roberts in the trash bin. That was real.

"Nothing for me," Max answered.

"No, thanks," Hollister added.

He watched as a polished nail touched a button and the woman spoke into the receiver. She turned her chair away to mask the words. When she hung up, she turned to them. "Paul's on a long-distance call to London. He'll be with you in a minute."

Hollister listened to the woman's voice, but he was staring at her breasts. Her nipples were pushing at the material of her blouse. When he raised his eyes, they met hers. She held his look for a moment and then returned to her reading. The look told Hollister he could have her. It gave him a sense of power. Paul DeSilva needed the office, the title, and a string of motion pictures to bring women close to him.

Hollister needed only two minutes of quiet waiting. He wondered if it were another of his fantasies. His magic look sure as hell hadn't satisfied Kim. Where was she? Why hadn't she called? The intercom on the desk buzzed. The woman picked up the receiver, spoke quietly, and then looked to the two detectives. "You may go in now."

Paul DeSilva opened the door. He was wearing a blue blazer and an open collared shirt that revealed a mat of curly hair on his chest and a collection of gold chains around his neck. He took Max's hand. "How are you? Come on in."

He shook Hollister's hand too then looked to Meg Rogers. "Hold my calls."

"Sit down fellas," DeSilva urged, closing the door.

The two detectives sat in comfortable chairs facing an executive desk. The walls were lined with awards and plaques. DeSilva rounded his desk and sat down in the high-backed, padded chair. Hollister decided why the man looked familiar. He looked like a younger Hugh Heffner.

"Just fuckin' shocking, isn't it?" DeSilva laced his fingers together to reveal a variety of gold rings.

"The good die young," Max said philosophically. "I'm Detective Baxter. This is my partner, Sergeant Hollister."

DeSilva studied Max soberly. "Didn't I see you in a movie a couple of years ago?"

Max smiled, straightened in the chair some. "Naw. I'm not an actor. People used to say I look a lot like

Alex Karis. Remember him?"

"Oh, yes, I knew Alex well. He co-starred in a film I did in Brazil a couple years ago, and you're right. There's an uncanny resemblance."

"What can you tell us about Shannon Roberts' death?" Hollister said, not interested in the bullshit.

DeSilva looked wounded as he placed an open hand over his heart. "What can I tell you about Shannon Roberts' death! You think I know something about her fuckin' murder?"

"You didn't answer my question," Hollister countered soberly.

"Hey," DeSilva said, rocking forward in his chair to slap his desktop. "You got fuckin' nerve, fella. Walkin' into my office to accuse me of knowin' something about a fuckin' murder."

"I asked you what you knew about Shannon Roberts' death," Hollister repeated slow and deliberate.

"I'll tell you what I fuckin' know," DeSilva said as if greatly offended. "I know I gave Debbie Cross one of her first fuckin' acting jobs. Yeah, that's who she used to be. Debbie Cross. I saw she had what it takes. I said, 'hey, if you're gonna make it in this business, you need a name and Debbie Cross isn't it.' Next thing I know she's co-starring in a sit com on ABC and calling herself Shannon Roberts."

"How long did you know her?" Max asked, playing the good cop.

"Hell, first met her at Universal. I was doing Logan's Gate. I used her in a couple episodes. That must be five, six fuckin' years ago."

"Did you ever work with her again after that?" Max continued.

"We saw each other around. I bought her dinner in New York once. We were always friends, you know. But I never hired her again until Memories in Blue."

"That's the picture she was working on?" Hollister questioned.

DeSilva stared at his desktop and shook his head. "One hundred and ninety-four million dollars plus change right down the fuckin' drain." He looked to them. "And that's just the bottom line of the budget. Figure in the first twelve to eighteen weeks, the picture may have grossed sixty, seventy million, pick up an Academy Award...I'd own this fuckin' town."

"You hired her for the picture?" Hollister asked.

"Hired her! The fuckin' picture was conceived and written for her. I never considered anyone else. There was no one else."

"How did she feel about the picture?" Hollister pressed.

"Same as me," DeSilva said, pushing back into his plush chair. "She was crazy about it. She knew this was the big one."

Hollister sensed DeSilva was lying. "There were no problems between you and Shannon over the picture, or anything else?"

DeSilva pointed a finger at Hollister. He looked livid. "Who's tellin' you this shit? That little Jewish rat of an agent she's got. If I were you, I'd check out that little pervert. Everybody in this town knows he's got a fifteen-year-old live-in."

"We're talking about the murder of Shannon Roberts," Hollister reminded.

"Yeah, so what the fuck you doin' in my office? You find her in a trash bin and here you are knockin' on my door."

"She was working for you, Mister DeSilva," Max said with a smile to ease the tension. "It seemed the place to start."

"Yeah, okay, but I don't like his fuckin' attitude," DeSilva said, shooting a look at Hollister.

"It comes from talking to assholes all the time," Hollister said soberly.

"There," DeSilva shouted. "That's what I mean." He pointed a finger at Hollister.

"He didn't mean it the way you think," Max burned a look at Hollister. "Tell us about the last time you saw Shannon?"

"Friday, here on the lot. Sound stage twenty-two. We were shootin' interiors. I stopped by to say hello. You know, just to encourage her. She looked fabulous."

"No hint of problems?" Max said.

"Nothing," DeSilva assured.

"How about drugs or booze," Max questioned.

"Neither," DeSilva answered without hesitation. "She was so clean it wouldn't surprise me if she was a virgin."

"Do you have any idea who may have killed her?"

"I don't know why he did it, but from what I hear, you got some two-bit actor in jail, don't you?"

"We have reason to believe there are others involved," Hollister granted, to read the reaction.

It had a sobering impact on DeSilva. He wet his lips and fingered one of the gold chains around his neck. "Others? What do you mean others?"

"That's all we can tell you," Hollister answered, hoping to add to his worry.

DeSilva pushed back in his chair. He looked shaken. "Hey," he said, forcing a grin. "I wish to God I could help, but what do I know about fuckin' murder? I haven't done a Hitchcock in years."

"When's the last time you talked to Shannon?" Hollister questioned.

"Friday. Just like I said," DeSilva answered defiantly. "Now unless there's something else, I've got a meetin' I'm late for."

"We'll need to talk to the crew, look at the dailies from the picture," Max said.

DeSilva pushed out of his chair, announcing the conclusion of the meeting. "Show you anything we've got. One hundred percent cooperation. Tell Meg what you need. She'll handle it."

Hollister and Max pushed out of their chairs. "Appreciate your help," Max said.

"Hey, come on, I want whoever's part of Shannon's fuckin' murder in jail," DeSilva said, draping an arm around Max's shoulder as he guided them to the door. "You know that's a good jacket. Where did you get it,

131

Cicero's in Beverly Hills?"

"Costco in Glendale," Max answered.

DeSilva shook their hands at the door. "Give me a call anytime. Ciao."

"So, what did you think of Mister DeSilva?" Max questioned as they drove by the guard house at the studio's main gate, ignoring a red sign that warned, All Vehicles Must Stop.

"More or less your basic asshole," Hollister answered. "Plus, he's a liar."

"You think he's a murderer?"

"Be nice if he was since he's such a sleaze."

"I liked his secretary. Great legs."

"Did she have legs?" Hollister smiled.

Max left for home as soon as they returned to the station. His thirteen-year-old had a softball game at five-thirty. Hollister lingered, going through another collection of telephone messages hoping to find one from Kim. There was none. He fought an urge to call her cell. He glanced at the clock. She'd still be at her realty office. Maybe all she needed was to hear he missed her? Maybe all this was just a cry for attention? Maybe she was waiting? But then he knew she wasn't. He turned his attention to updating the homicide chronology on their desk top computer and drafted an internal email to Lieutenant Stratton and Captain Harris with bullet points highlighting the investigative steps and summarizing their interview with DeSilva.

A detective from the Auto team walked by and tossed a copy of the L.A. Times onto Hollister's desk. "Film at eleven," the officer quipped and headed for the door. Hollister looked at the folded front page of the paper. A picture of a smiling vibrant Shannon Roberts filled a third of the page. Below it in bold print the headline read, FALLEN STAR. Hollister reached for the paper, studied the picture. Jesus, Shannon Roberts was beautiful. He wondered what she was like in life, whether her beauty was more than skin deep. Maybe his suspicions of Shannon Roberts' beauty, his distrust of the dead star he didn't know, was rooted in the fact his wife, the woman who had deserted him, the woman who was missing, the woman who hadn't called, resembled the fallen star.

Forty minutes later and two blocks from his home, Hollister started hoping Kim's BMW would be parked in the driveway. It wasn't. He switched his hope to the answering machine in the living room. There were two messages. One from a reporter at the Times, another from the producer of 20/20, but nothing from Kim.

Refusing to be a prisoner of hope, Hollister changed clothes and went to the work-out room. He vented his frustrations with weights, bicycling and rowing for forty minutes. He followed the sweaty workout with a dip in the back-yard Jacuzzi. He still felt empty. He ate more cold chicken and pretended interest in a truck pulling contest on ESPN. It was ten minutes of nine when the telephone rang. Hollister washed down a piece of chicken with beer, switched off the T.V. and bolted to the telephone on the kitchen counter. "Hello."

"Kim Hollister, please," a male voice said in his ear.

Hollister stiffened with suspicion. "Who's calling?"

"Dean Benson," the man answered. "Kim left a message with my answering service in regard to a condo I have advertised."

"She's not interested," Hollister said and hung up.

He slept on the couch. It was as if he refused to acknowledge the loneliness of the bedroom, hoping somehow the reality of it wouldn't touch him. He was wrong.

Hollister was the first to arrive at the squad room in the morning. He hadn't slept well. Maybe it was the case or maybe his approaching thirty-ninth birthday. He refused to consider Kim's departure as a factor. Here at the station he wasn't a deserted male pushing forty with a mid-life crisis. Here he was an experienced detective sergeant entrusted with a major homicide case. If that didn't prove he was a success in his chosen field, what the hell would? Fuck Kim!

He stopped the nagging thoughts by opening the case file on the Roberts' murder. He read it cover to cover. A cursory review of the facts and proximity made the unfortunate Garth Mead look like the killer, but that was too easy. Mead had no real motive. Garth Mead was little more than a pervert caught in the limelight. The silver Mercedes and its swarthy driver seemed the real key. Hollister wondered how good David Rollin's alcoholic recollection was. Was it a silver Buick instead of a Mercedes? Maybe even a BMW? And what about the driver? Was Rollins really describing himself, as alcoholics often did? But it felt right. Hollister listened to Garth Mead's voice in his memory. It was a convincing tone. "I swear to God I didn't kill her." Motive was what was missing. If they could find the motive someone wanted Shannon Roberts dead, they would find their killer.

Returning his attention to the paperwork on the desk Hollister thumbed through a stack of telephone messages. He was hoping to find one from Kim. "Lee, I'm so sorry! Call me, Please?" It was a fantasy. There was no message from Kim. There was a message from Raymond Ortiz, the follow-up investigator at the coroner's office. Thanks – Family & friends have been in touch regarding dispo of body. Hollister made a mental note to call Ortiz later. Who was calling regarding Shannon Roberts' body could be important? Murder, experience had taught, was seldom committed by those beyond the circle of family and friends. There was another message from a reporter he knew at a local TV station. No doubt what he wanted. And another message from Meg Rogers at Stonegate Studios. Please call. More bullshit from DeSilva, Hollister thought as he studied the telephone number. He folded the message and pushed it into a pocket. DeSilva could wait. Waiting would help push the cooperate button.

"Glad you're here," a harried looking Lieutenant Stratton said glancing into the Homicide cubicle and then crossing to Hollister's desk. "Got your email. Captain Harris doesn't like your wino wit. I'm not thrilled with him either. You've been on this two full days. You're gonna have to come up with something solid or Harris says it goes downtown."

Hollister shrugged it off, "So throw me in the briar patch."

Max arrived and joined them. "Morning, Crime Busters."

Stratton and Hollister ignored him.

"If it wasn't Garth Mead," Stratton continued, "you need to stay on this."

"You know how many hours of overtime we logged on the 'Man from Glad' last week?" Max protested, as he sat down beside Hollister. "My dog hardly recognizes me anymore."

"I'm only passing on the pressure I'm feeling," Stratton defended offering yet another telephone message. "And speaking of the Man from Glad, Vice put a pimp in jail last night. He's at Central. His name's Edward G. He claims he knows something about the 'Man from Glad.' Shannon Roberts was found with that trash sack over her head like the other 'Man from Glad' hits. Find a connection, find something!"

"The sack wasn't over her head," Hollister corrected.

"I saw her. Maybe it was over her head before she went into the dumpster?"

Hollister knew some of the pressure Stratton was facing was linked to his pending oral board for captain. Stratton was beginning the transition from cop to administrator. He was becoming management. His career had become his partner and it left little room for anyone else. Hollister and Max cleared their desk before leaving the station. Max folded an armful of computer printouts. "Twenty dollars if you can tell me how many Mercedes there are in LA County." Max dropped the sheaf of papers into a drawer.

"Let's see," Hollister paused to consider the question, "you count the number of millennials, divide by two, add a couple thousand Asians, throw in a shit load of dope dealers and multiply that by the number of days in the week."

"Let's just say there's a whole bunch," Max allowed, "and only God and a Kraut paint crew in Germany know how many of 'em are silver."

Max drove as they headed to the central jail. "You notice John seems a little preoccupied."

"It's called becoming a captain. First you have to become an asshole."

After showing their badges to a camera at the gate and parking, they were buzzed through the set of metal doors into the Central Jail's gray reception area, Hollister and Max checked their guns in small wall lockers and again showed ID to a uniformed sheriff's deputy behind a heavy glass. Max talked to the khaki clad jailor through a speaker on the counter. "Hollister and Baxter from Hollywood Homicide. We'd like to see Edward G. Booking number two-oh-two-oh-one-oh-four-three."

"Hey, Baker," the jailor barked into an intercom, "bring up Glass, oh, four, three. LA dicks wanna see him."

"Oh, four, three," a filtered male voice answered

over the intercom.

"Interview three," the face behind the mesh said, "down the hall on the left."

The room was small and stale. The door opened and a muscular black jailor stiff-armed Edward G. into the room. The man was dressed in a baggy orange jump suit. They were wrinkled and soiled. The shadow of a beard was turning his boyish face dark. He was frail and hollow-eyed. Hollister wondered how such a man operated as a pimp."

"Sit down," Max said.

"You got a cigarette?" Edward G. asked as he slid into a chair across the table from the two detectives.

"Look at me," Max said, ignoring the question. "I'm a two-hundred-and-twenty-pound lie detector, and the moment I detect a lie, we're walking out the door. You understand?"

Edward G. studied the two detectives. "What guarantee I got you'll make me a deal?"

"Look at it this way," Hollister suggested, "you got nothing to lose."

"Okay," Edward G. said. "I heard of these two guys out in the valley. They make kiddy porn. Low budget video tape shit. I hear they've been asking around for young stuff."

"What's their names?"

"Raoul and somebody. I'm not sure."

"What do they look like?"

139

"Raoul's a tall guy. Maybe thirty. Black greasy hair. Other guy's a fat bean, travels with him. Kinda no-neck, you know? I don't know his name."

"What kind of a car do they drive," Max continued. He was making notes. Hollister was watching Edward G. searching for hints of fabrication. He saw none.

"A blue Lincoln. Four door. Nice car. Looks like Raoul has bucks."

"You notice the license?"

"Come on, I ain't no fuckin' cop. I look at people. I don't look at numbers."

"Uh huh, well, where do these people live?" Max pressed.

"Once I was bullshittin' with Raoul and he said he had to drive in from the Valley. That's all I know."

"You don't know the address?"

"You don't ask addresses on the street," Edward G. answered.

"Well, when you found him a girl, how did you get in touch?" Max said matter-of-factly, deliberately leading the man.

"I called him," Edward G. said and then blinked as he realized his mistake. "But I didn't say I ever got him a girl," he added, straightening in his chair. "Don't put words in my mouth, man."

"What's the number, Eddie?"

"I don't know."

"Bullshit," Max spit at him slapping the table with a flat hand.

Edward G. jumped in his chair

"He's lying," Hollister said and started to push up out of his chair. "Let's go. He doesn't want to deal. He just wants to play fuck around."

"Okay, okay," Edward G. pleaded. "I'll tell you."

"You gotta do more than tell," Max warned. "You gotta testify."

Edward G. bit at a fingernail before he answered. "Three-three-nine, six-one, seven-oh."

Max jotted the number down.

"Does this make me a snitch?" Edward G. questioned with a look at the two detectives.

Hollister pushed out of his chair. "Look at it this way, for you, that's a step up."

At the police building, Hollister and Max took an elevator to Intelligence Division on the fourth floor. Max gave the attractive policewoman at the reception desk the telephone number Edward G. provided. "We need an address to go with this."

"Two or three days," the policewoman said. "We'll give you a call."

"Do you have any kids," Max tried to read the name on the I.D. card the woman wore clipped to her lapel.

"Hanes," the brunette answered. "And yes, I have two children. You selling Amway or something?"

"No," Max smiled, "I'm not selling anything. How old are the kids?"

"Girls," the brunette said, "Fourteen and sixteen. Why?"

"The people at the other end of that number have raped, sodomized and strangled two little girls. One fifteen. One seventeen. They put the bodies in trash sacks and dumped them in garbage bins."

"I'll have the address for you in twenty minutes," the brunette promised.

"Thanks," Max winked.

Thelma Washington never liked Monty Golden. He was a pervert and she didn't trust perverts. She often wondered why Shannon did. Thelma had only seen Golden twice, although Shannon talked about him, and with him, often. She even seemed to like him. On the two occasions when he had come to the house, once for a meeting and once on Shannon's birthday six months ago, he never spoke to her. Now with Miss Shannon dead he was back and with him was one of what he called his "personal assistants," an eighteen-year-old boy in tight jeans with bleached hair and a gold nose ring. They were upstairs searching Miss Shannon's bedroom looking for what he called important papers. Thelma damned herself for not hiding all of Shannon's jewelry. She'd thought about it, but afraid someone might accuse her of stealing, she'd not done it. Now it seemed it was too late.

Monty Golden's lie of searching for papers hadn't fooled Thelma for a minute, but she was uncertain what to do. She didn't think the police would do anything. A poor black maid accusing a rich white man of stealing wasn't likely to generate much excitement, then she remembered the card the two detectives had left her. When she called, the man said they were out of the office. "Don't you police have radios or something?" Thelma complained. "I need help."

"I'll see what I can do," the man promised.

Golden and the boy had been upstairs for over an hour when the chime at the front door sounded. Thelma had been waiting in the kitchen. She hurried to the front door. "Thank God," she said. Hollister and Max stood waiting.

"What's the problem?" Hollister was surprised at her reaction.

Thelma pointed to the stairs as Monty Golden and his young companion appeared. "They're into Miss Shannon's things."

"Officer." Monty Golden smiled displaying thirty-eight-thousand dollar-implants. He pulled an embossed business card from a pocket and offered it to Hollister. "Monty Golden, of the Golden Agency. Shannon's personal agent and close personal friend."

Hollister took the card and glanced at it.

"Him and that toe head was in Miss Shannon's things," Thelma accused, pointing a boney finger at Golden. "Lord knows what they was taking."

"Business papers," Monty defended with a nervous smile. "Just looking for contracts. I've got attorney's calling from MCA, Columbia. They want answers."

"Check his briefcase," Thelma suggested. "Look in there."

Monty shot Thelma a burning look. Hollister noticed he was wearing a toupee.

"What's in the briefcase?" Max glanced at the leather covered case in Monty's hand.

Monty tried for a look of innocence, but the sweat on his smooth Botox forehead was betraying him. "Contracts, papers...things."

"Then you won't mind showing us," Max said. Monty Golden paled even more. The nervous blond boy with him flashed Golden a look. "I told you," he cried, childlike. "I said leave the shit alone, but no, you had to take it."

"Shut up," Golden snapped.

"Open the briefcase," Hollister ordered.

Golden swallowed the lump in his throat and set the briefcase flat on a tabletop.

"Go on," Max urged.

Golden's fingers trembled as they snapped open the latches. He closed his eyes and lifted the lid.

"Lord," Thelma said. They stared at an array of gold, silver and diamonds. The collection of necklaces, bracelets, watches, pins and earrings lay in a tangle in the open briefcase. "It's not what you think," Golden seemed close to tears.

"Your ten percent, right?" Hollister said sarcastically.

"I bought most of this for Shannon," Golden defended, looking at the faces around him, searching for a hint of sympathy. "I wasn't stealing. I was going to make sure it was safe."

"Tell you what, Monty," Max closed the briefcase and pulled it away from Golden. "We'll relieve you of that great responsibility." Hollister took Golden by the arm and marched him to the front door. The blond boy followed. When they reached the door, Hollister looked at the youth. "Go find a job where you can keep your pants on, kid." The boy disappeared. Hollister turned to Golden. "What's left of Shannon Roberts is laying unclaimed at the morgue. I want you to do something about that."

"Why, yes, yes of course," Monty Golden answered.

"We're gonna want to talk. I don't want you hard to find."

"My, my office is on Sunset."

"I know where your office is." Hollister stiff-armed the man out the door, slamming it behind him.

"You know," Max said as they walked to the detective car parked in the front driveway of the Roberts' estate, "Hollywood is a land of illusions, isn't it?"

"Profound," Hollister answered. He wasn't in the mood for another of Max's philosophical views on life.

"You see pictures of Shannon Roberts in People magazine, the Enquirer, on TV. It's all smiles and glamour, the good life," Max continued.

"Uh huh."

Max climbed in behind the wheel. Hollister on the passenger's side. "But the reality is their lives are really screwed up. Nothing is what it seems. It's all phony."

"Shocking," Hollister was being deliberately sarcastic. He was annoyed with Max. He didn't want to compare his life with anyone. Why the hell hadn't Kim called.

Max started the car. "Me, I'd sooner have a piece of

the rock. Look at us," he said pulling the car in gear. "We got something. Someone at home who cares. Someone to share a life with."

Hollister was smarting with shame. He said nothing as the quiet tree-lined streets of Beverly Hills swept by. They were almost to Sunset when the radio called, "Six-William-twenty-two, meet Six-William-thirty on tac-two."

"Roger," Hollister answered. He switched frequencies and keyed the mike. "William-thirty, this is twenty-two."

"Yeah, twenty-two," Stratton's filtered voice answered from the radio. "The address you requested on the 'Man from Glad' came in. I'm in Tarzana on Van Alden at Ryder, behind the seven-eleven, just west of the freeway. Meet us Code-two?"

"Roger," Hollister answered, "We're on our way."

Dressed in casual street clothes, Lieutenant Stratton along with Detectives Parker and Torres were standing beside Stratton's SUV with big mud tires when Max pulled the detective car in beside them minutes later.

Stratton flipped open a yellow tablet as Max and Hollister joined them at the hood of the SUV. "Intelligence gave us the name Raoul Sandoval. Address, one-nine-six-four Green Rush Place. That's about two miles West on Van Alden. Tee intersection to the right. Cul-de-sac street. One way in, one way out. Raoul Sandoval has eight arrests for sale of pornographic materials." Stratton paused, when there were no questions, he went on. "I called SID prints, asked for a comparison of Sandoval and the three lifts we got from the trash sack the little girl's body was found in. We got a make. Little finger left hand. Index and thumb from the right hand."

"How about the sack from Shannon Roberts?" Hollister questioned.

"Nothing," Stratton answered.

"We still got 'im by the balls," Parker suggested.

"Figured we'd send you up there, Max. In my SUV you look less like a cop than any of us."

"Thanks," Max quipped.

"Go door to door looking for tree trimming work," Hollister suggested. "The SUV looks like it belongs to a tree trimmer."

"Tree trimmer," Max grimaced. "Shit, I was hoping at least to be a Kirby vacuum guy."

"Knock on a couple of doors, then the suspect's, see if anyone's home."

"Let's do it," Max agreed, taking off his gun.

Green Rush Place was tranquil when Max turned the SUV onto the cul-de-sac street. The driveways of the six and seven hundred thousand-dollar homes were dotted with BMWs, Audis, and Mazdas. The lawns were lush green and carefully manicured. A Japanese gardener with a Mexican assistant were the only ones visible on the street. Max drove slowly, studying the white numbers stenciled on the curb in front of each house. He found one-nine-six-four at the center of the cul-de-sac circle. The house was a Spanish ranch style with smooth stucco arches and an orange tile roof. A fan-folded, white curtain covered the front window and there were no cars in the driveway. The Bronco slid by and pulled to the curb several houses away.

Max keyed the portable radio lying beneath his seat. "Found the house. Nothing in the driveway. I'm gonna knock on a few doors."

A two click reply answered him. Hollister and Lieutenant Stratton were parked two blocks away on Greenbriar Drive.

Max, clipboard in hand, started four houses from Raoul Sandoval's home. He marched to a front door, deliberately eyeing the trees along the front of the house. He rang the bell and waited. A woman in her fifties opened the door. She had gray hair and bags under her eyes. There was a cigarette hanging from her mouth. It danced when she spoke. "You the pool man?"

"Got a problem with the pool?" Max smiled.

"No, you got a problem," the woman answered. "I didn't pay thirty thousand dollars to sit in cold water."

"Actually," Max said, clicking his ballpoint pen at the woman. "I'm not the pool man. I'm from Max's Tree Service; I noticed the locust trees in front could use a little TLC."

149

"They're not locust, they're Chinese Elm." The door slammed in Max's face.

Max clicked his ballpoint. "Could've sworn they were locust."

At the second house a talkative housewife ordered what the surprised Max estimated to be six hundred dollars' worth of trimming work.

"We don't want any," a gruff balding man said through a part in the double doors at the third house.

Max's nine-millimeter automatic was locked in the glove box of the SUV. He felt naked without it, especially now, walking to the front door of the suspected Man from Glad murderer.

He was nervous, even a little frightened, he confessed, hoping it wouldn't show in his voice. He wondered what he would say. There wasn't a tree in the front yard, just a collection of large tropical plants. He had no idea what the plants were. The front door was wooden planking to match the Spanish design. It looked massive and strong. Difficult, if not impossible to kick in, Max told himself. It was cool in the shade near the door. He took a breath, cleared his throat and pushed the doorbell. He heard the chime deep inside the house. His heart raced. He tried to will himself calm. Seconds dragged by. He pushed the button a second time. Again, there was no response. Max turned away.

He visited two more houses before returning to the SUV. He drove half a block and pulled to the curb again. He adjusted the rearview mirror so he could see the house without turning before he reached

150

down to key the radio. "The chicken's not on his roost. Advise?"

Lieutenant Stratton shifted in his position behind the wheel of the detective car and looked at Hollister.

Hollister picked up the mike. "Watch and wait."

Two clicks answered.

"Hope the sonofabitch hasn't run," Stratton said, propping a knee on the dash.

"You own a house in this neighborhood, you don't have to run," Hollister answered. "You can afford trouble."

"Why would a guy that makes skin flicks kill a fifteen-year-old and maybe Shannon Roberts?" Stratton wondered aloud. "There's a dozen women on Sunset that'll do anything for fifty bucks."

Hollister shrugged. "Maybe he's into snuff films."

"Who gets off watching a teenage girl get strangled?" Stratton wondered aloud.

"Who wants to watch a fifteen-year-old do anything?" Hollister countered. "I'll take a thirty-year-old any day."

"Like your wife?" Stratton smiled.

"She's thirty-four," Hollister answered, thinking about her.

"She's a good-looking woman," Stratton said, "you know your wife looks a little like Shannon Roberts."

Hollister ears warmed with embarrassment. "I can't see Shannon Roberts involved in kiddie-porn." He deliberately shifted the conversation away from his wife.

"It doesn't have to make sense in Hollywood," Stratton cautioned.

"Maybe the silver Mercedes will provide some answers.

"We gotta find it first."

"Yeah, I know," Hollister admitted. The conversation between the two men died as they settled for the wait. The day was long and hot, and nothing stirred at the residence of Raoul Sandoval. Hollister and Lieutenant Stratton made the first run to the gas station rest room near the freeway. Parker and Torres followed shortly thereafter.

Max, on the point on Green Rush Place was unable to move. He ate a beef stick and pissed in a paper cup. After five hours he was hot, stiff and uncomfortable behind the wheel of the SUV. Max was picturing himself in command at the scene of a major homicide when he fell asleep.

A car door slamming jolted Max awake. He blinked open his eyes and found the shadows stretching long on Green Rush Place. He glanced at his watch. Jesus! It was ten minutes to six. He massaged the back of his neck and looked at his rearview mirror. His heart jumped. Two men were walking with a slender girl in blue jeans from a Lincoln parked in the driveway of the Sandoval home. Max twisted in his seat for a better look. The shadows were heavy along the front of the house and the three figures were now nothing more than silhouettes. Max strained to see, but the shadows disappeared. He was certain they had gone inside. He reached for the radio under his seat. "Six-William-Thirty, two males and a female entered the location." His voice was high-pitched with excitement.

"Roger," Hollister's voice answered casually. "Stand-by."

Lieutenant Stratton straightened and massaged his buttocks. "My ass went to sleep," he complained.

"Time to go to work," Hollister said.

Stratton nodded agreement. "How do you wanna do it?"

Hollister was thinking tactics. "I'll call West Valley, have them send us a couple of radio cars. Max and two uniforms can take the front. You and I will take the back with Parker and Torres on either side. We'll move as soon as the blue suits get here."

It was nearly dark when the patrol car and two detective cars reached the intersection. They pulled to the curb and six men climbed out. The air was now cool and alive with the sound of insects.

They moved along the curb in the darkness. Leather squeaked as the men moved. Their footfalls were quiet on the asphalt. There was a quiet tension. Stratton glanced at Hollister as they moved "Maybe we'll get lucky and catch them at dinner."

"Maybe," Hollister smiled, he was worrying about a feeling of impending doom and Stratton was thinking about food. It eased the grasp the darkness seemed to hold.

"Where's the house?" Hollister asked when they reached Max and the SUV.

"See the arched window with the light on?" Max pointed.

"You got the front door," Hollister said softly. They were still a half block away. They moved on in the darkness.

The seven men paused at the mouth of the driveway. Hollister moved to Max. "Give us a minute to get into position."

Max nodded agreement and patted Hollister on the shoulder. "Watch your ass."

"We run into a dog or anything goes wrong, punch in," Hollister urged.

"Be my pleasure," Max said, raising one of his big shoes.

Hollister pulled his pistol from its holster and looked to Lieutenant Stratton. Stratton nodded and drew his gun. Hollister led the way up the driveway to the left side of the house. Parker followed after the two. Torres walked along the curb to the north side of the lawn and cut across the grass to the corner of the house.

The side of the garage was in night shadow and Hollister nearly walked into a six-foot-high wooden gate before he saw it. A sign nailed to the face of the gate read, "Beware of Dog." There was no choice. Facing dogs was part of the job. Hollister didn't like it, but he'd had to kill several of them. He took in a breath, readied his pistol and pulled on a string for an unseen latch. It clicked open. He waited a second, half expecting a snarling dog to throw itself against the gate. When it didn't Hollister pushed, and the gate swung open. It thumped against the stucco wall of the garage.

Hollister and Stratton followed a cement walk to the rear of the house where light from inside spilled out to illuminate a wooden deck with a hot tub.

As they neared the back wall of the house, Hollister could see the backyard fell away steeply into the dark void of a rugged hillside. He inched along the wall with his back to it, gun raised, and looked carefully around the corner. The dog the sign warned of was nowhere in sight. The muffled sound of rock music drifting from inside. Hollister signaled Stratton still as he moved cautiously to the corner.

The curtain for the slider was open. Hollister saw the reason for the bright lights. A teenage girl in a sheer nightgown sat with her legs gaping in a cushioned chair facing a video camera and flood lamps. The girl's head and eyes were rolling from side to side and she had a bewildered look on her face. Hollister recognized it. She was drugged.

A man, pressing an eye to the camera's viewer, was dark haired and Latin. Sandoval, Hollister guessed. He knew only seconds remained before Max and the two uniformed officers would be demanding entrance at the front door. He moved around the corner to Stratton. Two witnesses to what was going on were better than one. Stepping close to the lieutenant, Hollister whispered, "Take a look."

Stratton eased by Hollister and around the corner.

The lieutenant inched to the glass slider and looked inside. Sandoval was lifting the teenager's nightgown open, laying the thin folds of the sheer material aside to bare the girl. The tall Latin stepped back to his camera, looked to a hallway and snapped his fingers.

A big Doberman was eager as it pulled on a chain being led into the room by a short-masked man. The man was wearing a leather loin cloth and carrying a braided whip. Stratton watched in stunned silence as the dog moved for the drugged girl. The dog stuck its head between the girl's legs, licked her, and then raised itself trying to mount her.

Stratton grimaced. "You son of a bitch!" He cried and struck the tempered glass with his fist, stepping into plain view.

Raoul Sandoval spun from the video camera and grabbed for an automatic pistol lying atop a television set. He swung the muzzle of the gun to the slider and fired three shots in quick succession. Glass exploded. The first shot hit Stratton in the upper chest, buckling his protective vest. The second severed the carotid artery at the base of his neck and the third missed. John Stratton dropped his gun and grasped his neck. He turned and stepped toward Hollister. Deep red blood spurted from between his fingers.

The lieutenant collapsed in Hollister's arms. Their eyes met briefly. Stratton looked shocked, a look of bewilderment and disbelief. Hollister had seen the look before. Stratton tried to speak, but blood bubbled from his mouth.

"Shit," Max cried as the sound of the shots reverberated inside the house. He raised a foot to the front door and kicked. A jolt of pain shot through his knee and hip. The door held.

"Sonofabitch," Max grimaced, stepping back to try again. Two uniformed officers stood poised, guns ready, waiting for the door to open. Max kicked with all his strength. The brass deadbolt buried in the door held but the wood around it cracked loud with the impact. A shower of splinters and a cloud of plaster spewed into the entry way as the door sprang open and banged against the wall. The snarling, charging, Doberman came out of the shadows. A burst of gunfire lit up the entry way and filled the night with ear-splitting concussion. The dog was dead before it fell in an awkward sprawl at Max's feet.

In three different homes on Green Rush Place, worried homeowners grabbed telephones calling 911 to report the gunfire.

Hollister was kneeling with the wounded lieutenant when he saw the man step out onto the deck. He had a gun in his hand. Hollister raised his pistol and fired. Stratton jerked in Hollister's arms at the sound of the shot.

The air cracked beside Raoul Sandoval's ear. He turned, bounded over the rail of the deck and disappeared into the night.

Hollister laid Stratton down. Stratton's head rolled like a broken doll. His eyes were wide with fright. "You're gonna be all right," Hollister lied. He ran to the rail and looked down into the blackness. He could see nothing, but he could hear the man crashing through the brush far below. Hollister leaped over the rail into the darkness. He landed twenty feet below on a steep, dry, weed covered hillside. He lost his balance and fell forward down the incline into a jagged tangle of brush. The sharp, dry branches ripped at his face and hands. Hollister grimaced and rolled free. He tried to quiet his breathing to listen. A hundred yards down the hill a dog began barking near a row of backyards cut into the hillside. Hollister wiped a stinging palm on his trouser leg. It felt hot and sticky. Blood. He wasn't sure if it was his or Stratton's. A siren whined in the distance. A second dog joined in the barking below. Hollister moved down the hillside, slipping, falling, and sliding through the sharp brush and the darkness, until he reached the bottom. Light from nearby houses spilled over fence tops to illuminate nearby trees and rooftops but did little to erase the blackness that surrounded Hollister. His hands burned with a hundred pricks. He pushed to his feet and moved for a nearby cement block wall and the light beyond. The night exploded in a blinding hot flash. The shot surprised him. It was so close he felt the heat from the muzzle flash. His ears rang from the concussion as he fell heavily into the brush.

Hollister expected the pain to come and then a curtain of blackness would close over him as death swallowed him. The pain came but it wasn't from a bullet, it was from a jagged rock stabbing him in the side. The shot had missed. He was alive. Instinct told him to lay still. Sirens were closing from the distance. The slap of rotors and the sound of jet turbines joined with them to be punctuated with dogs barking. The earth smelled dry and hay-like. Memories of Ohio farmland drifted in. He fought the urge to move as the pain in his ribs roared for relief. The man had to be close by.

Raoul Sandoval had friends and, perhaps more important, he had money. All he had to do was get to East L.A. and the rest would be easy. Juanita could get the cash out of the safety deposit box. There was no way for the police to know of it. The sirens were closer. So was the helicopter. They would go to the top of the hill first. Police always did that. They drove like hell to the scene while the crooks drove just as fast in the opposite direction. It made no sense. He hoped the cop that chased him down the hill was dead. He couldn't see him but there had been no movement since he fired. Gun aimed in the direction his pursuer had fallen, Raoul stood up.

Hollister heard the movement and held his breath. A long silence followed. His lungs felt as if they were going to burst. He searched the darkness for the man. Nothing! Then he heard him.

Raoul moved to a cement block wall and pulled himself up. An illuminated swimming pool greeted him. Beyond the pool behind a sliding glass door a man sat in a recliner chair facing a television set. He was slouched and sleeping. Raoul swung his legs over the top of the block wall and dropped to the decking near the pool. He hoped the sliding glass door was unlocked. It would be simple to rob the man and steal his car. By the time the police discovered it, he would be long gone. Gun in hand, Raoul moved along the edge of the pool toward the house.

"Freeze or die!" Hollister's voice warned from the darkness. "Choice is yours."

Raoul stopped. He stood frozen. His back to the voice. For a moment Hollister thought the man was going to surrender. Then the Latin spun toward him and fired. Bits of gray concrete spewed as the shot pock-marked the wall. The concussion reverberated in the confines of the walled backyard. Hollister already had a careful aim on the man's upper body, with the pool's backlighting he looked much like a silhouette target. Hollister fired, one, two, three times. Two of the bullets hit Raoul Sandoval in the chest. The third broke off a gold capped incisor in his lower left jaw as it entered his mouth. Sandoval cartwheeled backwards into the deep end of the pool. A crimson cloud of blood billowed out into the illuminated blue clear water as he sank.

Hollister dropped over the wall onto the decking and looked at the body in the pool. It was turning slowly and drifting toward the surface. He glanced at the house. He could see figures running inside. The once sleeping man was now on a telephone. Shouts and voices were coming from adjoining yards. Hollister sat down on the decking with his back to the wall. He laid his gun aside. The body was back on the surface now. Floating face up - although Sandoval's back was arched, and his face was under water. Hollister looked at his stinging hand. It was trembling. He was glad he wasn't the one in the pool. He pulled a thorn from the palm of his hand and leaned his head back against the wall. He closed his eyes. Jesus, he was exhausted. He was on the verge of being ill. His arms and legs felt heavy.

"Move and you're dead," a voice warned.

Hollister opened his eyes. A balding man in a tee-shirt and slippers stood a few feet away from him with a shotgun. There was a second heavier man at his shoulder with a baseball bat. The police helicopter swung into orbit overhead and washed the night away with an intense blue light.

John Stratton was still clinging to life when Max carried him into the emergency room at Woodland Hills Hospital. Penny Wilson, the drugged sixteen-year-old, arrived a few minutes later by ambulance. Hollister was brought in by a patrol sergeant. Jose Mendoza was handcuffed when Detective Parker pushed him through the double doors into the emergency room reception area. His nose was bloody, and he was still dressed in the leather loin cloth. Parker and Torres had found the frightened Mendoza cowering in a bedroom closet.

The Sandoval home on Green Rush Place was cordoned off as the officer involved shooting team from the Use of Force unit, along with a team from the Scientific Investigation Division, went to work. The quiet cul-de-sac was jammed with a collection of police cars as well as a crush of reporters and minicam vans. Behind the wide yellow tape that warned "Police Line - Do Not Cross" a voice among the crowd of curious spectators asked, "Who got shot?"

"Someone shot a tree trimmer," a female voice answered.

A block away near the foot of the hill on LeFloss Street a second team of Robbery-Homicide detectives worked with a coroner's deputy removing the body of Raoul Sandoval from the swimming pool of Tom and Janice Spalding. The once blue pool water now had a distinct pink tint to it. Tom Spalding was already on the telephone talking to his attorney brother-in-law. He wanted damages for property as well as mental anguish. The city would later quietly settle out of court.

The P.M. watch commander at Hollywood Division dispatched a radio car to Lieutenant Stratton's Van Nuy's home to pick up his wife. Denise Stratton arrived at the hospital seventeen minutes after her husband's death.

An intern and a black nurse worked at removing splinters and thorns from Hollister's hands and chin. He was bruised and weary but had no serious injuries. He felt foolish getting attention when he knew John Stratton was somewhere in the hospital. As long as the doctor didn't come in, he had the hope the lieutenant was still alive.

The door to the treatment room swung open. It was Max and a doctor in a blood spotted surgical gown. The doctor looked tired. Max was red eyed and sober, but he forced a grin. "How you feeling?"

"How's Stratton?"

"I'm sorry. For all practical considerations," the doctor answered, "he was dead when they brought him in."

"You got the sonofabitch though," Max said patting Hollister's shoulder.

Yielding to the doctor's advice, the OIC of the officer involved shooting team agreed to interview Hollister at the hospital. They used the doctor's lounge on the second floor. Hollister told and retold the story. Minute by minute, time and time again. Lieutenant Brillion and Sergeant Oaks, Hollister's two interrogators, carefully compared each of his answers with the results of their on-scene investigation. The interview took two hours.

"It's not for us to decide the legality or the justification of an officer involved shooting," Lieutenant Brillion told Hollister when it was over, "but John Stratton was a classmate of mine and a damned good cop. I'm glad you killed the sonofabitch that shot him."

A deputy chief was standing in the hallway, talking with Captain Harris and Lieutenant Brillion when Hollister finally emerged from the doctor's lounge. The trio fell silent as he walked by.

It was two-twenty A.M. when Hollister and Max finally left the hospital. Traffic on the freeway was light. "I'm gonna miss John," Max said.

Hollister didn't answer. He didn't know what to say. He had never killed a man in one-on-one combat before and it wasn't impacting him the way he thought it would. Working homicide, he had often wondered how those that murdered felt. He'd seen the entire spectrum of emotions, deep heartfelt grief to cold indifference. Now he was among them and he wasn't sure how he felt. He'd stood close to death. It had struck John Stratton and Raoul Sandoval. Why not him? Why was it fate ended two

lives close to his but let him live? Was it God's decision? What was it he was living for? What did God want from him? Was God real? John Stratton knew the answer. Hollister wished he did.

Max dropped Hollister at his house, offering to come in.

"It's late," Hollister suggested not wanting to confess there was no one waiting inside. "Give me a break, Grandma."

"Okay, okay," Max granted. "I'm just damned glad it wasn't you. I mean I'm sorry for John, but I'm glad it wasn't you."

Hollister nodded silent thanks and climbed from the car.

"Pick you up in the morning," Max added.

Hollister took off his shirt and shoes before going to the refrigerator. He poured a Diet Coke and gathered a handful of Fig Newton's from a jar on the counter. Returning to the living room, he glanced at his watch. It was almost three, but he was wide awake. He turned the TV on, avoiding late night talk shows out of respect for John Stratton, it seemed he shouldn't laugh at anything this night. Hollister felt sorry that John Stratton was dead, but he wasn't sure that what he was feeling was grief. So, this was how a murderer felt? Bewildered! Several hours earlier he was chasing an armed killer through the dead of night. Now he was alone with a Diet Coke and a handful of Fig Newton's. The thought brought an audible laugh. He decided on the DVR. The television screen blinked on before Hollister realized it was the disk for "The Nude in the Woods." On the screen Shannon Roberts was doing what she seemingly did best, taking her clothes off.

In the turn of the century bathroom, Shannon was filling an ornate tub with water as she sat on a nearby stool, skirt pushed high, carefully peeling away a mesh nylon to reveal the smooth flesh of her upper thigh. Her blouse was unbuttoned and hung open. Although her breasts were covered, he could see the deep shadow between them. Hollister grimaced and pushed a button on the remote. The screen went black. Jesus, he was lonely. Where the hell was Kim? Why hadn't she called.

The national and state flags in front of the Hollywood station were at half-mast when Hollister and Max arrived the following morning. The pats on the shoulder and the congratulatory remarks started in the parking lot and continued until Hollister and Max reached the Homicide desk. There they continued. Good shooting, Hollister...Nice work, Sergeant.... Way to go, Sarge...You dumped the sucker, Pal.

Hollister wasn't sure what to say so he said nothing. He didn't think he'd done anything special. Quite the contrary, he felt some responsibility for John Stratton's death. He was the one that invited the lieutenant to take a look! He wondered if he would have reacted the same way. A nameless sixteen-year-old being assaulted by a Doberman. He suspected Stratton's reaction was strong because he was a father. Hollister was not. Although he wasn't comfortable with accepting Stratton's action as brave. there was a thin line between bravery and recklessness, and he wasn't certain where Stratton belonged. Getting yourself killed for someone who wasn't in a life-threatening situation didn't seem particularly wise.

The homicide desk was unusually quiet. The other detectives, in consideration of those in homicide, were answering all the calls. Parker and Torres arrived with a box of CDs. "We took twenty-two kiddie-porn cassettes out of Sandoval's house," Torres offered.

"Anything of Shannon Roberts?" Hollister questioned.

Parker shook his head. "Nothing but a bunch of homeless little girls."

"We found cassettes of the two kids killed," Torres added.

"You collected phone records, photos?" Hollister pressed.

167

"Got it all," Parker assured. "Had prints come in and dust. If there's a link to Shannon Roberts, it's not an obvious one."

"Shit," Hollister muttered, dreading another dead end.

It was Parker who went into Lieutenant Stratton's office. He returned with a fifth of Wild Turkey and plastic drink glasses. Torres passed the glasses while Parker poured. "John kept this in his bottom drawer for special occasions," Parker said pouring the liquor into the glasses. "I'd say this is a special occasion." He set the bottle down and raised his glass. "To Lieutenant John Stratton, a good cop, a good friend and a good boss."

They raised their glasses and drank. Parker poured another round. As he did, Torres stood. "What'd' say we take up a collection and send Max over to help the family until the funeral?"

"I'll second that," Parker said, raising his glass.

"Everyone in favor," Torres urged.

A loud "aye," filled the entire squad room.

Wallets were pulled out and emptied onto the table. Max gathered the collection of bills and counted them. "Thirty-six hundred and sixty-two dollars," he said, folding the wad of money into his pocket. "I'm sure Denise will appreciate it."

"If she needs anything, you call us," Hollister said. "We'll get it." He was feeling the warmth of the liquor.

"I will," Max nodded.

The intercom on the console buzzed. Parker picked

up the receiver. "Homicide," he listened, looked to Hollister. "Yeah, he's here. I'll tell him." He hung up. "Hollister, you're wanted at RHD. See Brillion."

The Officer-Involved Shooting team kept Hollister waiting in an interview room most of the day. The day was long and boring. Late in the afternoon the Shooting Review Board made its announcement.

"The shooting death of Raoul Sandoval by Detective Sergeant Lee Hollister has been found to be within the 'deadly force' policy of the Los Angeles Police Department. After a thorough investigation, the Shooting Review Board recommends that the District Attorney declare the shooting death a 'justifiable homicide'."

The following Thursday morning there were four funerals in Los Angeles. The service for fallen Police Officers John Stratton, Keith Canfield and Jesse Martinez was held at the First Baptist church in Van Nuys. Although they were to be interned at separate locations the grieving families recognizing the trio of cops, men having served together would want their final service together. Lieutenant Stratton lay in an open, satin-lined coffin in uniform. On his collar he wore the double bar insignia of a captain. Chief-of-Police Moore, upon hearing of Stratton's pending oral, had ordered him promoted posthumously. Jesse Martinez's coffin was closed due to damage to his skull. Keith Canfield's coffin stood beside his partner's. He looked at rest in his uniform. The service and the interment that followed in Northridge drew less press attention than expected. The death of a trio of police officers from the same LAPD Division was unprecedented, but there was competition.

It wasn't that the news directors of Los Angeles were callous, it was the sweeps. And there was no doubt the news event of the day was the funeral of superstar Shannon Roberts at Forest Lawn.

Hollywood was out in force. The fact was the entertainment industry loved a funeral. Most Hollywood stars and the hordes of wanna be's usually had only one camera to compete for, this day there were hundreds. The press flocked like moths to a flame. The famous, the infamous and the not so famous all came. Few were invited, or expected, but thousands came. It was a chance to see and be seen.

The twenty-two-hundred mourners pressed into the chapel where a golden casket sat in a sea of long-stemmed roses. CNN carried the funeral live.

The Reverend Del Torn delivered a stirring eulogy when he drew a parallel between Shannon Robert's brief stardom and the fiery shooting stars that sometimes light up the night sky. "We see them, we stand in awe, we reach for them, but we cannot hold them. They are brief, beautiful, and soon gone, but seldom forgotten."

Walt Altice, a lean tanned man in his mid-forties, with gray hair and a neatly trimmed beard, sat in his office, watching a cassette of the dailies from Memories in Blue on a computer, while sipping a glass of Jack Daniel's. Shannon Roberts' funeral had left him angry, bitter and depressed. The intercom on his desk buzzed. Altice gulped down the remaining liquor, stopped the DVR and picked up the receiver. "Yeah?"

A receptionist in the outer office spoke, "There's two LAPD detectives here."

"Fuck! Okay, send them in," Altice said.

Max opened the door and led Hollister into the office. Altice watched from his slouched position in a leather chair as he lit a cigarette. "Pardon me for not getting up," he said straightening some in the chair, "but I'm drunk."

"Little early in the day?" Max suggested.

"It's seven o'clock in London," Altice defended. "I'm an international drunk."

"I'm Max Baxter. This is my partner Sergeant Hollister. We're investigating Shannon Roberts' death."

"I thought that was over," Altice squinted at the two detectives. They sat down in front of his desk. "News said the man that killed her hung himself."

"We think there may be others," Hollister said.

Altice pushed straight in his chair and exhaled smoke. "Who?"

"We thought maybe you could help," Hollister answered. "You and Shannon were close."

"Yeah, we were close," Altice confessed as he rocked forward to lean his elbows on the desk. "This picture was going to be great," he said with pain showing in his face. "In spite of the fact that Paul DeSilva wanted to make it another of his tits and ass specials."

"You didn't want that?" Hollister probed.

"I don't do skin flicks. I got nothing against glistening female bodies, but it takes more than that to make a motion picture. You want a skin flick, go hire some horny TV director."

"What did Shannon Roberts want?" Max asked.

"Shannon was more than a set of tits." Altice looked at Max. "This was the first picture she was going to really act in. All the others starred her body. This one was..., well, it was fucking different. You could see it, sense it. She was really into..., well, what the fuck does it matter now?" He pushed back in his chair.

"How did Paul DeSilva feel about this change in course?" Hollister questioned.

"DeSilva would have his mother take her clothes off in a gas station if he thought it would make him a buck. He's a money grubber. He doesn't know Aero flex from Polaroid. The only reason he got this picture rolling was because of Shannon Roberts. He doesn't have any money. You can bet he's in hock up to his Italian eyebrows."

"What happens to the picture now?" Max asked.

"It's fucking dead," Altice said, stabbing his cigarette in an ashtray full of butts. "Everyone gets paid, except Shannon."

"Paid?" Hollister questioned.

"Yeah," Altice explained, "completion bond! Insurance! Nobody loses a fucking dime. Not me, not DeSilva, not the investors, no one."

"How much insurance are you talking about?" Hollister pressed.

"The whole package?" Altice paused to light another cigarette. "I'd say seventy-five to eighty million."

"The studio handles that?" Hollister added.

"This wasn't a studio picture," Altice explained, "so the executive producer is responsible."

"Who's that?" Max asked fanning the cigarette smoke that hung in a blue haze.

"Paul DeSilva," Altice answered.

"So, his picture didn't lose any money?" Hollister asked.

Altice chuckled making smoke come out of his nose. "Lose money? This is fuckin' Hollywood. Pictures lose money, people don't."

"How did Paul DeSilva and Shannon Roberts get along?" Max questioned.

Altice ran thumb and forefinger over his beard as he thought about the question. "DeSilva came over to the sound stage on Friday. We were shooting a scene where Liz, that's who Shannon was playing, comes home from her mother's funeral and walks around the living room where she grew up. She hasn't been in the house in years. So fucking DeSilva calls me aside and says let's shoot it in the nude. Can you believe that? The girl comes home from her mother's funeral and walks around the house nude! I told him he was fuckin' crazy!"

"What did he do?" Hollister said.

"He told me shoot it nude or walk."

"Walk?"

"Fired, get out, end of the road, the boot."

"Did you?"

"Fuck no. My commitment was to Shannon and the picture. Not that greaseball."

"What did you do?" Max asked.

"I told Shannon what he wanted and what I thought. She told DeSilva if he goes, I go."

"And?" Hollister prompted.

"He backed down and we did what we wanted."

"Do you think Paul DeSilva killed Shannon?" Max asked bluntly.

Altice shook his head. "He hasn't got the balls, and he'd made more money if the picture got made."

"When's the last time you saw Shannon?" Hollister questioned.

"Friday. She dropped me at LAX. I went to Vermont for the weekend. My mother lives there. She's ill. If I hadn't fucking gone maybe Shannon would be alive?" His eyes welled with tears. He made no attempt to hide it.

"Why do you say that?" Hollister added.

"DeSilva wanted to get together Saturday night. You know the three of us. Talk over the script. Friday scared him. He was trying to make peace."

"Maybe Shannon went without you?" Max suggested.

"I don't think she'd do that," Altice answered.

"But you don't know?" Hollister pressed.

"I don't know," Altice admitted.

"Do you know what her plans were for the weekend?" Max continued.

"It was a long week. First week of production. Shannon said she was going to sleep late and work out. That was it. I told her I'd call when I got back."

"Do you have any idea who killed her?" Hollister questioned.

"Yeah, I know who killed her," Altice answered soberly. "Guys who pay to see women take off their clothes. Guys who would never have the nerve to talk to a woman like Shannon Roberts, yet they'll watch her movies twenty times. The kind of guy who thinks if he ever met Shannon, she'd go to bed with him. The kind of guy that thinks because she took her clothes off in a motion picture, she'd be an easy lay. A lot of them go to movies and a lot of them make movies. Pick one, they all did it."

Monty Golden met the two detectives at the door of his office. He was dressed in baggy pants and a pastel jacket. His open collar revealed a collection of gold chains around his neck. He offered a hand to Hollister and then Max. It was clammy. He made the handshakes light and brief. "Nice to see you again, fellas," he said in less than a convincing tone. "Sorry to keep you waiting. I was on a call to New York. Either of you like a cup of coffee or a cool drink?"

"No, thanks," Max answered.

Hollister didn't answer; he was looking at the life

size poster of the scantily clad Shannon Roberts on the wall of Monty Golden's office. It was a movie poster and the copy across the bottom read, "The Nude in the Woods."

Monty closed the office door behind the two detectives and said, "Sit down, please." He returned to his desk.

Hollister and Max sat in chairs facing the executive desk. Behind Monty a floor to ceiling window revealed the sprawling panorama of downtown Hollywood. The walls of the tenth-floor office were covered with the autographed faces of Hollywood's famous. Max eyed them. "You represent all these people?"

Monty smiled. "One time or another. Many go through agents as fast as marriages. Except Shannon. I've been working with her exclusively for the past couple of years."

"Let's not bullshit each other," Hollister warned. The poster of Shannon Roberts annoyed him, and he wasn't interested in Monty's small talk.

"No, bullshit," Monty agreed. He was picking nervously at a thumbnail.

"When was the last time you talked to Shannon Roberts?" Max began as he tried to work his hulk into a comfortable position in the small chair.

"Friday. She called me when she got home from the studio. It was around six."

"What did she want?" Max continued.

"Some business about the picture," Monty answered with a shrug, inferring that it wasn't very important.

"That comes very close to sounding like bullshit," Hollister warned.

Monty Golden wiped at his mouth. He was beginning to glisten with sweat. Hollister noticed it. "There are people in this business who get very upset when you talk about things."

"If you're worried about what you tell us you've been watching too much television," Max offered to comfort him. "We don't tell anybody anything."

"Okay," Monty said. His voice was trembling. "Paul DeSilva called me on Friday and said Shannon was giving him problems with the script. He said he'd give me another two percent if I could get things squared away. He said he couldn't afford problems and Shannon was threatening to walk."

"And what did you do?" Max pressed.

Monty massaged the back of his neck. It moved his hairpiece slightly. "I...I called Shannon, left a message. She called me back. We talked. I asked her to meet with DeSilva. She didn't want to without Walt Altice, but she finally agreed."

Hollister's pulse quickened. The missing pieces of the puzzle were falling into place. "When was the meeting?"

"I don't know. Saturday sometime. At least that's what DeSilva wanted. He said he was going to call her."

"Did he?" Max demanded.

Monty nodded. "I talked to him on Saturday morning from Palm Springs. He said they were going to meet later in the day. I didn't ask where."

"Where do you think they met?" Hollister questioned.

"Paul DeSilva told me at her funeral they never did," Monty answered. "He said he tried calling, but all he got was her answering machine."

"She do drugs, drink?" Hollister continued.

"Never even saw her take an aspirin. Booze? I don't know, maybe. But she wasn't a drunk, if that's what you mean."

"Do you have any idea who may have wanted to kill Shannon?" Max asked, shifting in his chair again.

"I heard it was that nut that hung himself," Monty said. "I bet he got hot watching her films and tracked her down."

"It wasn't him," Hollister said.

"Wasn't him!" The suggestion startled Monty Golden.

"Who the hell is it?"

"We don't know," Max answered.

"What if it's some psycho prick that's unhappy over a deal and wants revenge?" Monty questioned as color drained from his face.

"That's show biz," Hollister answered.

It was nearly six o'clock when Hollister and Max returned to Hollywood station. A five-hour citation search at the traffic division was over and the net result was five license numbers of Mercedes ticketed for illegal parking in the Hollywood-Beverly Hills area on the two days before and after Shannon Roberts' murder. Neither man was saying anything about the odds of the license numbers of being of any value. The reality of that would come soon enough.

Parker and Torres had the homicide office crowded with a collection of shackled heavy metal punkers. The blue hair, nose rings, black leather, and shaved heads made it difficult to tell male from female.

Hollister and Max gathered the paperwork they needed and moved to what had been Lieutenant Brillion's office where they had room to work. Hollister laid out the list of names and addresses and picked up the first citation.

Date: 8/24 Time: 2320
Location: 2664 Oakmont Place, B.H.
Vehicle: Mercedes/Wht/86 License: 1cnb134/Ca.
Direction: Prked Rt/Cb-N/W
Offense: Bhmc-10647m - Blocking Driveway
Summary: R/C To Abv Address. Czn Rpts Abv Veh Blocking
His Driveway When He Arrived Home. Obs & Cite Bhmc-10647m
Weather: Clear/Dry Good Street Lighting.
Copy Of Citation Affixed Ext/Driver's Wind-shield.
Officer: M. Cunningham, 23459

Hollister noted the address and ran a finger down the typed list looking for addresses on Oakmont Place. Max pushed a coffee in front of him. Hollister paused to sip it.

"You and Kim wanna come over this weekend for a barbeque? Forget about police work for a couple hours."

"Kim said something about a meeting at her new branch this weekend," Hollister lied. His ears warmed with guilt. He hoped Max wouldn't see it.

"Careful she doesn't become all work and no play."

"I'll do that." Hollister returned his attention to the list. It was in alphabetical order and he was at the top of the second page when he spotted it. "God damn!" he blurted bolting aloud straitening in his chair.

"What!?" Max asked pushing close.

"Look at this," Hollister was excited. He turned the list for Max to see. "The citation was issued to a silver Mercedes on Saturday night at two-six-six-four Oakmont in Beverly Hills."

"Yeah," Max agreed.

Hollister stabbed a finger at a list of names and addresses. "Now look at this... Paul DeSilva, two-six-five-three Oakmont. That's straight across the fuckin' street."

"Ain't that something?" Max hooted.

While Max ran the license number through DMV, Hollister made a telephone call to the studio.

"Mister DeSilva's office," the voice of Meg Rogers purred.

"This is Sergeant Hollister calling. I'm returning a call from Mister DeSilva," Hollister said, trying for a professional tone as he remembered Meg Rogers' nipples under the thin material of her blouse. Kim's absence was taking its toll.

"I'm the one that called, Sergeant. I'd like to talk to you," Meg answered, speaking softer. "I have information that may be of interest."

"Would you like me to come to your office?"

"No," came a quick reply. "It's best we meet somewhere else. This evening, if you wouldn't mind?"

"Not at all."

"There's a place called Casa Del Sol on Ventura, say eight?"

"See you there."

"Got some good news and some bad news," Max smiled, returning to the Homicide office from Records.

"Start with the good news," Hollister suggested.

"I know who the driver is."

""What's the bad news?"

"The driver of the Mercedes is a frog," Max answered.

"A frog?" Hollister questioned.

"Yeah," Max agreed. "A snail biter, a wine sipper, a war wimp, you know...a fuckin' Frenchman."

"A Frenchman!" Hollister was surprised.

Max looked to note his notes. "His name's Phillip DePaul, French driver's license number, seven-one-seven-A-M-B. Address, nine-sixteen Avenue of the Elms, Apartment Four-C, Paris, France. He rented a silver Mercedes from Classic Connection Rentals at Los Angeles International airport two days before the murder. He returned it Sunday afternoon. We know on Saturday night it was parked in front of a driveway at twenty-six-sixty-four Oakmont Place in Beverly Hills, straight across the street from Paul DeSilva's house. The car was cited at twenty-three-twenty."

"What's DePaul look like?" Hollister questioned retraining his eagerness.

Max shook his head. "I talked to the clerk that rented the car. She can't remember. She said they get fifteen, twenty customers per shift. Many of them foreigners. But they have video."

"Video. That will take time. How did he pay for the car?"

Max looked to his notes. "American Express Gold Card number four-one-two-eight-eight-five-oh-three-three-one. Shit, I've never been able to get one of those," Max complained.

"Run him through R&I, CII and NCIC," Hollister urged.

"Done that," Max answered. "He's as clean as a snail track on a kitchen window."

"Let's get on the telephone to that policewoman in Intelligence," Hollister suggested. "The one that got us Sandoval's address. See what she can do with this Frenchman. Tell her to check with the FBI, Interpol and American Express. We need a physical description and a record, anything, and everything they can get. Tell her we'll buy her dinner and a new pair of panties."

"How in the hell can a French crook get a Gold Card and I can't?" Max grumbled as he glanced at his watch. "It's seven o'clock. It's not likely we're going to get any answers tonight."

The parking lot of the Casa Del Sol was crowded with cars when Hollister arrived at seven-forty-five. He found a space near the rear of the lot. He was glad to park the detective car there. He climbed out and headed for the gentle arches of the Spanish restaurant.

A long-padded bar stretched across the lounge and

Hollister was moving for a vacant stool when he spotted Meg Rogers sitting at an oval table. She offered a smile of recognition. Hollister walked to the table. "You're early."

"Sit down, said the spider to the fly." Meg smiled, gesturing to a chair.

Hollister eased himself into the cushioned chair across from the woman. The subdued lighting in the room mixed with the flickering light from a candle on the table to wash over her face. It made Hollister feel very Hollywood. There were younger women dotting other tables in the lounge, but Meg Rogers had a mature sensuality that could not be ignored. "You look good off duty," she said, "but you still look like a cop."

"And you look good without an office, but you still look Hollywood," Hollister countered adjusting himself in the chair.

"We all have crosses to bear." Meg smiled, stirring her drink. She was making him feel masculine and virile. His battered ego was absorbing it like a dry sponge.

A waitress in a mini skirt appeared out of the press in the room. She set a bowl of salsa and a basket of tortilla chips on the table. "May I get you a drink?" she said, with a look to Hollister.

"Jack and diet coke. Tall, please."

The waitress disappeared. "Would you mind if I got right to it?" Meg asked.

Hollister shook his head. "Not at all."

"Isn't that why we're here?" Meg questioned.

"You tell me."

The waitress returned with Hollister's drink. "To truth, justice, and the American way," Hollister said, raising his glass.

"All right," Meg leaned into the small table and spoke softer. "I've been with Paul DeSilva since he moved onto the lot to work on Memories in Blue."

"How long is that?"

"Almost two years. It took him over a year to put together the financing. The studio would only go seventy-thirty plus distribution."

"What's that in dollars?"

"Almost sixty-eight million for Paul to raise."

"Wow!"

"He couldn't even get the quarter million he needed for Shannon Roberts to commit to script."

"Why?"

"His last two pictures lost money. You lose money in Hollywood, you lose friends."

"But DeSilva got the money somewhere."

"Yes. From an Englishman by the name of George Franklin. I never saw the agreement, but from what I heard of Paul's side of the conversations, I know it was a short-term loan. Twelve months. Then they'd sell the film to the studio and recoup their investment."

"I don't know Hollywood deals, but it doesn't sound criminal."

"They were seven months into their twelve-month agreement and Shannon Roberts was walking off the picture."

"And if Shannon walked?"

"They lose their asses."

"And you think she was going to walk?"

"It happened Friday. Paul was in a rage."

"Do you think Paul DeSilva killed her?"

Meg took a heavy drink from her glass. "I don't know what to think. All I know is with Shannon Roberts dead, no one loses a dime. The insurance company holding the completion bond has to pay within sixty days."

"Can you prove any of this?"

"No, and I feel like Benedict Arnold telling you, but I had to. Paul DeSilva is an asshole."

"So why work for an asshole?"

"I'm forty-seven-years-old, Sergeant. I haven't had an acting job in three years. Maybe you haven't noticed, but youth is where it's at. They don't make Smokey and the Bandit pictures anymore, I've got two kids, one in college and a dead-beat X that sends them Christmas cards from Italy."

It was the first time Paul DeSilva had been out in months. The pressure he'd been under had been enormous, but now it was solved. Shannon Roberts wasn't going to walk off his picture. George Franklin's money man wasn't going to send someone to break his fingers and he wasn't going to lose every dime he had. Shannon Roberts' death had stopped it all. Hell, with the insurance pay-off he might even make a few bucks. And, Sixty Minutes as well as 20/20 were both after Shannon's final footage. The rights could be worth fucking millions if he could keep the insurance bastards from tying it up. Shannon's death was tragic, and he could, and had, truthfully said he didn't know who killed her. His rationale was she'd killed herself. It was fuckin' suicide to screw around with the better part of ninety million. People got killed for a hell of a lot less. At age fifteen, DeSilva, along with five other South Philly toughs, had beat an old man to death for twelve dollars. People got away with murder. It happened every day. Only in the movies did the cops solve every case. In reality he didn't think they were very smart. A detective wearing clothes from Sears! Jesus, who would believe that?"

He'd met the girl in the Blue room at the Burbank Studio cafeteria. She had a great set of tits and looked all of eighteen-years-old. Like others, she was working as a waitress until the right part came along. She'd done two walk-ons on daytime soaps and she knew who Paul DeSilva was. That was why she had her hand on his leg as he wheeled his polished Jaguar into the parking lot of the Casa Del Sol. "How about a little Mexican Chili to warm you up, girl?"

DeSilva held the girl by the ass as they walked to the entrance making small talk. She was young and firm and he was looking forward to getting her naked in his hot tub later.

"Let's see what's happening in the bar before we chow down," DeSilva said, pulling the door open. Tinny Spanish music drifted out to greet them. They moved inside to the archway that led to the step-down lounge. The lounge was crowded and noisy as the Friday night crowd drowned the week's regrets with tequila and pretended to have fun. DeSilva's eyes drifted over the crowd. He liked its frenzy. There was an excitement about it. He was searching, woman to woman, table to table, when he spotted them. Recognizing Meg Rogers was no shock. She was a looker. A bit old for his tastes, but still a looker. The guy she was with looked familiar but, with his back to DeSilva and across the room, he wasn't sure who it was. Then the man turned to speak to a waitress and DeSilva recognized him. Fuck! It was the police detective! His heart raced as his pulse pounded in his ears. The girl at his side felt DeSilva stiffen. "You all right?"

"Come on," DeSilva said, pulling the girl toward the door.

The shaken DeSilva drove ten blocks north on Ventura Boulevard before he pulled into a supermarket parking lot and dug out his cell phone. "Paul," the young girl pleaded, "tell me what's wrong, maybe I could help."

The girl was nothing but an annoyance now. "Just shut up," he said as his shaking fingers punched the number into the cell phone.

"You're scaring me," the girl whined.

"Shut up, and get the fuck out!" he snapped.

George Franklin was asleep in his third-story flat on Hampton Road in the North of London. At first, he thought the sound was rain on the window, but as it continued, he realized it was the chime of the bedside telephone. He pushed the satin comforter aside, baring the nude girl at his side, and swung his feet to the floor before picking up the receiver. "This is Franklin," he said, switching on a light to pick up a cigarette.

"We got problems, George," DeSilva's voice warned across the miles.

Franklin struck a gold lighter and drew on his cigarette. He was fully awake now. "What kind of problems, Paul?" Memories of DeSilva's earlier panic were flooding his mind. The man was proving to be a real liability.

"Meg Rogers is talking to the police," the excited voice said in his ear.

"You'll have to excuse me, Ol' chap," Franklin scratched at the mat of gray hair on his chest, "but I don't know who the hell Meg Rogers is."

"She's my fuckin' assistant, dummy. You've met her half a dozen times."

"I'm afraid you pay much more attention to assistants than I."

"You'll pay attention if she spills her guts to the

police. She knows everything," DeSilva warned.

Franklin stiffened. "Watch what you say," he cautioned. "What could this woman know?" Franklin questioned.

"Maybe she's listened in on our calls, looked at the contracts. Who the fuck knows?"

"You keep our agreement in your studio office?"

"Where in the hell do you want me to keep it, in the glove box of my car? Listen to me, Georgie boy, I'm not gonna take all the heat myself. I'm not the one who come up with this fucking master plan."

Franklin knocked an ash into a nearby tray. "Be calm, Paul," he urged as his mind raced putting together the plan. "Anything this woman may say to the police is simply hearsay. It's not evidence. You're overreacting. I want you to go to your office and remove our agreements. Get rid of them. Burn them. We don't need them anymore. I have copies. There's nothing the police can do, or prove, as long as you don't tell them anything. Do you understand that?"

"Don't talk down to me, you Limey prick. It's my ass on the line. How about if I make a deal with the cops for your Yorkshire ass."

"Don't threaten me, Paul," Franklin warned, stabbing out his cigarette. "If this girl frightens you, there are steps we can take."

"Then take the steps, George, because like I said, I'm not going to jail for some shit scheme you cooked up."

"What's the girl's name?"

"Meg. Meg Rogers."

"Where does she live?"

"Archway Drive in Studio City. Why?"

"I'll take care of it," Franklin assured.

"How?"

"If you don't know, you can't tell."

"I haven't told anyone fucking anything, have I?" DeSilva countered.

"Goodnight, Paul," Franklin hung up.

"Is there a problem, Love?" the sleepy nude asked, pulling the comforter up to her chin behind Franklin.

"Business," Franklin said pushing off the bed to walk nude to a robe draped over a chair back. He pushed his arms into the robe, tied the belt, and moved for a nearby study. "Go back to sleep. I've got to make a call."

Franklin put on glasses before sitting down behind an ornate desk. He lifted an address book from a drawer and thumbed through it. Then, picking up the telephone, he held it to his ear and dialed.

"Good morning, Operator. I'd like to make a call to Madrid."

FIFTEEN | TIT FOR TAT

It was six-fifty Friday evening when TWA flight one-twenty-two lifted off the runway in Madrid. Nearly eleven nonstop hours later the 747 touched down at Los Angeles International Airport. Abu Assad presented his French passport to the U.S. Customs official. "Enjoy your visit to the United States, Mister DePaul," the officer said after examining Assad's papers and luggage.

Assad climbed aboard an airport shuttle to the Classic Connection Rent-A-Car office. There he presented his American Express gold card. "I'd like a Mercedes, please," he said with a French accent. Twenty minutes later he was eastbound on Century Boulevard in a red Mercedes coupe. Abu was uneasy being back in Los Angeles, especially for follow-up on the original assignment. It was sloppy business, and if the money hadn't been so good, he would have refused. Businessmen. He had disgust for them. They always thought killing would solve their problems.

In reality it usually only created more. Killing only solved problems when in the hands of professionals. He did not consider his English employer a professional. He promised himself to do the job quickly. No lingering. He was eager to get back to the rented villa near Madrid. It was peaceful there. Unlike Paris, which had become an unpleasant place for an Arab to live. Terrorist fools had cost him so much. In Spain his dark eyes and olive complexion drew little attention. It was the same in Los Angeles, yet he had no desire to live there. He, as he suspected all Iranians did, dreamed of someday going home. Home to Iran. If only the Americans hadn't turned their back on the Shah decades ago, perhaps he'd still be there, working with his horses. His anger swelled. Killing another American for pay would not be difficult. Slowing for a red light, Abu glanced at his Rolex watch. It was nine-forty-five in the morning. He was tired. Jet lag, he concluded. He'd check in at his hotel, get a few hours' sleep, and then take care of business. His return flight was already reserved for Saturday evening.

The morning air was cool and heavy with moisture and its touch erased the fatigue that gripped Hollister's mind. The city seemed to ignore him as he jogged the twisting winding streets of the San Fernando Valley. The jogging was ironic he thought. A jogger, a wanna be unknown actor had set it all in motion and now he was dead, but he was not the reason the famed star was drugged, strangled and dumped in a trash bin. The reason was still elusive, unclear. The catalyst behind the death of Shannon Roberts seemed more and more to be Paul DeSilva. If she walked off his picture, DeSilva would be penniless. Her death cost him nothing. Padding his loss, it was likely he'd even make money. Then there was the Mercedes seen in the alley by the wino when Shannon Roberts was dumped. Was it mere coincidence that a Mercedes was ticketed across the street from DeSilva's home in Beverly Hills the night before? Hardly. But who in the hell was Phillip DePaul? If he was the killer, it wasn't likely he was traveling under his real name, which meant Intelligence Division wasn't going to come up with anything. Hollister dreaded the thought of another dead end. They were close. Maybe it was time to throw some shit in the fan. Time to shout fire and see who ran for the exits. Time to squeeze Paul DeSilva. DeSilva didn't know what they knew. If, as Director Walter Altice suggested, Paul DeSilva did hire someone to kill Shannon Roberts, maybe a squeeze would frighten him into a panic move. The more Hollister thought about the idea, the more he liked it. There was even a psychological edge to bringing DeSilva in on a Saturday. He would know the police were close to breaking the case, if they hadn't already. Hollister decided to call Max as soon as he got back to his house. DeSilva was about to have his weekend plans revised.

Paul DeSilva was walking to the Jaguar parked in the driveway. He was carrying a red leather golf bag and a full set of clubs. He had a midmorning round set at the L.A. Country Club with Glen Bowers from Cannon Films. If he let the little faggot win, he was hoping they would pick up an option he owned on a recent Taylor Gray novel. A police car braking to a stop at the curb in front of the house startled him. The black and white was followed quickly by two others. DeSilva's pulse jumped as he watched uniformed officers climb from each of the three cars. "Fuck!" he said, letting his golf bag fall to the driveway.

The two officers in the first car were wearing khaki uniforms. DeSilva recognized them as Beverly Hills cops. The other four were wearing dark blue. They were L.A.P.D. The six officers walked across the lawn to the driveway. DeSilva's mind was in a panic. What the hell had happened? Meg Rogers! That bitch. She'd done this. She'd told them. DeSilva's heart pounded in his ears. His knees felt weak. He was close to being physically ill.

"Paul DeSilva?" The officer was a big, broad-shouldered man with blond hair.

"Yeah," DeSilva answered as the others closed around him. One of the officers took away the golf bag. Another was patting him from behind.

"What in the fuck is this?" DeSilva demanded in less than a forceful tone.

"We're assisting LAPD," the blond-haired officer

answered. "They have orders to pick you up."

"Pick me up?"

One of the officers in a dark blue uniform read from a printed form. "You have the right to remain silent."

"I wanna make a telephone call," DeSilva protested.

"Not now," the blond-haired officer answered.

"If you give up the right to remain silent anything you say can and will be used against you in court."

"What the fuck's this about?"

"You have the right to speak with an attorney and to have the attorney present during questioning."

"You're the one that's gonna need a fuckin' attorney," DeSilva warned.

"If you so desire and cannot afford one, an attorney will be appointed for you without charge before questioning."

"Can't afford one?" DeSilva blurted. "I got fuckin' Nancy Grace's home phone number... and I'm gonna use it."

"Let's go," one of the L.A.P.D. officers said, taking DeSilva by the arm.

"Go! Where the hell are we going?"

"Hollywood Division."

"What about my fuckin' golf clubs, my open garage?"

"We'll lock it up," the blond-haired officer assured.

"You people are gonna fuckin' regret this."

The four L.A.P.D. officers pushed DeSilva toward the waiting patrol cars.

Max arrived at the station a half hour after Hollister. He found Hollister in the station coffee room. Hollister was thumbing through the sports section of the Times. Max sat down across from him. "Sorry to screw up your Saturday," Hollister said.

Max relaxed in a plastic chair. "Don't worry about it. You got me out of wallpapering a bathroom. Doris gets in these moods about every three months. Gotta do something to the house."

Hollister nodded agreement. "Read an article about instincts in Readers Digest. Claimed women have cycles of nesting instincts. You know, feathering a nest, papering a bathroom."

Max nodded agreement. "Might explain why she wants to fly south to the Caribbean every winter."

"What do your instincts tell you about Paul DeSilva?" Hollister asked.

"I think he's involved," Max answered.

"Me too. I think he knows who Phillip DePaul is."

"DeSilva here yet?"

"On his way," Hollister answered.

Paul DeSilva was frightened. The close confines in the rear of the police car and the burly Mexican officer beside him had quieted his protests. His mind was in a panic. George Franklin was a safe seven thousand miles away, and he was on the hot seat. Alone. Who in the hell could he call? Who would help? Murray Sellers, his agent at ICM. He would know a good attorney. He hoped Murray wasn't in Palm Springs for the weekend. The police car turned into the station parking lot. Paul DeSilva wondered if he'd ever be free again.

The interrogation room was small and spartan. The windowless walls were covered with acoustical blocks that were gray with age and abuse. The air was stale with the smell of nicotine and sweat. Hollister and Max let DeSilva wait for forty minutes before they entered. DeSilva bolted to his feet when Max finally opened the door. "I have the right to call my attorney."

Hollister could see the apprehension on DeSilva's face.

Max sat down at the small table. "I'm sure you want to talk to your attorney, but if you call him now, he's going to have questions about charges, writs. Why don't we talk first?"

"I don't have anything to say," DeSilva said, but he sat down.

Hollister sat in the remaining chair. The strategy called for him to be quiet.

"I have the right to remain silent," DeSilva said with a look at each.

"You also have the right to know what this is about," Max countered. "Our investigation has uncovered a lot... we're close to making an arrest."

"Facts," DeSilva blurted, "what kind of facts!?"

Hollister was watching, reading reactions. DeSilva

shifted in the chair, turning sideways to his accuser.

"We know how much your picture was insured for," Max answered.

"Ha," DeSilva mocked, "What'd'ya think? I'd make a fuckin' movie without insurance? This wasn't some B movie you'd find on cable next summer."

"We also know the problems you were having with Shannon Roberts," Max countered.

"Shit," DeSilva blinked. "Get me a phone and I'll call six producers that had problems with Miss congeniality. Doesn't prove dog shit."

"And we know about your short-term loans with George Franklin," Max added. "You want to tell us what happened when Shannon Roberts walked last Friday?"

DeSilva stiffened. "I know who told you all this shit," he said with a look at Hollister. "That unfaithful cunt is gonna find herself in the street. She won't be able to get a job as a stand-in for a whore."

Hollister didn't react. He knew he couldn't without jeopardizing Meg Rogers. DeSilva obviously suspected her, but Hollister wasn't about to confirm it. He held DeSilva's penetrating look.

The power at the table shifted slightly, "I saw you and Meg at the Casa Del Sol," DeSilva said smugly, "so let's quit the bullshit. I know how far you're gonna get with this bunch of hearsay bullshit."

Hollister knew it was time to pull the stops. "It wasn't Meg Rogers that told us about Phillip DePaul," he said.

"Who the fuck's Phil DePaul?" DeSilva questioned defiantly.

"He's the one that parked a silver Mercedes across the street from your house the night Shannon Roberts was killed," Hollister answered.

"Yeah, and I suppose you got fuckin' pictures of it?" DeSilva mocked. His confidence was returning, and he was beginning to believe he could lie his way out of the situation.

"We got something better," Hollister said, leaning toward DeSilva as he reached inside his jacket. "The parking ticket DePaul got when he blocked your neighbor's driveway."

DeSilva's face turned ashen. "I've got a right to a phone call."

"When you get your attorney, tell him we've got a witness that saw the same Mercedes in the alley when Shannon was dumped." Hollister waved the copy of the citation in DeSilva's face.

"I don't have to say anything. I want to make my telephone call." It was almost a plea.

"You want me to book him so he can make his call?" Max said to Hollister.

Hollister tucked the copy of the citation into a pocket and stood up. He was enjoying DeSilva's discomfort. "It's Saturday. I don't want to waste anymore of my day working on this shit. Let's let it wait until Monday. We'll get a warrant from the DA."

"Aren't you afraid he'll rabbit?"

"I didn't have a fuckin' thing to do with the murder. I won't run," DeSilva interjected.

Hollister studied DeSilva for a moment. "If Meg Rogers has so much as a bad dream, we're gonna take it personal. You understand?"

"Yeah, I understand."

"And don't plan any unexpected trips between now and Monday," Max added.

"I'm not going anywhere."

"I'll talk to the watch commander," Hollister said to Max. "Get a car to take him back to Beverly Hills."

"I'll get a ride," DeSilva said. "Just get me out on the street."

"Be my pleasure," Max smiled, pushing to his feet.

Oakmont Place was quiet and peaceful. The knurled Maples lining the parkway on both sides of the street covered the block with a patchwork of shadows adding to the tranquility. The only movement on the block was an occasional bird searching the manicured lawns for worms. The rich were carefully locked behind their doors basking in the privacy of walled backyards. It was a beautiful place, but it was not a friendly place. Wealth brought with it a paranoia forced by the reality of crime. The rich had learned to be careful. It had evolved into a life of things instead of people. In the ghetto the streets teamed with people. There was nothing to stay home for. In Beverly Hills the streets were deserted and quiet. There was no reason to go out. Detective Parker studied Oakmont

Place. He wasn't so sure the unseen wealthy were as fortunate as he once thought. He'd driven onto the block ten minutes earlier in a polished Cadillac borrowed from Narcotics. He made a pass to spot the address. It was a sprawling two story, vine-covered, Spanish adobe on the west side of the street. There was a late model white Jaguar in the driveway. On his second pass Parker drove by the house and pulled to the curb facing south a quarter of a block beyond it. Settling into the Cadillac's comfortable seat, he adjusted the rearview mirror until he had it framed squarely on the house and the Jaguar. Then keying a mike with his foot, he spoke to the receiver concealed in the sun visor. "William-twenty-two is on the point."

"Twenty-two, which side of the street are you on?" Parker's voice asked over the radio.

"West side. Facing south. A quarter of a block south of the target," Torres answered.

"Roger. I'll take northbound on the east side. That way we can roll either direction."

Two audible clicks answered.

Parker was driving a late model, Buick. Torres spotted him from his slouched position in the Cadillac as soon as the Buick turned onto the block from the south. "That sure is a sissy looking car you're driving." Torres said on the radio.

"Better than that pimp mobile you're hiding in," Parker defended.

Torres flipped Parker the finger as he drove by.

"Is that your IQ or the direction to the nearest school?" Parker asked over the radio.

Parker eased the Buick to the curb behind several other parked cars. Like Torres, he adjusted his rearview mirror and settled in to wait.

"Hey, Raul," Parker said over the radio. "What are we gonna charge Hollister for this stake-out?"

"Maybe next weekend in Vegas instead of standby?" Torres answered.

"You want to take the women along?"

"Why take them. There's lots of women there."

Behind the vine covered stucco walls Paul DeSilva was on the telephone. He'd walked seven blocks after leaving the police station before he spotted a cab. Fuckin' L.A. had no public transportation. The driver was a pimple faced Arab who charged him sixty dollars extra for going into Beverly Hills and the ride took twenty minutes. As soon as he walked through the front door he went straight to his study at the back of the house and called London. George Franklin didn't answer. The desperate DeSilva placed the call three more times before calling the international operator a "bitch" and hanging up in frustration. He dug out Franklin's office email address and sent a message there.

George,
It's an emergency. Call me ASAP.
Paul DeSilva.

Ten minutes later, after two more attempted telephone calls, he sent a second email to Franklin's iPad. The goddamned Limy was hiding and he knew it. Well the sonofabitch wasn't going to get away with it. He'd make a deal with the cops if he had to. Smart bastards. Fuckin' know-it-all's in cheap clothes and Aqua Velva. He tried George Franklin again without success and then called Murray Sellers at ICM. He got an answering service. He demanded they find Sellers. It was an emergency. He poured himself a glass of scotch, lit a cigar and paced as he waited for Sellers to return his call. There was hope, he told himself. He wasn't in jail yet. Shit, all the cops had was some revenge-seeking secretary. That bitch. Why did she do it? He never laid a hand on her. And then there was this pro that George Franklin brought in. A real smooth operator. Great references. Fuckin' idiot got a parking ticket. Real pro alright. Just another sheep-dip, sand-nigger. He'd turn the cops onto the bastard if he had to.

DeSilva poured himself another scotch as he thought about the young Arab. He was lean and dressed like some fruit actor. He had cold lifeless eyes with no emotion. What the fuck was life without emotion? He remembered the Arab's eyes when Shannon Roberts walked into the room. She was in a form-fitting Dan skin and the man didn't react at all! Maybe he liked men? Might explain why he was a killer. DeSilva had spent all afternoon trying to lure Shannon to the alleged script meeting. She was reluctant. She wanted Walt Altice with her, but finally she agreed. He picked her up twenty minutes later in the alley behind her house. What a gorgeous set of tits; too bad they were connected to a brain.

Franklin and the Arab were waiting in his study when DeSilva and Shannon arrived. George Franklin was introduced as one of the principal investors and the Arab as a French screenwriter. DeSilva poured all four a drink while they made small talk. He had to admit it was exciting knowing Shannon was sitting in the room with a man who was awaiting his cue to kill her. DeSilva had no idea how the Arab was going to do it. It wasn't until the news report that he learned she died of drugs and strangulation. Maybe the Arab wasn't so stupid after all. How could those nickel-dime cops prove he and Franklin were involved? Maybe it wasn't so bad after all?

DeSilva sipped his scotch and thought about the last time he saw Shannon Roberts. He and Franklin were walking out of the study. It was the Arab's cue. As they left the room, Shannon moved to a telephone at the end of the bar. She smiled at the Arab and said something about calling her maid. When DeSilva last glanced back she was talking quietly on the telephone. Too bad. She sure had a great set of tits.

SIXTEEN | SUNSHINE, PALM TREES AND DEATH

Hollister sent Max back to Doris and the waiting bathroom wallpaper. They would meet at the station at six-thirty to relieve Parker and Torres on the stake-out of DeSilva's house. After Max was gone, Hollister headed for Los Angeles International Airport. He had an idea on how to tighten the noose around Phillip DePaul's neck, a review of the video made at the rent-a-car agency. Then they would have a face for Phillip DePaul. There was no need to rob Max of more of his day off. He wasn't the one without a wife.

Saturday afternoon traffic was light on the west-bound Santa Monica Freeway. The sky was clear, and the sun had the temperature in the high seventies. Hollister glanced at the cars around him. Most were couples with kids. The Saturday syndrome, cramming a few hours of fun into a day off. Hollister looked at them and for a moment he envied them. They were together, laughing, smiling, talking, and going places. He was alone, in their midst, tracking a murderer. He felt foreign, like a trespasser. An imposter. They were looking for life. He was investigating death. Maybe that was why Kim left. Maybe she had seen he was alone. Maybe she realized he had always been alone. He wondered where Kim was. What was she doing? Was she alone? How long had it been? Six days. He held her breasts, kissed her neck and she left. Not a bad ending. Not great, but not bad. He wondered if he loved her. It was obvious she didn't love him. Maybe that was it. They simply came unscrewed. The thought provoked a smile. He certainly loved her physically. He ached remembering their lovemaking. There was irony in their lovemaking because, in spite of what the name implied, it had not been love. Jesus, it was a sobering thought. He was fast approaching forty and, although married twice, he was once again - alone.

Was it his fault? He hadn't left Kim. Hell, lots of men worked hard. Cops didn't have an edge on it. Kim simply used it as an excuse. Maybe it was fate settling the score. He had left his first wife, now his second wife left him. An eye for an eye. Whatever the hell it was he knew he had to tell Max. The mere thought of it made him flush with embarrassment. Pride was a bitch and so was the reality of telling someone your wife left you.

The International Terminal on World Way was crowded with a tangle of cars, buses and cabs. Hollister double parked until a car pulled from the curb, then he eased the detective car into the vacant space and pushed the selector to park. He pulled the coiled cord of the radio microphone and dropped it over the rearview mirror. He didn't want some eager airport cop impounding a detective car.

The Customs office was on the second floor. Hollister rode the escalator with a crush of smiling Japanese. They filled the air with short, choppy, phrases and laughter. Many had cameras hanging around their necks.

"Toyota," Hollister said to a dark-haired Japanese man that smiled at him.

Hollister showed his badge to a Customs Officer that glanced up at him as he stepped into the spacious administrative offices. Most of the desks were vacant. Saturday, Hollister concluded.

"Who's in charge today?" Hollister said to the officer who had returned his attention to the sports section of the Times.

"Deputy Director," the officer said without looking up. "End of the hall, on the right."

Crossing the office complex, Hollister noted every desk had computer terminals with large screens. The Feds didn't have the same money problems the city had. There was a glass-enclosed officer at the end of the hall. The upgraded furniture and carpet told Hollister it was the director's office. The door was open. A blonde woman in her mid-thirties was at a coffee pot in the corner when Hollister stepped in. "May I help you?" she asked.

"Hollister, LAPD Homicide. I'd like to talk to your

boss."

"My boss?" The woman turned to him. She was shapely and the conservative blouse she wore didn't hide it.

"The officer said I could find the deputy director back here." Hollister didn't allow his eyes to go below her neck.

"That's true," the woman agreed.

"I'd like to talk to him," Hollister added.

The woman crossed to the desk and set her cup on it. "You can't talk to him, but you can talk to me. I'm Janet Trainer, the Deputy Director."

"Sorry," Hollister said, feeling foolish.

"I'm used to it. What can I do for you? She moved around her desk and sat down.

"I'm looking for a Frenchman who entered, or departed, the country through LAX recently."

"Requests normally come through your Intelligence Division?" The woman said, as she studied Hollister.

"That would take time," Hollister defended, "and I don't have time. I'm working on a homicide."

"Sit down, Sergeant," the woman invited. "You're investigating a murder?"

"Yes," Hollister sat down in a chair in front of the desk.

The woman picked up a pen. "What's the name of the French citizen?"

"Phillip DePaul," Hollister said, digging in a jacket pocket. He pulled out a small notebook. "Date of birth is ten, six, eighty-three."

The woman made notes then gathered up the telephone. "Dave, come in here please."

A moment later a customs officer appeared in the doorway. The woman offered the slip of paper. "See what we've got on this individual?"

"Right." The officer took the paper and moved away.

Janet Trainer picked up her cup.

"Where do you work, Sergeant?"

"Hollywood."

"It must be very interesting, but I can't imagine working there full-time," the woman said with professional interest.

"Airports are very interesting, but I can't imagine working in one," Hollister countered.

"It's all in what we get used to, isn't it?" The woman returned his smile.

Hollister nodded agreement. "I hope I never get used to murder."

"Are you married?"

"Separated," he admitted for the first time.

"Did the job cause it?"

"I don't know," he granted. "How about you, are you married?"

"Used to be. He was in Customs too. He took off with a stew from United. Fly the friendly skies."

"Working in airports can be hazardous." Hollister smiled.

The woman nodded agreement.

The uniformed officer returned and offered a computer printout to the Director.

"You're going to find this interesting," the woman said after a quick read. "DePaul did leave the country through LAX on Sunday. Air France, flight one-oh-six, non-stop, LA to Paris."

Hollister pulled out his notebook. "What was the flight number again?"

"One-oh-six," the woman repeated with a glance at the printout. "But there's more."

"More?"

"Phillip DePaul came through Customs this morning at eight-fifty-eight."

"What! This morning?" Hollister was shocked.

"Arrived on British Air, flight one-twenty-two, non-stop from Madrid. Still traveling with a French passport."

Hollister was on his feet, his heart racing. The killer was back in Los Angeles. What the hell did he want? How could he find him? "Can I have that?"

The woman folded the printout and offered it.

"Can you get me a picture of him?" Hollister asked.

"Color or black and white?" The woman smiled.

The afternoon on Oakmont Place was quiet. A black maid walked a poodle, a Mexican gardener trimmed a hedge, an occasional car drove by. Torres and Parker were fighting individual battles with boredom. When the red Volkswagen turned onto the block Torres sank several inches lower in his seat as the car rolled toward him.

Torres was careful not to turn his head as the car passed but his eyes were watching. Female Caucasian, early-twenties, dark hair, light complexion, sunglasses, on the pudgy side. This wasn't Volkswagen country, so he was betting the girl was a servant or co-ed coming home for the weekend. He was surprised when the car slowed and swung into the driveway of Paul DeSilva's home. Torres keyed the floor mike. "Hey, we got something."

The radio clicked twice in answer. Parker was watching.

Ruth Fowler was dressed in tight jeans and a tee-shirt. Although she was twenty pounds overweight, youth was yet to let her sag. She climbed out of the Volkswagen and walked toward the front door. She hadn't expected to hear from Paul DeSilva again. She didn't understand what happened at the restaurant that upset him, but it didn't matter now. He had called. He was sorry. Could she come over? She was thrilled. My God, from Bath, Maine, to Beverly Hills. Maybe this would be her home someday. She drew in a breath and pushed a doorbell at the front door.

"Fuck," Hollister growled, pushing through the automatic doors of the international terminal onto the sidewalk. There was a citation on the windshield of the detective car. He knew clearing a citation was a pain in the ass. A form fifteen-seven with a detailed explanation of the circumstances to justify the violation along with the detective commander's signature and a request for a citation cancellation. Throwing it away, better known as the "ghetto toss", was likewise hazardous. The citation would automatically go to an arrest warrant and result in an investigation. Paying the citation was no option either. Parking in a "No Parking Anytime" at LAX had to be at least a couple hundred bucks. He headed for the car. What asshole would ticket a police car. He rounded the front of the detective car and grabbed the citation off the windshield. He wanted to see who this prick was. He bet it was a woman. "Have a nice day," the officer had written across the otherwise blank citation. Hollister's anger turned to embarrassment. He smoothed the ticket, stuck it in a pocket and climbed into the car.

Hollister drove the circular World Way, working his way through the heavy flow of traffic, looking for signs indicating "Rental Car Return." Finally, he spotted the sign and moved into the left lane to follow the arrows.

The Classic Connection car rental office was beside the sprawling Hertz complex. Its smaller parking lot was lined with a collection of polished Bentleys, Rolls Royces, Porsches, a Corvette and a line of classic Mercedes. Several of the Mercedes were silver. Hollister wondered if he were looking at the car that took Shannon Roberts on her last ride. He parked beside a Rolls Royce.

"May I help you," a perky brunette smiled when he reached the service counter. Her name tag read, "Kim."

Hollister pulled the silver and gold badge from his belt and displayed it. The perky smile faded. "Oh."

"I'd like to know if you rented a car to a man named DePaul. He's a Frenchman. He may have been in early this morning."

"I just came on at noon," the girl balked.

"Check anyway?" Hollister ordered.

"What was the name?" The girl stepped to a computer terminal.

"DePaul," Hollister answered. "Phillip DePaul."

The girl's fingers moved on the keys. The computer beeped. the girl watched as the results appeared on the screen. Hollister watched her eyes, waiting. "Yes," she said, seeming relieved she had found it. Hollister had his pen poised. "DePaul, Phillip," the girl read, "one day. LA return... Mercedes coupe...red. California license One DLB Nine One Four...declined deductible...paid with an American Express credit card... erified and approved."

"When's the car due to be returned?" Hollister pressed. "It's a one day," the girl explained. "It's due for return tomorrow."

Hollister wrote on a page of his notebook and tore it out. "This is my cell number. If the car comes in, you must call me. Immediately! Understand?"

"Is he dangerous or something?" the brunette questioned. She was frightened.

"Only if he knows you've talked to me."

"I won't tell."

Parker spotted the red Mercedes the moment it turned onto the block. It didn't stir suspicion. A Mercedes in Beverly Hills wasn't an uncommon sight. He pretended to be reading as the car rolled by. The driver had dark hair and an olive complexion. Arab or Indian, Parker concluded. The man was searching for something. Parker's eyes went to the rearview mirror. His heart jumped when the brake lights flashed on in front of DeSilva's driveway. Parker keyed his microphone and spoke softly without moving. "Hey, taco breath, we got something."

"I see him," Torres' voice answered on the radio. "Already got the license number."

The white Jaguar was parked in the driveway. Assad knew it was DeSilva's car. The red Volkswagen parked beside the Jaguar added a complication. Someone was with DeSilva. That wasn't necessarily bad. Sometimes it was best to kill two when you were really after one. Police then had the problem of deciding who the real target was. Plus, it muddied the motive as well. Assad parked at the curb in front of the house and climbed out.

Entry was simple. First, he would try the door. Many left their homes unlocked during daylight hours. If it were locked, he'd simply ring the bell. DeSilva knew him. He was certain he'd open the door. That was all he needed. Assad walked to the archway that covered the front door. He listened for a moment. Hearing nothing, he reached for the brass knob. It twisted without resistance. He opened the door and stepped quietly inside.

The speedometer in the detective car hung near seventy-five-miles-an-hour as Hollister weaved in and around the slower traffic on the freeway. If Philip DePaul was Shannon Roberts' killer, then Hollister knew where he was going. Paul DeSilva's home. The fact that Torres and Parker were staked on the house eased his mind, but still, he wanted to be close. He'd park a block away and contact them on Tac One. The detective car couldn't be risked in close. What the hell did DePaul want? Non-stop from Spain? Why was he coming back? It made no sense. Hollister tramped harder on the accelerator.

The first floor of the sprawling house was quiet. Assad moved quietly from room to room. He was in the dining room when a toilet flushed upstairs. When he reached the bottom of the open staircase, he heard a girl's laughter on the second floor. He started up the curved staircase.

Paul DeSilva had the big tub built especially for such occasions. The tub was sunken into the tiled bathroom floor and big enough for four bathers. DeSilva's personal record was seven. That was a real night to remember. Now there was just him and the chubby waitress from the studio. He couldn't remember her name, so he was calling her honey. He called the girl after talking to the attorney Murray Sellers referred him to. What was his name? Saul Howard. Scare tactics, that's what he called what the cops were doing. The attorney claimed if the police really had a case, they would make an arrest. It was all bullshit. He had nothing to worry about. He was innocent until proven guilty and this was America where the law protected him from harassment. Fuckin' K-Mart cops.

He had Saul Howard's personal number and bail money if needed. There was no need to waste the weekend, so he called the girl. She was there forty minutes later, and twenty minutes after her arrival, DeSilva had her mildly drunk and nude. The Jacuzzi jets were on in the tub, the water was hot and soapy, and the nude girl was scrubbing DeSilva's hairy chest.

"Lower honey, lower," DeSilva leaned his head back on a folded towel and closed his eyes. The girl's hand moved slowly down his chest over his stomach. He tensed, anticipating her touch. "Paul," the girl said. Her hand stopped moving.

"It's okay, honey," DeSilva said without opening his eyes. He took her hand and pushed it toward his erection.

"Paul," the girl resisted and pulled away, "someone's here."

DeSilva opened his eyes. He recognized the Arab immediately. "What the fuck!"

The pudgy waitress sank lower in the water.

Assad ignored DeSilva's question. He had already decided how to do it before the girl spotted him. He stepped to a nearby mirror backed countertop.

"Get your ass outta my house." DeSilva reached for a towel beside the tub. "You wanna see me, call like you were fucking civilized or something."

Assad picked up a hair dryer lying on the marble countertop. Switching it on he turned and casually tossed it into the soapy water of the bathtub.

The lights in the bathroom blinked and went out as a circuit breaker tripped. Paul DeSilva was standing when the jolt of electricity surged through him. He bit his tongue, shook his head, and fell, eyes wide, with a heavy splash into the water. The pudgy waitress trembled, tried to speak and then fell face forward into the water.

The Jacuzzi jets offered a few final bubbles as their power source fell silent. The bathroom was quiet. Assad studied the two bodies in the water. When he was satisfied there was no movement, he turned and walked from the room.

Outside the air was thick with an exchange of

radio traffic. "Hey, Raul, you notice the driver of the Mercedes looks Arab or something?"

"It ain't a silver Mercedes," Torres answered.

"Maybe he took it to a one-day paint center."

"And maybe it ain't him."

"You wanna bet it isn't?"

"We go with him, we might lose DeSilva."

"He's got the little brunette bimbo to keep him busy. Let's follow the red Mercedes a couple blocks, jam him. If he doesn't have a French accent, we let him go," Parker urged.

"I don't like it," Torres argued.

"You wanna tell Hollister we just let the frog go?"

The exchange died when Assad appeared from the front of the house and walked toward the waiting Mercedes.

"Au revoir," Parker said as Assad climbed in behind the wheel of the Mercedes.

Torres laid flat on the front seat of the Cadillac and listened for the sound of the Mercedes as it passed. He waited fifteen seconds before he sat up to peer over the dash. The red Mercedes was making a turn at the end of the block. Torres turned to where Parker was parked. The Buick was swinging in a tight U-turn to follow. "Shit," Torres hissed as he straightened behind the wheel and reached for the ignition.

"I knew you'd come to your senses," Parker said as he roared by Torres' Cadillac heading for the corner where the Mercedes had disappeared.

Torres pulled the Cadillac in gear and followed.

He felt uneasy about what they were doing. Hollister hadn't said anything about a plan for the French suspect if he arrived, but he had warned them not to lose DeSilva, but what if it was the Frenchman? What would they do with him? He hoped Parker had some ideas.

The red Mercedes drove leisurely through shaded blocks of plush residential housing before turning south on Cannon Drive. "Come on by," Parker urged over the radio. "Let's jam him at the next intersection."

"If it's the Frenchman, what do we do with him?" Torres questioned, keying the mike.

"I'll take him to the station and call Hollister. You get back on DeSilva's house."

"Roger," Torres said as he gunned the Cadillac by Parker's Buick and then passed the red Mercedes which was now only several car lengths ahead. The driver seemed to pay no attention to Torres as he passed the car. When he was well past the car, Torres eased the Cadillac back into the same lane in front of the Mercedes.

Jamming called for sandwiching the suspect's car. One in front, one behind, blocking any escape. When executed properly, it was quick and easy. The element of surprise was an important ingredient. Parker and Torres had added an extra touch to their jamming technique in the truest sense of the word. The car following would bump the suspect's car from behind just before they jumped out, weapons in hand to yell, "Police." The unsuspecting drivers, without fail, would look to their rearview mirrors or turn and then, the officer from the front car would have his gun screwed in the suspect's ear.

"Okay, we got a red light," Torres said, looking to the intersection of Cannon Drive and Wilshire Boulevard. He glanced at the rearview mirror. "Shit," he grimaced. The red Mercedes was switching to the left lane.

"No, sweat," Parker said over the radio. "He's got a car in front of him. It's still Plan A. I'll pull up tight and bump him. You move in."

"Roger."

Assad was watching the man in the Cadillac as well as the Buick behind him. He wasn't certain until he changed lanes and the Buick changed with him. They had been with him for five blocks. The doubt was gone now. They were police. He slowed for the light, willing himself calm. Did they know of DeSilva and the girl? How long had they been with him?

Who the hell were they? There was a SUV paused at the traffic signal in front of Assad or he would have run the red light. He was confident the Mercedes could outrun the two big American cars. The Cadillac with the Latin in it pulled to a stop beside the SUV. The Buick was close behind. He could see the man's face clearly. Assad eased the Mercedes to a stop a car length behind the station wagon. As soon as he stopped, the Buick thumped into his car from behind, rocking the smaller Mercedes. Assad kept his eyes locked on the Cadillac. The driver's door sprung open and the Latin rolled out, gun in hand. As he crossed the space between the Mercedes and the SUV, Assad tramped hard on the accelerator. The Mercedes roared and jumped forward. The front bumper hit Torres between the ankle and the knees, breaking both of his legs and slamming him forward to smash against the back of the SUV with a sickening crunch. Torres fired a shot as he flailed at the hood of the Mercedes. The windshield disintegrated in a shower of glass. Torres heard his leg bones crack and break. Something popped loud in his lower abdomen and he felt like a child wetting his pants. A warm, salty, taste filled his mouth. The hood of the Mercedes was warm as his hand slid across it and he fell.

"Noooo!" Parker shouted, jumping from the Buick with gun in hand. He had watched in horror as the Mercedes lunged, crushing Torres against the SUV. He raised his pistol and fired a volley of shots.

The crack of the nine-millimeter combined with flying glass and bits of leather as the bullets ripped through the Mercedes. Falling across the center console, Assad jammed the selector into reverse and tramped hard on the accelerator. The Mercedes spun its wheels on the pavement sending out a howling scream and billows of blue smoke as it leaped backwards.

Parker jumped and rolled aside on the asphalt as the Mercedes roared backwards slamming into the front of the Buick. Glass, chrome and steam spewed from the impact. On his back in the street Parker popped an empty magazine from his pistol and grabbed for another strapped to his belt.

Assad sat up and pulled the Mercedes into drive. Torres, pelvic bones broken, and legs crushed, was trying to crawl away from the rear of the SUV on his elbows dragging his bloodied and twisted legs like a slug. The Mercedes lunged forward turning to the left. The twenty-seven-hundred-pound car powered over Torres's upper torso, crushing, tearing at his clothes and breaking him as it thumped over his body.

Parker rolled onto his stomach and fired. Three of his shots hit the SUV. The sixty-two-year-old driver filled the inside of her car with screams. The remaining two shots ripped into the rear of the Mercedes puncturing the trunk lid. The bullet riddled car roared into the intersection and disappeared east on Wilshire.

Parker dropped his pistol and scrambled to the side of his fallen partner. Parker's stomach convulsed. Torres's face was bloodied and fried with blisters and torn flesh from contact with the hot muffler on the underside of the Mercedes. Blood ran from his nose and mouth. His eyes were open, but they were crossed, and one was blood red. His arms and legs were twisted into awkward positions. A jagged leg bone stuck through his trouser leg. Tears streamed down Parker's face.

"I'm sorry, goddamned, I'm sorry." Parker reached out to touch Torres, but he couldn't. Parker pushed up and ran to the open door of the damaged Buick. Sinking into the seat, he grabbed the microphone. "Officer needs help, shots fired, officer down... intersection of Cannon and Wilshire in Beverly Hills!" his voice was breaking. "I need a fucking ambulance!"

"All Units, all frequencies... officer needs help... Cannon and Wilshire in Beverly Hills," the female voice from Communications responded. Her voice was tense but controlled. "Shots fired... officer down. Unit reporting, your identification?"

"Just get me a fucking ambulance!" Parker screamed, striking the dash of the car with a clenched fist.

"All units, all frequencies, six-zebra-twenty-two reports the suspect from the officer involved shooting at Cannon and Wilshire is eastbound on Wilshire in a red Mercedes. The vehicle has bullet holes and TA damage."

Hollister was eastbound on the Santa Monica Freeway when he heard the broadcast. His stomach muscles tensed. He knew it was Parker and Torres. His heart swelled into his throat. He moved into the right-hand lane and exited the freeway at Robertson Boulevard.

Assad knew he had little time. The policeman that shot at him undoubtedly had a radio and by now a description of his car would be broadcast across the city. Even if that were not true, the fact the car had bullet holes and no front or rear windshield made it obvious. There was blood on his cheek. He guessed it was from flying glass and not a bullet wound. Allah was still with him. He forced himself to drive carefully for several blocks before he turned south on a street where an overhead sign read Robertson Boulevard.

Hollister turned his head lamps on and laid on the horn as he raced north on Robertson. He cursed the detective car for not having red lights or siren, as well as the motorists reluctant to get out of his way. He was praying Parker and Torres were alive. It brought back the stark memory of a prayer offered for John Stratton the night he was shot in the neck. God seemed busy with other things that night as the lieutenant lay with blood spurting from his jugular. Hollister was approaching Pico Boulevard when the red Mercedes sped by in the opposite direction. Without hesitation he twisted the wheel hard to the left and stood on the brake pedal.

The detective car swung in a tire-screaming one-hundred and eighty degree turn across three on-coming lanes of Robertson Boulevard to come to a near stop facing southbound. The air came to life with horns and screeching tires as frightened motorists took evasive action.

Hollister floored the accelerator and watched the speedometer as it climbed to near eighty miles an hour. He was closing on the Mercedes. It was a block ahead. He cursed the microphone of the radio falling onto the floor, out of reach, on the passenger's side of the car. Too great a risk to reach for it. Great fuckin' design. Hollister flashed by slower cars on the right. The brake lights on the Mercedes flashed. The car slowed and swung right to disappear from his sight.

The detective car roared to where Hollister had last seen the Mercedes. He braked the car and looked. A driveway led into the mouth of a subterranean apartment garage. Hollister twisted the wheel and gunned the car down the incline into the shadows of the garage. The ceiling of the garage was low and laced with overhead insulated pipes and lights.

Fading yellow arrows on the floor directed the traffic flow. Hollister followed them as he drove up and down the aisles. His eyes, growing accustomed to the half-light, searched frantically for the Mercedes. They found nothing. Hollister's heart pounded like a drum in his ears. The only sound he could hear was the yelp of his tires turning from row to row. He was beginning to believe he turned into the wrong driveway. He was tense with fear, frustration and anxiety. His palms were wet on the plastic of the steering wheel. He turned the corner of the last aisle and spotted the Mercedes. It was parked in a lane near a doorway where a sign announced, "Elevator." The driver's door of the Mercedes was standing open. Hollister braked to a stop close behind the car, pulled his nine-millimeter from its holster and climbed out.

The rear of the Mercedes was pocked with bullet holes. Its rear window and windshield were gone. Hollister glanced inside the car as he moved by.

Gun in hand, he pushed open a door that led

to the elevator and stairs. The Frenchman had at least a thirty second lead. Hollister hoped he'd find someone that saw the man, someone he could have call for back-up. Maybe they could trap the bastard in the building. Hollister stepped through the door and moved for the elevator. He heard movement behind him and started to turn but it was too late. A clenched fist slammed into Hollister's neck at the base of his skull. The impact knocked him forward. He felt foolish. The embarrassment was much greater than the pain. His head slammed into the doors covering the face of the elevator. He felt the metal doors buckle and bend inward. He was stunned. His vision was gray, and his ears were ringing. He knew he had to hold onto his gun. The cement floor was cool and gritty against his cheek. He didn't remember falling. He blinked, tried to see.

Assad moved quickly to Hollister stepping hard on the hand that held the gun. Drawing back his foot, Assad kicked the man hard in the groin. Hollister grasped and drew up his legs. Assad reached down and wrenched the gun from Hollister's hand. He kicked time and time again first into the man's head and then his stomach. Blood ran from Hollister's' nose. Assad took aim at Hollister's head. The chime of the elevator sounded. Assad paused. The buckled metal doors groaned as they parted to reveal a young couple in tennis shorts. A second froze the moment and then the women filled the elevator with a shrill scream. Assad turned and bolted away.

Hollister coughed and opened his eyes. The oxygen mask was uncomfortable. His mouth was full of saliva. He swallowed and coughed again. The ceiling was close, within his reach. It was white with row after row of dots. He felt he was moving. The vibration, the noise. A bolt of fear shot through him. "Relax," a paramedic pushed Hollister down on a gurney. He blinked his eyes and looked. He was riding in an ambulance. He relaxed, trying to ignore the flame in his groin, sucking in the cool oxygen.

"We're almost there," the paramedic said, pumping a blood pressure sleeve wrapped around Hollister's arm. Hollister didn't care where they were. He just wanted sleep. Sleep to escape the embarrassment and questions he was certain were coming. He had played the Frenchman's fool, made the John Wayne pursuit and got his ass kicked in the process. He tried to think about the moment. He couldn't remember it. In addition to being a fool, he was stupid. Where was his gun? He tried to remember. His mind refused to focus. "My gun?" He tried to sit up again.

The paramedic pushed him down. "Relax. They'll find your gun."

There was the answer. The Frenchman took it. Not only did he take his gun, he took his pride. Hollister closed his eyes. He could see the Frenchman. He was handsome and tanned, dressed in a white dinner jacket, walking to a polished white Mercedes. Who was the girl with him? She turned and glanced at

Hollister with a teasing smile as she took the French-man's arm. What! It was his wife, Kim! She turned and moved with the Frenchman toward the waiting car. Hollister ran after them. His feet were like lead. His gut was aflame. Finally, he reached them and grabbed her by the arm. She turned and her eyes found his. It was Shannon Roberts. He closed his eyes and turned away. "Lee," the sultry voice called. He looked to her. It was Kim again. Hollister reached for her, but the Frenchman pulled her into the car. He tried to reach her, but someone was holding him, telling him to be still. They were in the car now. The Frenchman was smiling, laughing. He had Hollister's gun. He had it all. They pulled away. Hollister felt powerless, foolish.

Abu Assad tossed the nine-millimeter pistol into a bed of ivy outside the apartment building. He crossed the street, cautious not to run or look back. He walked to the corner and turned east. He had covered a block before he heard the sirens. Then there were more. He turned another corner. The sound of helicopter rotors sent a wave of panic through him. There was a service station on the corner. Again, he fought the urge to run. He cut across the station's parking lot and stepped into the men's restroom just as the police helicopter appeared overhead.

The water pouring into the grimy grease stained sink was cool. Assad used it to rinse the dried blood from his cheek. He took off his jacket and stuffed it, along with his French passport, into the trash can. He mussed his hair and rolled up his sleeves. He was studying his image in the mirror when a bald man stepped into the small restroom. He glanced at Assad and moved into the single stall to bolt the door. Assad listened, drying his hands on a paper towel. The man's belt jingled as he lowered his pants. Assad tossed the paper towel and stepped outside.

A blue Toyota was parked outside the door of the rest room. Assad glanced around and then moved to the driver's window to look inside. The keys hung in the ignition. He opened the door, climbed in, started the car and drove away.

Assad found an Auto Club membership kit in the glove box. He took a map of California from the kit and studied it as he drove. Interstate Five ran as a solid line from Los Angeles to where it ended at Tijuana and the border with Mexico. Using the scale on the map, he computed it as a hundred-mile drive. In a little over two hours he would be out of the country.

The trauma team at Cedars Sinai Hospital emergency room worked on Raul Torres' broken body for two hours before the exhausted team leader said, "Mark death at twenty-two past the hour." He walked away from the treatment table to pull off his bloody gloves. A nurse joined him. Pulling off her mask she said, "Don't take it so hard. He was a dead when they brought him in."

"He still is," the doctor said, wiping at his face.

Hollister vaguely remembered looking up into a lamp in the treatment room. Someone was manipulating his balls and asking him if it hurt? He didn't care. He wanted sleep. When he woke hours later, Max was in the room with him. Hollister recognized his partner's big shoulders. He was standing, looking out the window, his back to Hollister. Hollister tried pushing himself up in the bed, but pain stopped him. There was a plastic I.D. bracelet around his right wrist, and he was in a gown. He looked to his wrist for his watch. It was gone. "Max," Hollister said, "what time is it?"

The surprised Max turned. "You're awake."

"Did they find him?" Hollister questioned as he lay back on the inclined bed.

"Not yet. He stole a car at a Shell station at Pico and Holt. We've got an APB out."

Hollister didn't want to ask, but the compulsion to know demanded it. "Parker and Torres?"

Max averted his eyes as if to ready himself. He returned them to Hollister's. "Parker's okay, at least physically. The sonofabitch ran over Torres. He's dead."

Hollister wiped at his face. The headache was making him weary. He didn't know what to say. The responsibility he felt for Torres' death settled over him like a smothering blanket of guilt. "What happened?" he said weakly, with a dry mouth.

"The Frenchman showed up at DeSilva's house. When he left, Parker and Torres followed. They tried to jam him a couple blocks later. Things went wrong."

Hollister nodded. The details weren't important. Nothing would change the fact that another cop was dead. Somehow it made Hollister feel very old.

"Have you picked up DeSilva?" Hollister asked, thinking of the clear connection they had between DeSilva and the Frenchman.

"No," Max answered, "but the coroner did. He's dead too."

"Dead?" Hollister said in disbelief.

"After Parker told us they followed the Frenchman away from DeSilva's house, I went back after him. I found him naked and dead in an upstairs bathtub. There was a girl with him. The Frenchman dropped a hair dryer in the water."

"Jesus!" Hollister said as he closed his eyes, weary with it all. It was dark when he woke. The door to the hallway was open and light spilled in, but it was quiet. He guessed it was late. He reached to a nearby stand. His watch was in the drawer. He held it close to his face in the faint light. It was ten minutes after one. A doctor had talked to him earlier. His injuries weren't serious. A concussion, bruised testicles.

So, what, he mused, they weren't getting much use anyway.

Marshal and Davis followed the doctor's visit. Marshal had brought a pint of Seagram's VO. They offered their sympathy, their encouragement, a few bad jokes and left. They had a cop killer to find. Lieutenant Brillion and Sergeant Oaks from the Officer-Involved-Shooting team came in early in the evening. They wanted to know if Hollister could provide a description of the Frenchman. Hollister had to confess he never saw the man before he was hit from behind, but there were pictures of the Frenchman in his car. "You're a lucky man," Sergeant Oaks told Hollister when the questions were over.

"Why don't I feel lucky?" Hollister answered sarcastically.

Captain Harris and Lieutenant Prescott were Hollister's final visitors. Hollister hadn't seen Prescott in several years. The lieutenant's first official day as the new officer-in-charge of the Hollywood Homicide unit wasn't until Monday morning, but the death of a detective and the injury of another was ample cause to call him in early. Prescott was a dark-haired, handsome, robust man with intense eyes when they worked Narcotics together. Now the lieutenant's hair was streaked with gray and the robust look had yielded to a gaunt, fatigued appearance. Hollister wondered why the man had aged so much. It made Hollister wonder how he looked to Prescott. It wasn't likely Prescott was the only one growing older. The lieutenant still had his inquiring dark eyes and, as they found Hollister, he winced with the guilt they provoked. Where's your gun? Why did an officer die on a stake-out you sent him to? But Prescott asked none of it. Instead he said, "How are you, Hollister?"

"Good, Lieutenant," Hollister answered.

"We've got the entire homicide unit working on the case," Captain Harris explained. "They got lifts off the Mercedes. Maybe we'll get a true ID on this Frenchman."

Hollister didn't really think they would be that lucky. The police seldom were.

"We've got an alert out on the Toyota," Lieutenant Prescott added, sounding very authoritative, like he'd worked on the case for weeks. Hollister felt powerless, as if he'd been declared impotent and pushed onto some sidetrack.

"Max tells us the suspect took your gun," Captain Harris said, adding to Hollister's feeling of despair.

"It's missing?" Hollister answered defensively. He wished he could stand up. He didn't like defending himself on his back.

"Well, get some rest," Harris suggested. "We're glad you're all right." His tone was sincere.

"Thanks," Hollister offered in reply.

It was late when Max returned. Hollister was still awake. They shared a drink from the bottle of VO Marshal smuggled in. It was rare the Mormon Baxter drank, but he looked haggard and eager for relief. Over ice, the alcohol tasted good and Hollister enjoyed the warmth it brought to his aching stomach.

"No word on the stolen Toyota," Max said, pouring himself a second drink in a paper cup.

"This guy's good, Max," Hollister said thinking about the Frenchman.

"Yeah, but he's still just an asshole, and all assholes fuck up eventually."

"We hope."

"Parker's taking Torres' death hard," Max said, staring into his cup.

"Who the hell wouldn't? Pour us some more," he said, aiming his empty cup at Max.

After a third drink Max left, promising to return in the morning. A nurse in glasses came in and offered Hollister a drink of juice. He declined and she turned the room light out. Four hours passed. Sleep had helped. The pain was nearly gone from the base of his skull and he felt stronger. Even the ache in his balls was subsiding. Hollister swung his feet to the floor and eased his weight onto them. He found his clothes hanging in a small closet on the far side of the room.

The feelings of frustration and fear that haunted Hollister had powerful roots and, as he dressed in the darkness of the hospital room, he remembered them. He searched for his badge and found it in a trouser pocket. He gave a sigh of relief. It felt good in his hand. He was a police sergeant. His badge granted him the authority, but his gun was gone. He vowed this time would be different. This time he would find the French sonofabitch that killed Torres, Canfield and Martinez. He'd find him and he'd kill him. No matter the cost... Hollister pulled on his pants, pulled his shirt over his head and moved for the door.

Max Baxter didn't leave Hollywood station until near midnight and he was back at six A.M. He checked the Teletypes and crime reports that came in during the night. There was nothing involving a Toyota or a suspect fitting the Frenchman's description. It appeared someone had already been through the reports once. Max assumed it was the Officer-Involved-Shooting team. Pushing the reports aside, he called the airport detail at Los Angeles International and then U.S. Customs. There was no record of Phillip DePaul exiting the continental United States since the APB alert. Max hung up. He was frustrated but determined. They were playing the game by the Frenchman's rules. They were chasing. The Frenchman was running. Time and tactics were on the Frenchman's side and, if he was clever enough, they would never find him. Max gave up on the idea of finding the man with the dragnet and dug out the wealth of personal papers collected from DeSilva's home. He had to find a way to get ahead of the Frenchman. They had to take the game plan away from him. Max searched until he found the red leather address book. He flipped it open. It was predominantly female names, addresses and telephone numbers but Max found one he was searching for. He picked up the telephone, checked the law enforcement directory beneath the plastic cover on his desk pad and dialed. He was excited with his idea.

"US Customs," a female voice answered.

"Records, please."

"One moment." The line clicked on hold briefly.

"Records, Carlson."

"Carlson, it's Baxter from Hollywood detectives. I talked to you earlier."

"Right, checking on the Frenchman."

"I've got another name I'd like you to run."

"What is it you're looking for?"

"Entry into and out of LA over the last couple of weeks," Max answered.

"If our twenty-six-million-dollar computer can't tell you that, we'll ship it back to China. What's the name?"

"Franklin. George Sinclair Franklin," Max said.

"Citizenship?" Carlson questioned.

"British," Max answered

"Hold, please?"

Max could hear the plastic clicks of a computer's keyboard and then an electronic chirp. The man answered sooner than Max expected. "Got a hit," Carlson said.

"When?" Max questioned eagerly.

"Entry into the United States, AM Saturday, August, twenty-fourth. Exit the United States, PM, August, twenty-six, both through Los Angeles International."

Max scribbled the information on a pad. "You've made my day, Carlson."

Max hung up and pulled DeSilva's address book in front of him. He ran a finger down the page to...

"Franklin, George, Sinclair, 6147 Hampton Road, number 337, London, England. Home 011-44-01-342-2498, Officer 011-44-06-429-7810, L.A. 213-276-225l, room 1143.

Max recognized the 213-area code as the one assigned to the Los Angeles area. He picked up the telephone and dialed again.

The telephone rang four times before a sultry female voice answered. "The Beverly Hills Hotel. May I help you?"

"Security, please?"

Max listened to an instrumental version of Moon River as he waited on hold. It ended abruptly with a male voice interrupting. "This is Ted Fisher, may I help you?"

"Ted, this is Max Baxter, LAPD, Hollywood Homicide. I've got a suspect by the name of George Franklin. He's British. I think he was staying in your hotel on Saturday the twenty-fourth. I need to know what telephone numbers he called in Beverly Hills."

"George Franklin. The twenty-fourth," the security officer repeated as he made a note.

"Right," Max confirmed. "May have been in room eleven-forty-three."

"You calling from Hollywood station?"

"Yeah."

"I'll call you back."

The security officer was using the call back to confirm that Max was who he said he was. Many impersonated the police on the telephone. Max sat waiting, tapping his foot, trying to be patient. He sorted through the assortment of DeSilva's papers and found a telephone bill.

DeSilva's residence telephone number was on the face of the bill. Max studied it, hoping his suspicions were correct, then he looked at the amount due, $773.68. Max shook his head. DeSilva's telephone bill was half of Max's monthly house payment. He tried to think of what it would be like to be rich. His mind kept drifting to motorhomes and the mountains of southern Utah. The telephone on the desk rang. Max grabbed it up. "Hollywood Homicide, Baxter."

"It's Ted Fisher, Max," the security officer from the Beverly Hills Hotel said. "Our records indicate show George Franklin was in suite eleven-forty-three on the twenty-fourth. He made three calls. Two to a local number in Beverly Hills. One to West Hollywood. You want them?"

"Yeah," Max answered eagerly, readying his finger over DeSilva's residence telephone number.

"Two-seven-six-four-one-five-nine and eight-five-five-eight-two-four-three," the security officer said.

Max smiled and slapped the desktop with excitement. The numbers matched. He had a positive link between George Franklin and Paul DeSilva on the eve of Shannon Roberts' death. "Thanks, Ted." Max said and hung up. He was still grinning when the uniformed watch commander stepped through the door. "You got something on the stolen Toyota, huh?"

"No," Max answered. "Got something almost as

good."

"Yeah?" the lieutenant said, sitting down on the edge of the desk across from Max. "I saw Hollister in the parking lot earlier gassing a detective car. Thought you guys must have wrapped it up to call him in."

Max was shocked. "Hollister! What time was this?"

"Still dark. five, five-thirty, maybe."

Hollister had found a couple of Wilshire Division patrol cops in the hospital's emergency room waiting area. They were taking a statement from a robbery victim. When they finished, he badged them and bummed a ride to Hollywood station.

The detective squad room was quiet when Hollister arrived. He gathered the Teletypes from records and sat in the homicide office to read them. Max had done a good job writing the want on the Frenchman. Hollister's ears burned with the heat of embarrassment when he read the teletype on the assault on himself and the theft of his gun. Now every cop in the city would know he got his ass kicked and his gun stolen. How bad could life get. First his wife left him and then he lost his gun. Kim leaving might be the lessor of the two. There was little else that could be done before daylight. Hollister returned the reports and walked to the parking lot where he gassed his detective cars and drove home.

He shaved and showered and put on fresh clothes before he got out the blue steel nine-millimeter pistol Kim had bought him when he made sergeant. It was in the back of the bedroom closet in a shoe box with a box of ammo. The gun was glistening and black in his hand. Hollister tried the action. It was smooth and quiet. He loaded the magazine with cartridges from the box of ammunition.

Maybe it was the gun in hand or the sense of loss he felt that made him think of Parker. Hollister had a two partner. The man had died in his arms after losing control of their car during a pursuit. The anguish was not something police training prepared you for, or one that could be understood by anyone else other than those who had been there. Surviving your partner's death was not easy and Hollister felt an obligation to Parker. Hell, more than an obligation it was guilt. He looked at his watch. It was almost six A.M. He called Hollywood Division and got Parker's home address from watch commander.

Hollister drove fast into the night and the spread of desolate high desert north of Los Angeles. The purple night sky in the east worked at yielding to a lighter blue. The darkness was lifting from the rocky hills to take on browns and grays as dawn drew near. Nearly an hour slipped before he drove by the sign that told him he was entering the Lancaster city limits.

The GPS on Hollister's iPad read two-four-one-six Juniper Road six miles. Hollister made the announced turns and followed Juniper Road until the pavement ended. He doubted he was going the right direction. Every place he passed looked like a dump. It was growing warm. He passed a faded mailbox. It was numbered two-three-six-two-oh. Hollister was encouraged. He drove on. The homes, a collection of dusty shacks and shabby mobile homes surrounded with broken fences and rusting hulks of cars, lined the road. Every ranch seemed to have horses and goats. Dust covered everything. The only green was weeds growing in every trace of shade.

Finally, Hollister saw the sign. "Parker's Paradise Ranch." It was carved out of ornate wood and covered with dust. "You've arrived at your destination," the iPad announced. Hollister turned in the driveway and followed it several hundred yards to a double-wide mobile home where a Ford pick-up sat parked near the trailer's open door. The bed of the pick-up was stacked with strapped-on suitcases and boxes. Parker stepped out of the mobile home as Hollister pulled in. He had an open can of beer in hand. Spotting Hollister, Parker sat down on the top step outside the open door. Hollister climbed out of the detective car, glanced at the pick-up and walked to Parker.

"Hey, Sarge," Parker called, "You make a wrong turn somewhere? Last I heard you were in the hospital?" He was dressed in a tee-shirt, jeans and boots.

Hollister noticed Parker was slurring his words. The beer in his hand obviously wasn't the first one.

"Planning a trip?" Hollister questioned.

"Going home," Parker said, forcing a smile. "Little town. Bastrop, deep in the heart of Texas."

Hollister could see Parker's eyes were bloodshot and puffy. "Home. Isn't that where you're at?"

Parker took a drink from the can of beer and wiped his mouth on a sleeve. "This. Naw, this is fuckin' fantasyland. Ain't nothing real about it. This is what you get after a divorce."

"This shit storm will pass you know," Hollister suggested, studying Parker soberly.

"Frankly, as the man once said, I don't give a damn... You want a beer?"

Hollister ignored the offer. "Now's not the time to make decisions."

Parker shrugged. "I'm not making any decision right now. I made it yesterday when the doctor walked out of the fucking emergency room and told me my partner was dead."

"You're a good cop, Parker. A natural. You won't be happy if you walk away."

"Being here sure as fuck hasn't made me happy. I've been waiting on it. You know that sense of accomplishment, a thank-you from some fucking citizen I laid my ass on the line for, maybe justice in court. I've been waiting on it for almost twelve fuckin' years. You know how many times it's felt good? The only good thing about this job got killed yesterday. An ex-wife and a dead partner. I've had enough." When Parker finished there were tears in his eyes.

"You think I like it?" Hollister questioned. "It's a job someone has to do. Thanks, or no thanks."

Parker looked at Hollister. "Yeah, I think you like it. I don't understand why. I thought I did. I once thought I wanted to be like you, but I can't. It just isn't there. I wanted it to be. I wanted to be the best fuckin' detective in the LAPD, but I just don't have it."

"I feel that way every time I look in the mirror," Hollister said. "Yesterday I got my ass kicked and my gun stolen. You think I don't have a belly full of doubt? Shit, I think I invented it. But I can't quit. I can't let that fuckin' Frenchman get away with killing Torres, Canfield and Martinez. You know the difference between a good cop and a bad cop, Parker? The good cops don't quit."

"I didn't quit," Parker defended, throwing his empty beer can into the dust. "I just fuckin' gave up."

"What about the Frenchman? You gonna let him walk away?"

"I don't have any fight left in me."

"What would Torres do?" Hollister pressed.

"I'm not Torres. I'm the cop that was with him when he got killed."

"And I'm the cop that sent both of you out there. I need your help, Parker," Hollister pleaded. "If you leave now, my ass is grass. Stick it out until we wrap this thing. I need this one. We can't let the sonofabitch do this to us."

Parker wiped his chin on a sleeve, his eyes went to the dirt. He lowered his head to stare at his boots. The sun was higher and hotter. It was quiet for a long moment. Hollister waited. A crow sounded somewhere in the unseen distance. Parker looked into the distant desert, then to Hollister. "How long you figure?"

It was mid-morning when Hollister returned to Hollywood station. The half-mast flag reminded him this was not a normal Sunday. Several news mini-cam vans still lined the curb in front of the station. The reporters were looking for follow-up stories from Saturday's murders. The body count of related murders was now six. Sundays were traditionally slow news days. This was not one of them. Hollister parked the detective car among the collection of nondescript sedans and headed inside.

"Got it. Four ten, British Air flight one zero six," Max said into the telephone as Hollister stepped through the door. Max was in shirt sleeves, standing at their desk. He did not look pleased.

"The prodigal returns," Marshal said sarcastically from a desk where he sat. There was a handcuffed young black man across from him.

"We'll pick them up at the counter," Max said into the receiver and hung up. He gave Hollister a hard look. "Let's talk," he nodded his head toward the lieutenant's office.

Hollister walked into the lieutenant's office and switched on the overhead lights. Max closed the door behind them. "Where in the hell have you been? You leave the hospital you don't answer your cell?"

Hollister sat down in the chair which was once Lieutenant Stratton's. "What's the problem?" he could see Max was agitated.

Max made no attempt to hide his angry. "The problem is you....You come here, check out a car and go who-the-hell knows where. You don't tell me. You go to the airport and talk to customs. You don't tell me. You sure you want me as a partner?"

The accusations were true. Hollister was uncomfortable with the embarrassment it brought. He looked everywhere but at Max.

"You act like you're pissed off at the world. Then you become the Lone Ranger."

"It hasn't got anything to do with you, Max," Hollister assured.

"The hell it doesn't! For the past six hours I've been lying about where you were, betting my ass you'd show up. That's got a lot to do with me."

"I went out to see Parker," Hollister said, taking a deep breath.

"And you couldn't tell me you were going to do that."

"Okay, I've been HUA. I'm sorry." Looking up at his bigger partner.

"It's not just today. What's going on?" Max pressed.

"Kim left me," Hollister confessed.

Max's shock showed on his face. "Damn, I'm sorry. When?"

"Last Sunday. Same day Shannon Roberts died."

"Why didn't you tell me?"

"I...what the hell could I say?"

"I'm really sorry," Max paced awkwardly in the small confines of the office.

"You've got nothing to be sorry for. I'm should have told you."

"What happened?"

"She just left." Hollister shrugged. "Took all her shit and walked. I got home and found a note. Haven't heard from her since."

"She want a divorce?"

"Odds favor that."

"Jesus, I really liked Kim."

"I'm sorry I've been a pain in the ass."

"Lee, damn it, I can't help you if you don't tell what's going on."

"I'm sorry."

"And quit being sorry."

"Okay."

"My brother-in-law Jake's an attorney, you know?"

"I'm not ready yet."

"I'm really sorry to hear this."

"Max, stop the pity. It sounds girly."

"I wasn't pitying you. I was worried about Kim."

"Kim will get by."

"How are you feeling?"

"Terrific," it was sarcastic.

Max sat down to study Hollister's face. "Maybe we should give this one up. If we can't stay focused."

"I'm focused. We need to get this bastard."

Max was quiet for a minute, thinking about his words carefully. "You once told me there was a line we couldn't cross. That line that makes a case personal. We're cops, Lee. We're not out for revenge. We're after justice."

"I'm okay with that," Hollister assured.

"You think you're up to a trip?"

"A trip?"

"London," Max answered. "I'll tell you about it on the airplane." He moved for the door. "I've gotta go buy some socks. Pickup my passport. Be packed and back here by three o'clock."

"London? Max, what the hell's going on?" Hollister pushed up out of the chair.

Max glanced at his watch and then Hollister. "Go get your passport and some decent clothes. Be back here by three. See you then," Max said and was out the door.

The passport Assad carried was bought in Mexico City. It cost him two hundred and twenty American dollars. After driving across the border into Tijuana he'd sold the two-year-old Toyota and the policeman's gun for six hundred dollars. Flying Aero Mexico from Tijuana to Mexico City didn't require a passport. Once in teaming Mexico City, it took him only two cab rides and three hours to have a new passport identifying him as Ricardo Cortez, a citizen of Spain. The Mexican Custom's official stamped the passport without question when he boarded the non-stop Italian flight to Rome.

In Rome, feeling the security of European soil beneath his feet, Assad took a cab into the city. He dined in a sidewalk cafe and bought a hand carved horse at an open-air market. The anxiety of the chase faded quickly, and he once again relaxed.

The flight from Rome to Madrid was nonstop and Assad was looking forward to getting home. There was much he wanted to do at the villa. Perhaps when it was finished, he would invite his uncle from Teheran. It had been a long time since he'd sat and talked with family. A chime sounded and the seat belt sign flashed on as the aircraft began its descent into Madrid. Assad obediently buckled his seat belt.

The Spanish Custom's Officer carefully searched the small bag Assad carried before waving him through. Once again, his passport was stamped without a second glance. He pushed through the gate. It was raining outside. It made the night air smell fresh.

Assad hailed a cab and climbed into the back seat before giving the bearded driver directions. The cab was warm and smelled of wine.

The villa was in the hills south of Madrid, overlooking a two-hundred-year-old vineyard. The road wound its way through the village of Espel before snaking back and forth up a steep hillside. The roadway was a glistening black with the rain and the village was quiet. The cab's aging engine labored as it climbed the hill.

Assad watched the sweep of the windshield wipers. Ahead, around the next turn, would be the villa. As the cab's headlamps reached out through the darkness, he saw the car. It was parked a short distance from the driveway to his villa, the only car on the street. As they drew nearer and the headlamps illuminated the rain streaked sedan, he saw two silhouettes. A bone deep chill swept over him. What was it his Marine instructor taught so many years ago in Northern Virginia? "If you think something's wrong, it is! Trust your instincts. Don't underestimate your enemy. It will cost you your life." Assad tapped the driver on the shoulder. "Do not stop."

The flight over the pole to London was long and quiet. After three glasses of champagne which the Mormon Max claimed as soda had him relaxed and in his usual good mood. Hollister decided it was time to ask questions. "I take it we're on our way to see George Franklin?"

"Bloody good guess, ol' chap," Max answered with less than a convincing English accent. He went on to tell Hollister about discovering George Franklin had entered the country the day before Shannon Roberts was killed and left the day after. A key missing link was found when Max checked the calls he made. Two were to Paul DeSilva, both before the murder and another to the LeParc Hotel in West Hollywood. Following a hunch, Max had gone to the LeParc and

searched the guest registration records for the weekend Shannon Roberts was killed. He found what he
hoped for. Phillip DePaul had checked in on Friday
night and out on Sunday afternoon. Max checked
the telephone records and found the Frenchman
had called the Beverly Hills Hotel. The hotel George
Franklin was staying in. The records showed the
Frenchman called Franklin once before the murder
and once afterwards. Max had also talked with the
parking valet at the LeParc. The valet remembered
the Frenchman, a big tipper, who drove a silver Mercedes. Combining his findings with the information
Meg Rogers provided to Hollister on the financing of
the film, and Shannon's threat to walk, gave DeSilva
and Franklin motive. The links to each other and to
the Frenchman proved the conspiracy.

The return of the Frenchman and the murder of
Paul DeSilva added weight to the evidence of a conspiracy gone sour.

"I had Beverly Hills PD impound DeSilva's Jaguar. I impounded the silver Mercedes DePaul rented
when Shannon was killed, and the red one he drove
during the shooting with Parker and Torres," Max
explained. "Frenchman's prints have gotta be on them
somewhere. SID is on it. Maybe we'll find some DNA
from Shannon on one of the cars?"

"Why DeSilva's Jaguar?" Hollister questioned.

"Not likely Shannon got into the Frenchman's car
is it? Whoever picked her up at her mansion had a
familiar face. Bet on DeSilva."

Hollister nodded agreement. He was impressed with his partner's work.

"Plus, we're getting nowhere chasing the Frenchman," Max continued. "Why chase a shadow when we know someone who can tell us who he is, and maybe where he is?"

"Compass points at George Franklin?" Hollister agreed.

Max nodded. "Yesterday morning while a certain partner was not available, I asked for a meeting with Lieutenant Prescott, Captain Harris, and Deputy Chief Searcy. I laid out the case and said we wanted to go to London and get a co-conspirator, George Franklin."

"What did they say?"

"None of them were willing to put their ass on the line so Searcy called the chief. The chief said we should go get the sonofabitch. Then Prescott called the DA. DA laid it out to a judge; got an arrest warrant, sent it to Scotland Yard and now we're on our way."

Hollister smiled and relaxed in his reclined seat. "If you're trying to impress me it worked."

"Chief did put six men from robbery homicide on the case. But we got the fun part."

Abu Assad sat under the dripping roof of the train station in the village of Espel until three o'clock in the morning before he stole a bicycle and started up the road to his villa. The rain had almost stopped.

The sedan parked in the street earlier was gone but Assad stood in the heavy shadows a half block away and watched. When he was satisfied, he pedaled the bicycle to the villa next to his. There he opened a side gate and went into the rear yard. Again, he watched and waited from the shadows. When it appeared all was quiet, he climbed over the wet board fence and went in his back door. He did not turn on any lights.

Most of all Assad felt betrayed. Those who had made him what he was, seemingly now wanted him dead. He was suffering the same fate as the beloved Shah. He packed in the darkness in near silence. He included the cash taped to the bottom of a dresser drawer. He had no idea where he would go, but he knew he must. They would come back. The bastards. May they be damned by Allah. He was lifting socks from a dresser drawer when his hand brushed the wad of plastic explosive. His hand paused, allowing his fingers to explore the shape, feel the texture. He picked it up from the drawer as the idea took form.

He set the booby trap at the top of the stairs to the villa's musty wine cellar. A small barely visible thread traced across the top, set a half inch above its worn wooden surface. The intruder's foot would apply the pressure with the first step. He knew they would come back and when they did, they would pay heavily. He would teach his loyal American friends a lesson they would never forget.

The shapely stewardess was working in the curtained galley. Hollister could see her high heels and calves. He stepped to the curtain and parted it. The stewardess's eyes swept to his. She had her jacket off and the top thee buttons of her blouse were open. He could see the shadow of her cleavage and the swell of her breasts.

The girls breath quickened. He could see it in the rise and fall of her chest. She wet her lips with a quick flick of tongue, closed the stainless cabinet where she worked and turned to face him. Neither spoke. The woman stood with legs apart drawing the material of her uniform skirt tight across her stomach. Hollister stepped to her. She raised her face to his. His hands searched her body as they kissed. She was braless. Her breast was warm and firm in his hand. She moaned and molded her body against his. When their lips parted, she kissed along his neck to an ear. Hollister pulled her skirt up.

"Where's your gun?" the sultry voice whispered in his ear.

He ignored the question and cupped her buttocks in his hands.

"I'm not that kind of girl," she said and pushed away from him. Surprised, Hollister looked at her. His heart raced. It was Shannon Roberts. He turned to move from her. She reached and took him by the arm. Hollister looked to her. Now it was Kim. "Where's your gun, Lee?" She smiled, squeezing his arm again. Hollister was suddenly awake. Max had him by the arm. "Put your seat belt on," he said, "we're about to land."

Hollister looked out the window. Far below lay a patchwork of green fields, rolling tree-covered hills and country roads. It looked peaceful. Hollister's first impression of England was good. The runway was wet when the big craft set down on it to send up billows of spray.

The busy international terminal at Heathrow was teaming with a cosmopolitan sea of travelers. Hollister wasn't sure what he expected, but he was surprised at the steady stream of turbans, headbands, colorful African clothing and black faces.

"This is great," Max beamed as they moved along the line toward the Customs station. "Wish I'd brought my camera."

"Pardon me, gentlemen," an English voice said. Hollister and Max turned. The man was dressed in a belted raincoat and a hat. His face was lined with character and the hair at his temples was gray, although a neatly trimmed mustache was solid black. "Would you be with the Los Angeles police?"

"We would." Max extended a hand. "I'm Detective Baxter. This is my partner, Sergeant Hollister."

"Glad to meet you," the man said shaking Max's hand, then Hollister's. "I'm Inspector Conley from Scotland Yard. I'll be assisting you with your inquiry. Now, if you'll follow me, I believe we can hurry things along a bit."

The Inspector spoke with the Customs officer and after a look at passports they were escorted through.

"I've booked rooms for you at the Metropole," Inspector Conley said as they climbed into his small unmarked car. Rain was falling steadily. "It's a nice hotel. Sorry about the weather," he added glancing at Max in the back seat who wiped the water from his face. "I'm told it never rains in California," he smiled.

Hollister rode in the front seat. He felt vulnerable on the left side of the car as they drove into the soggy heart of busy London.

"Would you gentlemen like to freshen up before we get on with it? We're only a few blocks from your hotel."

"We'd like to get on with it," Hollister answered.

"Let's stop by the Yard and I'll have the local constables bring Mister Franklin in."

Hollister and Max waited in a fourth-floor office while the inspector went to alert the patrol. When he returned, Hollister said, "I hope he hasn't rabbited."

"He hasn't," the inspector assured, sitting down behind his desk. "He's been under surveillance since we got the call from your DHQ."

Hollister and Max exchanged a pleased glance.

"I also took a bit of a look into our records on Franklin." He opened a file. "Seems he's been on the fringe of a number of investigations linked to monetary schemes, sharking and suspected money laundering. Nothing that's led to an arrest, but he's been in a few times for questioning."

"What kind of business is he in?" Hollister questioned.

"The name of his company is ITM. That's for International Trade and Marketing. From what I've been able to learn, he's basically an import, export broker."

"Would that give him access to substantial amounts of cash?" Max asked.

"From what little we know of the business; I would say yes. There are quarantine periods, embargoes, customs inspections and even fluctuating markets that might mean weeks or months with funds and merchandise sitting and waiting on the right condition or clearance. Add a degree of dishonesty to that and you've got time and money as an ally."

"We have reason to believe Franklin may have used someone else's money, a lot of it, with the hope of making a quick buck without getting caught," Hollister explained.

"That seems to be one of Franklin's traits," the inspector agreed. "I also took the liberty of reviewing Franklin's international telephone calls. I understand you're trying to link him to a Frenchman?"

"Phillip DePaul," Hollister answered soberly. He's killed six people. Three were police officers."

"I wasn't able to locate any record of calls made to France, but I did find several made to Madrid. The most recent in the early hours on Saturday."

"Madrid," Hollister said straightening in his chair. "The Frenchman came to LA on a nonstop flight from

Madrid. How can we get an address?"

"I thought you might want that," the inspector said, looking to his notes. "So, I called a friend in government. The address is seventy-six Sabadell Road, in the village of Estel, just south of Madrid. They went out to have a look about the place, but he seemed not to be home."

Hollister made notes. He was excited. Even if the Frenchman wasn't there, he knew he could find a lead on where he might be. There were always curious neighbors, address books, matches, calendar dates, and travel tags on luggage. He'd find what he needed. He'd find it and track down the sonofabitch that took his gun and kill him. He tore the paper in his notebook by bearing down too hard with his pen. He hoped Max and the inspector hadn't noticed. Hollister closed the notebook.

He was no longer interested in George Franklin. Franklin was excess baggage. They could drop him and come back later. He wasn't going anywhere.

"Of course, I cannot confirm the number, or the address, belonging to your suspect, beyond doubt," the Inspector cautioned.

"Our suspect came to LA from Madrid, it's a pretty safe bet," Hollister defended. He didn't want to hear any doubt.

A rap sounded outside the inspector's door.

"Come in."

A round-faced brunette opened the door. She was in uniform. "Pardon me, Inspector, but DCI Brown says to inform you that Mister Franklin has arrived."

George Franklin knew something was wrong. Very wrong. The arrangement called for the Frenchman to telephone after the assignment was complete. He had not called. Franklin could only hope that Paul DeSilva was dead. That would insulate him from everything. Then he would be just another film investor. An investor who could demand the prompt return of his money. The police would soon tell him what the detention was for. He had that right. Maybe they were talking to all the investors. That's how he would play it. Ignorant and shocked. He didn't have to fake his shock when Hollister opened the door to the small interview room. He recognized both men as Americans. The British Inspector with them spoke first. "Mister Franklin, these gentlemen are from the Los Angeles Police. They would like to talk to you about a criminal matter in the United States."

George Franklin's mouth went dry with fear.

"I'll step out," the inspector said, and closed the

door.

Hollister sat down facing Franklin. Max sat down beside his partner.

"I don't know what...," Franklin stammered awkwardly.

Hollister cut him short. "Before you say anything, I've got something to say. We're in a hurry. We don't have time to waste on bullshit, so we're gonna tell you a few things we know about a call you made to the Frenchman in Madrid. We know about his flight to Los Angeles. We know he killed Paul DeSilva. A police officer staked on DeSilva's house saw the Frenchman enter and leave. That's Saturday. Secondly, we've got records of the Frenchman calling you at the Beverly Hills Hotel. He called you once before Shannon Roberts was killed and once afterwards. And you called DeSilva from the Beverly Hills Hotel and the Frenchman at the Le Parc." Hollister leaned across the table, closer to Franklin's slate gray face. "And you know what else we've got, George? We've got someone who knows your ass was on the line. In other words, we know it all. Your only hope to keep from buying a nonstop ticket to a fucking gas chamber in California is to blame it all on the Frenchman. You know why, George? Because Saturday he killed another cop."

"It's true," George Franklin blurted. His voice was high pitched. "It was DeSilva's idea. He planned it all. I didn't know anyone would be killed."

"Hold it!" Max barked. Franklin fell silent. He was trembling.

"You have the right to remain silent," Max warned. In the nearby monitor room, the savvy Inspector Conley pushed a record button. Now the official interrogation would begin and if ever played in court, or listened to by a battery of defense attorneys, it would sound very civil, formal and lawful. Hollister had, as the saying went, primed the witness. Now it was Max's job to follow-up and listen to the lies that followed. Without fail, half-truths, like the tips of icebergs would appear and equally without fail, they would later send the liar sinking in his own trap. "If you give up the right to remain silent, anything you say can and will be used against you in a court of law."

Hollister, his role as the bad cop over, left the room. Max, the good cop, took over. After the shaken and frightened Franklin listened to his rights, he eagerly waived them.

The interrogation went on for an hour and forty minutes with Max skillfully bringing out the inconsistencies in Franklin's fabricated story without meeting him head on. When it was over, Max closed the tablet on which he was making notes. He stood up. "I'm afraid I'm going to have to ask the police to hold you."

"What?" the shocked Franklin blurted. "I've told you everything I know."

"But we didn't tell you everything we know," Max smiled, and stepped out the door.

Hollister was waiting when Max came out of the interview room. "I've got us booked on a six o'clock flight to Madrid."

"Madrid!" Max cautioned. "We had permission to come to London. No one said anything about Spain."

"Max," Hollister pleaded, "We couldn't foresee Franklin telling us the Frenchman lived in Spain. We can't ignore that. We have to go; the sonofabitch has killed six people, three of them cops. Cops we knew. Cops who would do the same for us. We can't come this close and walk away."

"Did you call Lieutenant Prescott?" Max questioned.

"What for?" Hollister argued.

"He's the boss, Lee."

"He's also seven thousand miles away...we're here."

"I don't like it. We should call," Max cautioned.

"Bullshit, if we call, they'll spend all day talking about it, discussing it, calling the District Attorney. The fuckin' Frenchman is gonna walk away."

Max shook his head. "He may not even be there?"

"I can feel it," Hollister pleaded. "He's there."

"We should call somebody?" Max was wary.

"We've got his address. We'll check and see if he's there. Then we call."

Inspector Conley took the two detectives to a pub not far from Scotland Yard. They sat in the back and feasted on fish and chips and warm beer. "You people have a problem with refrigeration?" Max asked as he paused from a hearty drink of his second mug.

"No, we just can't seem to keep beer long enough to chill it." Conley smiled.

A game of darts between the inspector and Max nearly made them late, but Conley badged them through security and customs at Heathrow and they reached the gate just as the final boarding call was given. "We'll need a warrant to hold Franklin, you know."

"I'll call the District Attorney in Los Angeles as soon as we get to Madrid," Hollister promised.

The inspector shook their hands. "I'm glad I was able to help."

"Don't lose that number I gave you and tell Missus Inspector we'll get her a great seat at the Rose Parade," Max said and then they were into the jetway.

The plane was crowded, and their late boarding meant they were separated. Max sat on an aisle beside a British Naval officer. Hollister, several rows behind over the wing, sat in a center seat between a priest and a young Spanish woman who was breast feeding an infant. He tried to sleep but the smell of a dirty diaper and the baby kept him awake. It didn't seem to bother the priest.

The security at the Madrid airport, like most, was designed to intercept those carrying weapons onto the aircraft. Hollister expected the Custom's inspection would result in the discovery of their firearms, but the disinterested official who took their passports stamped them and waved them through.

They had no trouble finding a rental car counter.

Hollister took out the MasterCard issued to the City of Los Angeles. "We'd like a car," he said in slow careful English as he presented the card to a dark eyed twenty-year-old behind the counter.

"You're American?" The girl smiled, picking up the card. Her English was flawless.

"Yes," Hollister answered.

"I'm a sophomore at Hunter College in New York. I see you're from Los Angeles."

"Yes."

"What kind of car would you like?"

The rental was a Volvo and Max looked cramped on the passenger's side of the small car as he studied the map provided by the clerk. "How am I supposed to read a map in Spanish? The only two words I know are alto and cerveza."

They followed the directions the Hunter co-ed gave and forty minutes after leaving the airport their headlamps illuminated a small roadside sign that announced Alpe'a Estel.

"Watch for Sabadell Road," Hollister urged.

The number seventy-six was painted on a small post in front of the villa on the hillside. After parking a short distance away, the two detectives sat and watched. The street was dark and quiet. A night wind swept up over the hillside vineyards and breathed through the olive trees lining Sabadell Road. The rustle of the leaves was the only sound.

"Think he's in bed?" Max whispered.

Hollister glanced at the luminous face of his watch.

It was ten minutes to one. "Let's go see."

Max hesitated, "Lee, we should call the local cops. We're so far out on a fucking limb it ain't funny."

Hollister looked to him. "This prick ran over Torres in the street. He shot Canfield and Martinez and the only reason he didn't kill me is because somebody wanted to play tennis. And that's not counting Shannon Roberts, Paul DeSilva or the little girl in the tub. If you need any more than that just wait in the fucking car."

Hollister climber out of the car.

"Shit," Max muttered and followed after his angry partner.

The small rear yard, carved from the hillside, had an uneven brick surface. A cluster of leaves scraped along the bricks in a gust of wind. The weathered door sat an eighth of an inch from its frame, exposing a less than high quality metal tongue of its lock. Hollister pulled out his plastic I.D. car and pushed it into the space between the locks bolt and the door frame. The lock opened silently. They drew their guns and stepped inside.

Max, as agreed, remained just inside the back door, silent, with gun ready. Two men moving about in a strange dark house looking for a killer was too great a threat. Hollister moved slowly from room to room, eyes searching as they tried to draw forms from the darkness. The floor groaned under his weight in the kitchen and again in the hallway. His breath rushed from flared nostrils and he was covered with sweat running down his back. Finally, he found the bedroom. He stood and stared into the room for a long time listening for the sounds of the man breathing. There were none. He inched into the room. The floor groaned under his feet again. He paused and then went on. Reaching the bed, he stretched an arm and carefully felt its surface. It was smooth, quilted and cool. No one had been in it. "Damn," Hollister hissed.

Max was almost invisible in the hallway. Hollister walked to him. "He's not here. Let's see what we can find." A feeling of futility and defeat was settling over Hollister. It seemed Max was right; the sonofabitch was gone.

"I'll start in the bedroom," Hollister said.

Hollister was at the mouth of the bedroom when a light flicked on behind him in the kitchen. He stepped into the room and switched on a bedside lamp. A carved wooden horse sat on a dresser top. An airline ticket receipt lay beside it. Hollister picked it up. It was an Air Italia receipt and the name on it read Richard Cortez. He folded the receipt and stuffed it into a pocket.

In the kitchen Max was finding little of interest. The sink was dry and dotted with dead bugs. The yellowed refrigerator held several mold-covered dishes and a bottle of what he guessed was wine. He looked in cupboards. For the most part they were empty. There were no dirty dishes or fresh food to suggest recent visits. He moved to the hallway. Hollister was still in the bedroom. "Find anything?"

"Not much."

"Same here," Max said reaching for the door leading to the wine cellar. The dry hinges groaned. Max searched for a light switch. A single shade less bulb winked on at the bottom of the stairs. A musty damp smell rose up to meet him. He did not see the thin wire stretched across the top step. His foot missed it as he descended the creaking stairs.

The small wine cellar was covered with spider webs, broken bottles and a pile of rotting, forgotten, boards. Max took a quick look around, turned and started up the stairs. His left foot depressed the trip wire at the top of the steps. The explosion was violent. The small villa shuddered under the concussion. Window glass exploded outward. The lights went out.

Hollister had no idea how long he had been laying on the dusty floor. His ears roared and he felt numb and disoriented. Then he thought of Max. "God no!" he cried and pushed to his feet. He was dizzy. His ears rang and felt as if they were stuffed with wax.

"Max!" he called in the darkness groping along a wall through a collection of thick dust and debris. He tripped and fell. Something sharp stabbed at his hand.

"Max!" There was no answer.

Hollister couldn't hear the electronic pulse of an approaching siren as the first of the fire trucks arrived. The house was a sea of dust that choked the breath from him. Broken boards and plaster blocked his path. He tore at them, desperate to find Max, yet afraid he might. Flashlight beams sliced through the dust-laden air. The firemen came in through the broken front door. They were yelling to one another, shouting commands. Hollister heard little of it and understood none of it, and then they were on him, pulling him toward the door. Hollister struggled, but there were many of them. He gave up and they carried him out the door into the cool clear night air.

"My partner's in there," Hollister shouted as they forced him onto a stretcher. They were answering him, but he could barely hear them. More emergency vehicles were arriving. The night was full of flashing red lights and the sound of radios. Hollister collapsed onto his back. He was close to throwing up. He gasped in air. "Not again," he cried just before an oxygen mask was pushed over his face.

Hollister relaxed and sucked the soothing oxygen into his lungs. After several healing breaths he sat up. Four helmeted firemen were carrying Max on a stretcher from the shattered villa. Hollister tore away the oxygen mask and pushed up to follow after Max and the firemen.

Max's eyes were open, but they were glazed, and his head rolled from side to side. Blood was running from his nose and ears. Hollister moved to Max's side and laid a hand on his arm. A fireman carrying Max pushed Hollister aside and barked something in harsh Spanish.

The four firemen lifted Max into the mouth of a waiting ambulance. Hollister pushed through the midst of the men and climbed into the ambulance. The doors slammed shut. The ambulance jerked as it lunged forward, its siren pierced the night.

Hollister sat on a side bench and watched as a paramedic in the ambulance went to work on Max. An overhead light revealed blood dripping from the bottom of the stretcher to pool on the floor. The paramedic cut away a soiled towel a fireman had wrapped around Max's left foot. As the blood-soaked folds were snipped away, Max's black shoe fell with a heavy thump to the metal floor. A severed foot was in the shoe. Hollister grimaced and clamped his eyes shut. His stomach convulsed.

At the hospital they examined Hollister's ears and eyes and sponged his face clean. "Where's my partner?" An attractive nurse escorted Hollister through the corridors of the hospital until they reached an alcove with several chairs and a couch. There was a man curled and asleep on the couch. The nurse pointed to a set of wide double doors across the hall. Cirujia, was stenciled on the face of the doors. Hollister nodded understanding and sat down to wait.

He tried to organize his confused thoughts. He refused to allow himself to think of Max's shoe in the ambulance. He patted his pockets. His cell phone was gone. There was a telephone on the wall. He knew he had to call Los Angeles. Max's injury had to be reported. He tried to compute the time difference. He looked at his watch. It was five minutes after two in the morning. He couldn't remember if L.A. was nine

271

hours ahead or behind. What the hell, who cared? He wished he had more information. Was it a bomb? Was it natural gas? How serious were Max's injuries? A severed foot was pretty fucking serious. Poor bastard. Where was the suspect? The French sonofabitch. Why were they in Spain? Hollister knew he was in serious trouble. That didn't seem to be anything new. Where the hell was Kim?

Clicking heels on the polished hard floor of the corridor warned Hollister someone was coming. He stood up. There were three of them. They rounded the corner and came toward him. All in uniform and all three armed. They were sober. When they reached Hollister, a man with the mustache gave several sharp commands in Spanish. Hollister understood none of it. The dark eyes held Hollister's. The officer glanced to the man on his right and spoke. The man moved around behind Hollister and patted him down. Hollister held his arms out to accommodate the search. The officer said something in Spanish when his hand found the pistol on Hollister's side. He lifted Hollister's jacket and removed the gun. The young officer spoke to Hollister again. He seemed angry. Hollister reached into a pocket and pulled out his badge case. He opened it and held it in front of the young officer's face. "Policia de Los Angeles," the young officer said studying the gold and silver badge. His two companions crowded to his shoulders to look.

The young officer spoke again. This time is was friendlier. Hollister nodded and put away his badge.

The officer holding Hollister's pistol offered it to him. Hollister took the gun and returned it to his holster.

A nearby elevator chimed, and two men stepped off. They were obviously Americans. The taller of the two was tanned and polished looking, a diplomat Hollister guessed. The second man, although in a dark suit and tie, had the short-cropped hair of a Marine. They moved quickly to join the three Spanish officers and Hollister. The tanned man spoke with the mustached officer in fluent Spanish. Although the exchange was sober it seemed the men knew one another. When it was over the young officer clicked his heels together, saluted, then turned and marched away with his two men following.

The tanned man turned his attention to Hollister. "Jim Forrester from the US Embassy." He offered a hand. "This is Dan Crocket an associate. I understand you're an American citizen."

Hollister shook their hands. "I'm a police officer from Los Angeles. My name is Hollister, Lee Hollister. I'm a sergeant assigned to Hollywood Homicide."

"You're a long way from home, Sergeant."

"It feels that way."

"There's a doctor's lounge on the third floor," Forrester said. "Let's go there and talk. Dan, tell the nurse where we'll be and that we want to be notified the minute the sergeant's partner is out of surgery."

The chairs in the lounge were leather and soft and Hollister enjoyed them as much as he did a cup of strong coffee. He gave Forrester a quick chronology of the case and how it led them to London and then onto Madrid in the hope of finding the Frenchman. "I don't know what it was," Hollister concluded. "I didn't hear the explosion."

"The police say it looks like a bomb," Forrester told him.

"Could you ask the police to help me locate the Frenchman?" Hollister said.

"Trust me," Forrester answered. "They want very much to talk with him. They take illegal explosives here in Spain very serious."

"I need to call the States. Let them know what's going on," Hollister said.

"It's customary to be informed when police from the states are in Spain on business," Forrester offered.

"Time was an issue," Hollister defended less than convincingly.

Forrester nodded. "Of course. Let me have the hospital operator place the call. Then you can pick up in here."

It was a few minutes after seven P.M. but Lieutenant Prescott was still in his office in the homicide squad room. The day had started solemnly with the shooting death of an eighteen-year-old pizza delivery man who refused to give up eight dollars and twenty-two cents to an armed robber. Marshal and Davis were out at the scene on Melrose. This was the third Pepperoni murder. An armed suspect was ordering pizzas and robbing the delivery men. His latest was the eighteen-year-old black L.A. City College freshman. With three delivery men dead there was a growing howl and cry from the press for action. Action was always confused with the number of detectives investigating the crime. Police work was becoming as much public relations as it was fighting crime. With Hollister and Baxter in London, the thin blue line investigating death in Hollywood had grown even thinner. It seemed being OIC of Hollywood Homicide was going to be tougher than Prescott anticipated. The telephone on his desk rang. He pushed aside a report and picked up the receiver. "Homicide, Prescott."

"Lieutenant, this is Hollister."

"Hollister," Prescott rocked back in his chair. He envied the sergeant for having the good fortune to be working on the Shannon Roberts' case that got him out of the country.

"How's the weather in London?"

"I...I'm not calling from London," Hollister confessed. Prescott heard the sober tone in Hollister's voice.

"Where are you?" Prescott questioned, readying a pencil to make notes.

"Madrid," Hollister answered. "We got a statement from Franklin and an address on the Frenchman. We came here to get him. He booby trapped his house."

"Booby trap! Are you all right?"

"Max is in surgery, he lost a foot."

"Goddamn, Hollister," Prescott grated. "Who

275

authorized you to go to Spain?...and your partner is injured!" Did you get the Frenchman?"

"No," Hollister answered meekly. He knew he was in a world of shit.

"Give me the name of the hospital you're at?" Prescott ordered.

"Saint Justine," Hollister answered. "I'm with an official from the US Embassy. His name's Jim Forrester. He suggests you channel all communications through the Embassy."

"Jim Forrester, okay," Prescott was busy making notes. His mind was racing ahead. "Are you injured?"

"No."

"What time did this happen?"

"Three, four hours...I'm not sure."

"Where did this happen? There's going to be a lot of questions on this end?"

There was an awkward pause.

"Lieutenant," Hollister answered, "a nurse just walked in. Max is out of surgery. This can wait."

"Hollister, wait a minute. I..." A dial tone sang in Prescott's ear. "Goddamnit," the lieutenant muttered as he slammed the telephone.

Rolls of rose-pink wallpaper stood in the corner. A soak pan was on top of the counter and Doris was on a step ladder putting up a fresh cut in the corner. It was to be a surprise for Max when he came home from England. She was certain he'd like it. He liked flowers.

"Tommy, get the phone," Doris yelled, hoping her son would hear.

"What?" came a muffled adolescent reply. The telephone continued to ring.

"Answer the phone!" Doris barked. There was a wrinkle in the strip of wallpaper, and it frustrated her. She tried smoothing it with the pad of her hand. It worked.

"Mom!" a voice called.

"What?"

"It's for you."

"I'm busy. Take a message."

It's Dad."

Doris hurried off the ladder, out of the bathroom, and into the bedroom to pick up a bedside receiver. "Max," she said eagerly.

"Hello, Sugar," the familiar voice of her husband said in her ear. Doris thought he sounded tired.

Hollister sat in a chair beside Max's hospital bed. Jim Forrester had placed the call and left the room. Hollister felt awkward to the conversation between husband and wife. He didn't have a wife to call. Marriage. It sucked. Hollister's eyes moved to the sheet that covered Max. Only one foot showed beneath the sheet at the bottom of the bed. An IV was taped to his right arm. His face was dotted with small cuts and bruises. His eyes were blackened. "Yeah, London was great...No, it rained. Uh huh. Fish and chips," Max's voice was slow and drugged.

Hollister was beginning to feel tired. He was sorry they ever came to Europe. Fuck the Frenchman. Let him go. Who gives a shit? Finally, the fucking French had won, and it was going to cost his job, but unlike Max his penalty was less. At least he still had both his feet. The taste of his coated teeth was bitter. Life was being a real son-of-a-bitch. He'd lost his wife, the French man, his gun and now for certain, his job.

"Listen, Hon," Max said, cradling the receiver to an ear on the pillow. "Someone from the Department is gonna call you... Uh huh, to say I've been hurt. No! No! I'm okay. How would I be calling you if I wasn't? My foot. The left one. Can't I tell you about it when I get home? Madrid. Yes, in Spain. Yeah, it's real pretty.

I'll bring you something… A couple days. I'm not sure. Don't worry and I'll call you again in the morning. I love you too, Sugar. Tell the kids I said hi… Goodnight." He made a kissing sound into the receiver.

Hollister took the receiver from Max and placed it in the cradle beside the bed. "She okay?"

"Fine," Max said. "Just fine. She's a rock." He looked toward his feet. "I can't tell it's not there. It feels like it is."

"I'm sorry, Max. I'm sorry about this whole fuckin' mess."

"You want my pity? I'm the one that's a foot shorter," Max said angrily. He tried to suppress it but couldn't. It seemed an emotional release He turned his attention to the window as tears formed and ran down his cheeks. He brushed the tears away, sniffed. The quiet was awkward. Both men knew it was a time of change, a time of trauma, a quiet before a storm they both knew was coming. Hollister didn't know what to say. His ears burned with embarrassment. "I'm gonna be at the Embassy. They want me to stay there."

"I think I'll wait here," Max said. Again, his tone was sober.

Hollister followed impulse and stepped closer to the bed to squeeze Max's meaty hand. Max didn't react. Hollister withdrew his hand. "Get some rest," he offered, wishing he hadn't said it. Max nodded and again looked to the window. He sniffed but said nothing. Hollister turned to the door.

The room at the American Embassy was comfortable and quiet and Hollister collapsed into bed. It was a labor to pull away his shoes. He was physically and mentally spent. He laid down on the bed and closed his eyes. His legs twitched and his ears were ringing. A confused montage of strange faces and dark rooms kept haunting his sleep and he tossed and turned until a heavy knock sounded at the door. Hollister looked to the strip of light at the base of the door. "Yes," he called.

"Sergeant, it's Jim Forrester."

Hollister pushed from the bed and opened the door.

Forrester was sober. "The hospital called. There's a problem with Detective Baxter."

Twenty minutes later, Hollister paced in the hallway outside the surgery suite. He was haggard and worried. Jim Forrester was a few feet away talking with a doctor just out of the operating room. It was a sober tense exchange. When it ended Forrester walked to Hollister. He looked worried.

"I'm afraid it's not good. Apparently, his leg starting hemorrhaging during the night. By the time it was discovered he'd lost a substantial amount of blood and was in shock. They're considering additional surgery to remove more of the leg."

"Goddamnit!" Hollister roared in anger. "Don't they make rounds? Don't they check on their patients?"

"Keep your voice down, Sergeant," Forrester warned. "This isn't Los Angeles."

"I wanna see him," Hollister demanded, as if somehow that would help.

"They just got him through a second cardiac arrest. Now's not the time to make demands," Forrester warned.

It felt as if someone were turning a knife in Hollister's stomach. He turned and walked on weak knees to a nearby window. The sun was beginning to show itself in the east and an eerie half-light hung over the sprawling city. Traffic was light in the streets below. Hollister knew Max was going to die. He silently cursed fate and wondered why he had drawn such wrath. If only Kim hadn't left him. That's when it all went bad. Damn her. Tears welled in his eyes, but he felt no sorrow, just a soul-deep anger. Anger and a bone-deep thirst for revenge. He could hear Forrester talking to someone, and then they were beside Hollister.

"Sergeant," Forrester said. "I know this is a difficult time, but there are two pressing matters we must discuss."

Hollister ignored him continuing to stare out the window.

"First, there's been a call from Deputy Chief Searcy in Los Angeles. He's ordered your immediate return."

"Fuck him," Hollister said without emotion.

"Secondly," Forrester continued, "we've just learned from a reliable source the Spanish authorities have plans to detain you for the investigation of the bombing. There's concern that it may be linked somehow to Basque terrorists."

"That's a crock of shit. They can't hold me," Hollister said with a hard look at Forrester.

"Well, there are established protocols and treaties that address armed law enforcement personnel crossing international boundaries. You have violated a number of these agreements. I can't speak for the Spanish government, Sergeant, but as I said, this is not Los Angeles."

Hollister knew resisting was futile if they wanted him out of the country. "Can I see Max before I go?"

"I don't think that's possible."

Hollister returned his eyes to the window.

"We've reserved a seat for you on a flight that leaves in thirty-five minutes."

"I can't just leave my partner here."

"You have no choice. If you stay, you'll likely be arrested."

It was eleven-thirty in the morning when the American Airlines flight from Madrid settled toward the runway in Los Angeles. The thump woke Hollister. He'd slept most of the flight. A deep dreamless sleep that clung to him like an alcoholic hangover. Now he looked out the window at the first view of Los Angeles. Sprawling concrete runways, taxiways, parked aircraft, a distant terminal and an ever-present smog.

A sea of smiling faces lined the entry way. Eyes searched for loved ones coming off the flight. It made

Hollister feel lonely. He followed the arrows on the floor and the wall as well as those ahead of him at the Custom's inspection gates. It was there Parker's voice called, "Hey, Hollister."

Hollister turned and looked. Parker moved to him. He was shocked at Hollister's appearance. Hollister was unshaved and wrinkled. There were dark circles under his bloodshot eyes and his once square shoulders were hunched. "Need a ride, Big Fella?" Parker teased.

Hollister didn't answer. He followed silently as Parker led him toward the Customs gate.

"Any word on Max?" Hollister questioned as they climbed into a detective car parked at the curb in front of the International Terminal. Customs had taken over an hour as Hollister tried to explain his reasons for being in Spain. Finally, after a supervisor was called and Parker made his own call to the Chief of Police's office.

"Chief Moore's office. How can I help you?" a pleasant female voice answered.

"Yeah, this is Clint Parker. I work Hollywood Homicide. I need to talk to the Chief."

"You say you're from Hollywood Homicide, Mister Parker?"

"It's Detective Parker, Lady and it's damned important."

The female voice remained calm. "Well, Detective Parker, I suggest you first follow the chain of command and call your supervisor at Hollywood Division."

"Lady, you've heard of Shannon Roberts' case. If you haven't, what the hell are you doing in the Chief's office? Now, you let me speak to the Chief or you'll be talking to your supervisor, trying to explain why I called the LA Times instead of him."

"One moment please."

Parker was put on hold. Waiting, he listened to an instrumental version of "Over the Rainbow." He was about to end the call when a voice answered, "This is Chief Moore."

"Chief, this is Parker from Hollywood Homicide. I'm at LAX picking up Sergeant Hollister. Customs' clowns have been holding us in a detention room for nearly two hours. We got better shit to do. Since when is it hard for an American to get into America?"

The chief didn't know who the young detective with a distinct southern accent was, but he had been briefed earlier in the morning on the Roberts case. He knew what had happened in Spain. "I'll see what I can do," the chief assured Parker. He hung up. A few minutes later the telephone in the detention room rang. "Alright, you can go," a sober customs officer announced. It all added to Hollister's sense of doom.

Parker's detective car was waiting at the curb in front of the terminal in a red zone posted no stopping. An irritated looking helmeted uniformed motor officer was standing beside the car making notes in his ticket book. "I've got a tow truck coming. Who the hell are you?"

Parker headed for the driver's side of the car.

"Brooks and Dunn," he called sliding in behind the wheel to start the car. He was all smiles. "Oh, and the chief said to welcome you home." He added glancing at Hollister as he pulled the car in gear and sped away into the heavy traffic.

Hollister wasn't smiling. "Any word on Max?"

"There was a notice in the squad room this morning, said he was still in Intensive Care. Condition was stable."

They drove east on Century Boulevard from the airport. Hollister dug in a jacket pocket. "I've got something I want you to do. And, I want it done quietly. You understand what that means?"

"Yeah, I understand, quiet."

Hollister unfolded the thin airline ticket receipt he'd taken from the Frenchman's villa in Spain. He studied it as he spoke. "I want you to talk to Janet Trainer. She's the Deputy Director of Customs at the airport. Find out where this guy's been lately."

Parker nodded. He took the receipt and stuffed it in a pocket. "You know fucking customs is gonna love me asking shit of them."

Lieutenant Prescott was in the homicide office when Hollister rapped on the door. "Come in," Prescott did not get up. "How was your flight?" He finished signing several reports before he gave Hollister his full attention. Hollister sat down in a chair across from the lieutenant's desk. He ignored the question about the flight. He wanted Prescott to get on with it. "You look like shit, Hollister."

Even through the cloud of fatigue Hollister sensed it. He was about to be taken off the case. They wouldn't meet him head on. They couldn't. How could intelligent, experienced, management level personnel label him a Jonah? No, it had to be more subtle than that.

"This case has been difficult. Loss of good men," the lieutenant continued. Deputy Chief Searcy had ordered him back from Spain. Where was the area commander? Where was Captain Harris? None were there. There were no questions about the case. No questions about Max. The simple truth was they no longer cared what Hollister thought. He as a jinx. He was cursed. No one had said it, but it was a collective unspoken message. Get rid of him.

"We think you should take some time off, Lee. Get some rest. You've got a couple hundred hours of overtime on the books. In the interim, responsibility for the case has been assigned to Robbery-Homicide. They got resources to handle matters like this."

Hollister challenged the lieutenant's words with a hard look. "Who the fuck is 'we'?"

Prescott studied Hollister for a moment. "We've known each other for a long time, Hollister. I don't want to fight with you on this. No one does. Go home. Forget all this shit."

Hollister drove east on Hollywood Boulevard. The collection of towering signs and shops lured the seemingly endless flow from the sidewalks lining the wide busy street. Tour buses packed with expectant tourists, bikers with shaved heads and the countless ego cars jammed bumper to bumper. The intersections were crowded with whores, runaways, would-be starlets, punkers and pimps. The air was filled with the pulse of rock and heavy fumes from the glut of internal combustion engines. Hollister saw the street hustlers, the robbers, the rapists and the murderers. The cast was on its marks and the curtain was up. It was only a matter of time until shit happened and when it did, someone would call the police and eventually they would respond. Eventually. Sometimes no one called. Sometimes no one cared. It gave birth to a new thought. Hollister was paid to care. He was paid to be the conscience of this City of the Angels. Those too busy with their individual pursuit of happiness simply paid him, and other cops to do what they wouldn't, or couldn't, do. It made him feel cheap. "Protect and Serve," the ageless motto of the L.A.P.D proudly proclaimed on the side of every police car seemed to be more of an admission of guilt than service. For a brief moment Hollister felt like a whore. He was doing something everyone wanted to do at one time or another and he was being paid for it. Making the policeman's bond with whores closer was the fact both were usually cursed by those who paid for their services. He was part of it. A part the Chamber of Commerce would never talk about, a part few ever thought of, a part many would rather forget, but nonetheless, a part.

Along with the bittersweet knowledge that he was a part of it came the realization that his rightful inheritance could not be taken away from him without a scandal One could not turn on a whore without risk. Thus, he knew it was unlikely the L.A.P.D. would fire him. Official action would be taken. They were hungry for it, but their moves had to be, and would be, subtle, self-serving and cautious. He was a rogue cop, a maverick. He was outside the Jack Webb mold and he knew the management team had to muster their forces to squelch him. He wasn't properly interfacing with the support services designed to aid and assist a contemporary field investigator as presented in Special Order 90-107C. He was thinking and acting on his own and, if a detective sergeant was allowed to do that, then the great tax-paying public may discover they really didn't need a towering headquarters building full of high paid commanders, deputy chiefs, assistant chief, and an arm of administrators. It seemed the mid-East wars weren't really over after all. The same lead-footed bureaucracy that had cost a dedicated few a victory was now running the L.A.P.D. To them it was more important to be part of the team than to win the war. Well, Hollister promised, he wasn't going to roll over and play dead by "taking some time off." He had to be the victor. It was important, more important than his career, even more important than his life. Fuck the L.A.P.D. and Kim. He didn't need either, but then why the hell did it hurt so much?

Hollister felt grim and wrinkled and he was eager to get home, but there was one stop he had to make first. He had to see Doris Baxter.

Max Baxter's house sat at the end of a cul-de-sac in the hills of Glendale. It was a two-story blend of stucco and dark wood. The familiar pick-up truck with camper shell in the driveway made the house easy to find. The grass needed to be cut and there was a bicycle beside the front walk. Hollister parked at the curb and climbed out. A lawn mower buzzed a few houses away. The neighboring homes were pleasant and looked much like the Baxter's. Hollister wondered what it would be like to live in such a neighborhood. It had a peaceful quiet allure to it. Wally and the Beaver coming around the corner on their way home from school wouldn't have surprised him at all. He moved for Max's front door not really sure what he would say. Hi, Doris I'm sorry your husband's foot got blown off and that his heart stopped. Walking to the front door, Hollister hoped wouldn't die but he refused to pray about it. He was secretly worried God wouldn't listen to him either.

A small dog barked somewhere inside the house when Hollister rang the bell. His pulse quickened. The lock on the door clicked and a rather attractive nineteen-year-old woman with a baby in her arms opened the door. Hollister thought he had the wrong house. When he hesitated, the woman spoke. "Yes?"

"I... I'm looking for the Baxter's," he said.

"They're not home," the woman looked at Hollister's unshaven face and wrinkled appearance.

"I'm...I work with Max. I wanted to see Doris."

The young woman seemed wary. "Doris went to Spain."

"Spain! When?"

"Last night. I'm her sister. I'm watching he kids. Her husband was hurt."

"Yeah, I know. Thanks." Hollister turned away. He felt even more alone. Lieutenant Prescott obviously knew Doris Baxter was flying to Spain, but the prick had said nothing. The prick who has information, has control. The contest continued. Why the hell were they fighting him? Didn't they know the Frenchman was the enemy, not him.

Max had someone that cared about him. Hollister thought about that as he drove home. Someone that would fly halfway around the world to be with him. Hollister envied that. He wished someone loved him that much. Maybe he hoped, prayed Kim would be there, but he already knew the answer.

Once home Hollister showered and fell into bed. The combination of jet lag and stress were weighing heavily on him. His last thoughts were of the Frenchman. Hollister wondered if he were tired and worried? He supposed not.

The ring of his cellphone woke him. His sleep

had been deep and dreamless. Maybe it was Kim. He reached for his phone in the darkness. "Hollister," he said picking it up.

"Sorry to wake you," Clint Parker said. "But Max will be landing at LAX about three hours from now. The Imperial Highway Terminal. Want me to pick you up?"

"I'll be waiting," Hollister said, swinging his feet to the floor.

At the airport an ambulance, its emergency lights sending out pulses of red light, sat parked on the apron of the taxiway, waiting as the twin-engine Westwind jet appeared out of the darkness. Its turbines filled the early morning air with noise.

Hollister stood close to Clint Parker as they waited. "Whose airplane?" he asked above the noise.

"Some Mormon that owns a chain of grocery stores," Parker answered. "He flew Doris and a doctor over to bring Max back. Got some surgeon lined up at the UCLA Medical Center that thinks he can save Max's leg."

The sleek corporate jet braked to a stop nearby and the noise began to subside. The two detectives and the waiting paramedics crowded around the door as a steward folded down the stairs.

The first one off the aircraft was Doris Baxter. She was a plump brunette in her early forties. She looked tired. Hollister was waiting at the bottom of the steps.

"How is he, Doris?" Hollister asked, as two paramedics scrambled up the steps and into the small cabin.

"He, he's in a coma," Doris answered. Her attention went back to the open door of the aircraft.

The two paramedics appeared in the doorway. They carried Max in an awkward cross hands saddle. He was wearing a hospital robe and his footless leg was heavily bandaged and in a stiff splint. His head bobbed as they moved. At the bottom of the stairs they lifted him onto a waiting gurney. His face was pale and unshaven. The doctor with him was at his side carrying an I.V. line that led to Max's arm. They wheeled Max toward the ambulance. "Hey, Max." Hollister patted Max on the shoulder.

Max offered no answer. The paramedics lifted him into the ambulance. His wife and doctor climbed in after them. The doors swung shut and it pulled away, siren piercing the darkness.

It was daylight by the time the small caravan reached the UCLA Medical Center in Westwood. Max was wheeled to the Intensive Care Unit of the fourth floor. Doris went to the Admissions Office while Hollister and Parker sat in the waiting room not far from the ICU nurses' station.

"Wanna go down to the cafeteria, get some coffee?"

"Sure." They were moving for a nearby elevator when a nurse intercepted them. "Either of you, Detective Parker?"

"That's me," Parker answered.

"Telephone. You can take it at the nurses' station."

Hollister returned to the waiting area. He was glad Max was back on American soil. He felt responsible for Max's injury. No, it was more than responsibility, it was guilt. His fuck-up cost Max a foot and almost his life. Goddamned Frenchman. He killed more than a Hollywood sex symbol. He'd killed three cops, Paul DeSilva, DeSilva's girlfriend and two careers. Hollister's and Max's.

Max's career was over because there were few one-legged cops. Hollister's was over because he'd caused it. He had often wondered how it would end. He could never really see a graceful retirement. The traditional dinner and bullshit speeches, but this way was hardly better. He wasn't leaving in disgrace, but in defeat. It was a painful reality. Turned out the L.A.P.D. or a demanding wife, weren't so different after all.

Parker returned in a rush putting an end to Hollister's thoughts. "Got some good news." He smiled.

"What?"

The call was from the American Embassy in Mexico City."

"Yeah?" Hollister didn't understand.

Parker glanced at notes he had made. "Janet Trainer told me Ricardo Cortez left Spain for Mexico, so I called our embassy, told 'em we were looking for a cop killer. They just called me back. Cortez rented a car in Mexico City. They just found the car at the Estero Beach Resort north of Ensenada."

"Ensenada," Hollister growled with delight. "The sonofabitch is in Mexico!"

"At least his credit card is," Parker agreed.

Hollister grabbed the paper from Parker's hand. "Don't say anything to anyone about this." He turned to walk away.

Parker grabbed Hollister by the shoulder. "You're going down there after him, aren't you?"

"That's none of your business," Hollister warned soberly.

"The hell it isn't. Raul Torres was my partner. Wasn't for him and you I'd be halfway to Bastrop, Texas."

"Listen," Hollister said, trying a different tactic I'm not going down there as a cop. I'm going as a tourist."

"Well, hell," Parker said with a brazen smile. "I grew up with Mexicans. I speak Spanish better than most beans do. You're gonna need me."

"Anyone ever tell you you're a pain in the ass?"

Hollister and Parker returned the detective car to Hollywood station. Without going inside, they climbed into Parker's Ford pick-up and headed south on Interstate 5. They stopped to buy gas, two six packs of beer and a handful of beef sticks. In five hours, they were eighteen miles south of Tijuana and the Mexican border.

"You know," Hollister said popping open a can of beer, "when we crossed the border carrying guns, we stepped into shit."

"That's why I wear boots." Parker smiled.

"You're gonna drop me in Ensenada and turn around and go home," Hollister suggested.

"Like dog shit on a sneaker," Parker protested. "No way, Jose. I told you I'd stick around until the Frenchman got his ticket punched. Wasn't for that I'd already be salesman of the month at my Daddy's dealership in Houston. I earned this ringside seat."

"This is major league, Parker. It's gonna get tough

out afterwards."

"Seeing Torres get run over by that snail biter was major league too."

Hollister nodded. "Choice is yours." He finished the can of beer. His thoughts were already in Ensenada. The Frenchman would be waiting there. He would be expecting them. The bomb in Madrid proved that. Hollister wished he knew the man by sight. It would give him an edge he didn't have. He wondered if the Frenchman would recognize him. The answer would come soon enough. There was a growing bitterness in Hollister's mouth that the beer couldn't erase. He remembered it. The same taste had been with him on a rock hillside in Iraq. It was fear.

Mexico Highway One was the pride of the Mexican Department of Highways. Its four divided lanes followed the picturesque green rocky, coastline for a hundred miles from Tijuana to Ensenada, providing tourists, and their all-important American dollar, easy access to the jewel by the sea. Once a commercial fishing port, Ensenada had grown into a world class tourist attraction. Major cruise ships and private yachts crowded the quiet bay that fronted the city and a steady stream of motor homes and campers brought the sun worshippers south to crowd the wide native beaches. It was a quiet, beautiful place, but more important to the tourists, it was cheap.

"Twelve kilometers," Parker said, as the flashed by a sign for Ensenada.

They rounded the base of a rock outcropping to

find Ensenada sprawling in all directions, from the bay dotted with freighters, tankers and cruise ships, to the hills that stretched toward the green inland mountains.

"How do we find Estero Beach?" Parker questioned as he slowed for a red light. The air was rich with the smell of fish and salt air from the harbor.

"Ask."

A sign above a service station read, "Pemex." Parker pulled to one of the pumps.

"I'll fill it," Hollister said. "You get directions."

"Si, Senor." Parker smiled as he climbed out.

Hollister watched the flow of traffic as he pumped gas. There was a myriad of taxi cabs and colorful busses belching smoke and packed with brown faces mixed with American cars, motorhomes and campers. It seemed there were as many Americans as Mexicans in Ensenada. Hollister tried to remember the last time he'd been here. It was he and Kim and another cop and his wife. What the hell was the guy's name? Ward. Greg Ward. Worked motors, Had a good-looking wife. Hollister remembered because the four had gone skinny dipping in the ocean. He later learned Ward was now divorced too. It all seemed a very long time ago. Almost as if memories from another life.

"Hey, Amigo," Parker said, returning from the gas station's small office. "I got zee directions to Estero Beach. South of town, right on the beach."

The towering white arch stood over the long driveway entrance read, "Estero Beach Resort." Hollister's pulse quickened as they drove toward the reception office. He thought it looked like a sprawling Howard Johnsons. Parker pulled the pickup to a stop near the office and the two men climbed out. The afternoon sun was high in the clear sky. It was hot and humid.

A chime sounded as they stepped into the office. It was cool and air conditioned. A woman with long black hair and dark eyes was behind the reception counter. "May I help you?" she said in English.

"Got anything on the ocean?" Hollister questioned.

"Si, a cabana with two twins. Es a nice room, two-eighty-five a night."

"We'll take it."

The girl set a registration form and pen in front of Hollister. He offered a credit card in return.

As Hollister filled out the form he said, "We're meeting an associate here. Ricardo Cortez. Has he checked in yet?" The question was casual.

The woman looked to a list of guests. "Si," she answered. "Yesterday. The senor es in one-oh-six."

Each of the cabanas facing the windswept beach had a parking space. Hollister and Parker passed one-oh-six. Hollister glanced at the room. "No car."

The cabanas stood in a line facing the ocean. The two detectives found their room was only five doors from DePaul's.

"How do we find out if Frenchie's in there?" Parker questioned as they stepped into their warm room. The air was warm and humid. Hollister crossed to an air conditioner and pushed the button. The machine hummed and began to fill the room with musty smelling cool air.

"Call him," Hollister said. "You speak Spanish. Call and ask if Rosa's there. He'll think it's a wrong number."

"What do I do if Rosa's there?" Parker teased, moving for the telephone between the two beds. He picked it up and dialed. "Room one-oh-six, por favor. Gracias." He waited. Hollister watched silently. Finally, Parker hung up. "No answer."

A wide flagstone patio, dotted with small round tables and ornate wrought iron chairs, fronted the cabanas. Oil glistening bodies and colorful shirts sat at the tables, enjoying the sun and tropical drinks, while watching the surf break against a stone wall. Hollister came out of the room first, sleeves rolled up. He slipped on sunglasses and walked to a table in the midst of the others. After he sat down Parker joined him. Parker was shirtless and tanned. A waiter in a white jacket appeared. He sat a bowl of salsa and a basket of tortilla chips on the table. "A drink, Senors?"

"Dos Margaritas grandes, por favor?" Parker said.

"Si, Senor." The waiter moved away.

"Told ya you'd need me, didn't I?" Parker smiled.

They sat in the afternoon sun and drank and sweated and waited. No one returned to room One-oh-six. Tourists drifted in and out of the collection of patio tables. Parker and Hollister remained throughout the afternoon.

Hollister glanced at his watch. It was nearly six o'clock. "What if this sonofabitch doesn't come back?" He was fighting his impatience.

"I was just about to ask you the same thing," Parker countered.

"We gotta make it happen," Hollister grated in frustration as the waiter returned to the table again. "Senor, habla English?" Hollister questioned.

"Jess," the waiter smiled revealing a gold tooth.

Hollister pulled out a twenty-dollar bill. "A

friend of mine, by the name of Andrew Jackson," he smoothed the wrinkles from the bill. The waiter watched. "Would like to know where the man from room one-oh-six went."

"One-oh-six, jess," the waiter snatched the bill from Hollister's' hand. It disappeared into a pocket. He picked up their glasses and moved away.

"Parker went inside to relieve himself and to put on a shirt. The breeze, coming in off the ocean, was turning cool. Hollister watched a brown pelican make a steep dive into the ocean. Parker returned at the same time the waiter did. As the man set fresh drinks on the table he spoke in halting, broken English. "Senor Cortez…he and a senorita have a date. The went, how you say?…to dinner."

Hollister nodded. "Where did they go for dinner?"

"Senor, you ask where he went, not where he is?"

Hollister went to his pocket a second time, he pulled out a collection of bills and counted through them. The waiter watched. "Forty-eight dollars;" Hollister said, "think you can find out where he is?"

"Jess," the waiter said, reaching for the bills. Hollister pulled them out of the man's reach. "First you find out. Then I pay."

The waiter looked displeased. He turned and marched away.

"So much for foreign relations," Parker picked up his fresh drink.

Hollister laid the money on the table.

They waited. Hollister was beginning to have

doubts. He dreaded the thought of driving back to L.A. after being unable to find the Frenchman. He pushed the thought aside and watched a sail on the horizon far at sea.

"Here comes 'Frito Bandito'," Parker said, as the waiter reappeared. The man was smiling. When he reached them, he said, "Senor DePaul esta en el Cuevos de Los Tigres."

"Cuevos de Los Tigres?" Hollister questioned. "What's that?"

"The Cave of the Tiger," Parker answered.

"El ristorante," the waiter added. He reached for the money on the table. Hollister pushed a hand over it.

"How do we know this?"

The waiter's smile was gone. "The senorita, with the man, she works here. My boss, he made the arrangements. He says Dinner at six."

"What's the senorita look like?" Hollister asked.

"She have red hair, big," he gestured for her breasts, "and very young."

"And DePaul?"

"Tall, he wear a blanco jacket."

"And this Cave of the Tiger. Where is it?" Hollister asked.

"Norte," the waiter pointed. "Toward Ensenada. Look for the El Tigre. Follow the signs. Es muy facil."

"Gracias," Hollister said as the waiter took the money. Hollister looked to Parker. "Give me the keys."

"I'll drive," Parker answered.

"No," Hollister disagreed. "You stay here and watch the room. I'll check the restaurant. If he's there I'll call you. We can't risk missing him. You can take a cab over there."

"Promise?" Parker demanded.

"Promise," Hollister answered.

Parker dropped the keys into Hollister's waiting palm.

Ever since crossing the border Hollister regretted involving Parker. This wasn't the kid's fight. This was between Hollister and the Frenchman. He tried all afternoon to think of a way to get rid of Parker and now it was done. Parker would still face punishment for being on the fringe of it. Absent from duty, failure to notify a supervisor, conduct unbecoming an officer, carrying a firearm into a foreign jurisdiction, but he would survive. He'd still be a cop.

Driving north toward downtown Ensenada, Hollister watched the roadside signs intently. Most he could not understand, but finally he spotted one with an orange and black striped tiger that read, "Cuevos do los Tigres." An arrow pointed to the left. The Cave of the Tiger restaurant sat on pilings on a rocky bluff overlooking the sea. Waves, breaking with the afternoon tide, were smashing into the rocks to send cascades of saltwater into the air in front of the restaurant's wide windows. The parking lot was lined with cars, jeeps, pick-ups, campers and motorhomes. The tourists knew this was "the" place for sunset dining. The sun was a golden orb hanging low in the western sky above the ocean. Hollister damned himself for not asking what kind of car the Frenchman was driving as he parked the pickup beside a dirty camper from Arizona. He patted his waistband to ensure the nine-millimeter was securely in its holster and climbed out of the pick-up. He willed himself calm. There was no more room for mistakes.

Live music greeted Hollister as he stepped into the lobby. Two white-haired men in tuxedo's were playing guitar and singing as they strolled from table to table. The headwaiter was dressed in a ruffled long-sleeved white shirt and a black bow tie. "Buenos noches, Senor." He smiled as Hollister reached him.

Hollister's eyes were searching. The dining room stretched across the restaurant facing the ocean. It was several steps below the lobby and a horseshoe-shaped bar. The dining room was a sea of faces and a stream of waiters and bus boys who moved in and around the tables. The air was thick with the clink of dishes, music and cigarette smoke. The smell of spicy Mexican food permeated the cool room.

"Are you dining this evening, Senor?" the head-waiter inquired.

Hollister now had a feel for the room although he hadn't spotted the Frenchman or the girl. "No," Hollister said, "just came in for a drink and the sunset."

The headwaiter gestured to the bar. "Try fresh oysters with your drink. Es muy bueno."

The open bar overlooked the dining room. It provided Hollister a view of the room. He could see anyone entering or leaving. If Phillip DePaul was in the room. He had no escape. Hollister ordered a drink and began his visual search. He looked for white jackets and red hair. He found several but not together and then, near the windows at the far end of the dining room, he spotted them. The Frenchman was sitting with his profile to Hollister. The young red-haired Mexican girl was across from him. She was in a sleeveless dress and thin. Hollister felt his heart race. He took his eyes off the man to calm himself. He sipped his drink. Don't drink too much, he warned himself. After countless Margaritas throughout the afternoon without any food he knew he was on the edge of being under the influence. The Frenchman was no fool. Their encounter in Los Angeles proved that. He tried to think of a way to do it. Maybe the crowded restaurant was an asset. Just walk over, shoot him in the head, and walk out in the resulting pandemonium. He'd investigated many such crimes and seldom were a room full of witnesses able to give a valid description. The Frenchman deserved no warning. This was no game or sport. There were no rules of etiquette. This was good versus evil, and the only important thing was winning. Nothing else mattered, Hollister told himself, but he didn't believe it, no matter how hard he tried. He couldn't kill the man in cold blood. No matter how much he ached to, he knew he couldn't. He as a cop. Not because the City of Los Angeles called him one, but because he was, and no matter how hard he tried he knew he couldn't escape it. "Sonofabitch," he muttered into his drink. He released the fantasy of killing the man and started to think of his capture. He turned to look at the Frenchman. His heart leaped. He was gone! The chair at the table where he had been sitting was empty. The red-haired, big-breasted, girl was still there, but the Frenchman was gone. Hollister's eyes searched frantically. He found him, walking behind a couple leaving the restaurant. As the Frenchman neared Hollister, he passed behind him, moved down the bar and into the men's restroom.

Hollister knew the moment had come. His heart raced like a rabbit. He welcomed the flow of adrenaline. It erased the grip alcohol was gaining. He waited until the man disappeared inside the restroom before he pushed off the stool.

The restroom was small and dim. The air was stale and heavy with the smell of urine. The Frenchman was stepping away from the urinal, zipping his pants and moving to a small sink to wash his hands, when Hollister entered.

The Frenchman was Hollister's size. Maybe ten or fifteen pounds lighter, and younger. Hollister stepped to the urinal, drew his gun. He could hear the water running into the basin. He drew in a breath and turned.

Assad was rinsing his face. His eyes were closed. Hollister grabbed and handful of hair and jerked his head upright and slammed it against the mirror. He pushed the barrel of his pistol into the man's neck just below his ear. "You move, you piece of shit, I'll scatter your brains" Hollister jerked on his hair. "You understand?"

"Yes," Assad grimaced, trying to find the man's reflection in the mirror. He hoped it was no more than a robbery.

"I'm the cop you sucker punched in LA, asshole," Hollister grated in Assad's ear. "Give me an excuse to kill you."

"Sir," Assad said through clenched teeth. Hollister's weight was forcing Assad's groin into the hard edges of the sink. "I've never been to Los Angeles. You are mistaken."

"Right," Hollister twisted the handful of hair tighter, "and I'll bet you've never been to Spain."

"My name's Carlos Garcia," Assad plead. "I'm from Santa Maria, California."

Hollister released Assad's hair. "Don't breathe," he warned. With his free hand Hollister patted Assad's upper body for weapons. He found a small automatic pistol in an inside jacket pocket. "You on the police force in Santa Maria, asshole?"

Hollister tossed the gun into the water of the nearby urinal.

Assad felt Hollister's hand go into his back pocket. Hollister pulled out a wallet.

"Phillip DePaul," Hollister said flipping through the wallet. French driver's license, American Express card. Hollister tossed the wallet into the stained urinal with the gun.

"Officer," Assad said, watching Hollister's image in the mirror. He knew he had to stall, to distract. He was relieved to learn the man was a police officer. At first, he thought he was an agent and that death was a heartbeat away. Although the officer had a gun, Assad knew he wouldn't be shot behind the ear and left on the gritty floor of the restroom. Policemen were trained to protect life, not take it. He knew he had not lost all of the advantage. "I have money. A great deal of it. I am willing to pay you."

"I don't want your fucking money," Hollister answered, jerking him away from the sink. "Just your ass."

"You don't understand. I work for the US government."

"So do I. Now, we're gonna walk. I'm going to be a step behind you. If you run, I kill you. You understand me?"

"Yes, yes, I understand," Assad said as he straightened his jacket and ran a hand back over his hair. The officer let him get away with movement. Now all he needed was a distraction. He was certain he could take the man. This time he'd shoot the American bastard in the mouth.

"Move," Hollister ordered from behind.

Stepping out of the restroom, into the air-conditioned restaurant Hollister realized he was covered with sweat. He stayed within inches of Assad, guiding the man toward the lobby. They passed the headwaiter whose attention was on an arriving couple. In the restaurant the strolling minstrels were strumming their guitars. Many were singing along and clapping to the rhythm. Hollister kept his eyes on the back of the man's neck and his finger firmly on the trigger of his gun.

Assad knew the further he went with the man the less chance he had of escape. Strike in the first minutes, his training had taught him. He drew in a breath, stopped abruptly, and spun his left arm up chopping into Hollister's throat.

Hollister grabbed the Frenchman's jacket as he fell backwards pulling him down atop him. The hand holding the gun squeezed and the sharp crack of the shot sent a shock wave through the restaurant.

Assad went for the hand that held the gun. He slammed Hollister's hand against the base of a large potted plant. The gun fired a second shot as the broken clay cut deep into the back of Hollister's hand. Hollister's fingers opened in pain and the steel pistol rattled across the uneven tile floor.

Assad's attention was on the gun as it slid away. Hollister slammed a bloodied fist up under Assad's jaw. Assad rolled away. He came to rest on his knees a few feet from Hollister, facing him. Both men scrambled to their feet, sizing one another, knowing the first move was likely the last. Assad could see that the policeman was dazed. The blow to his throat and a hand dripping blood gave him the edge he prayed for.

At the headwaiter's desk the frightened man was hiding behind a post, spewing a string of frightened

Spanish into a telephone.

Assad spotted a Spanish saber hanging with an ornate helmet on a nearby column. In one swift move he was to it, pulling the saber loose. Hollister dove for the pistol on the floor. He grabbed it, rolled over and fired as Assad brought the sword down at him. The pistol shot sent a jolt through Assad's body. He stood frozen, a confused, bewildered look on his face. The gun fired again. Assad shook, moved a hand to his chest as blood poured out through his white jacket. The saber fell to the floor. Assad sank to his knees, reaching out toward Hollister. Hollister fired another shot into the base of Assad's neck. Blood spurted from Assad's mouth as he fell backwards in a lifeless awkward sprawl.

The headwaiter and several others were cowering near the reception desk. Hollister looked to them, tossed the gun to the headwaiter's feet. Blood was dripping from the back of his hand. He felt nauseous. Sirens were whining in the distance, growing closer.

The dim cell block smelled like a sewer and it was alive with the smell of human waste, flies and roaches. They had taken Hollister's watch, his wallet and his badge case. He tried sitting on the damp floor, but something crawled under his shirt. He decided to stand.

A metal lock clicked loud at the end of the cell block. Light flooded in as the door swung open. Two uniformed policemen swaggered down the walkway and unlocked the cell. They spoke in Spanish and gestured Hollister out.

The worried Hollister, with his blood bandaged hand, followed the officers from the cell. They walked in front, chatting and laughing, seemingly indifferent to any threat he might pose. He remembered one of them from the restaurant. A swarthy little sergeant with a low slung forty-five. Ten or twelve officers had responded. He'd been handcuffed, pushed outside and rushed away in a police car.

The interview at the police station after the shooting had listed until three in the morning. Hollister told the story again and again, in great convincing detail. The police did not seem to question it. It seemed their work was done. The revenge-seeking L.A. policeman had killed the man.

Hollister expected the brotherhood of the badge would have meant something to the police in Ensenada, but his treatment seemed more like that of any other criminal. Obviously, the Mexican police weren't concerned with foreign relations.

The second-floor detective squad room was bright with sunlight. Hollister squinted as he was led into the room. Then he saw Parker. He was standing near the open door of the detective commander's office. Parker's usual air of Texas confidence was gone. He looked worried and tired. "Nine-millimeter gift to El Capitan bought us ten minutes," Parker said, as Hollister and his escorts reached him. Let's talk." He gestured to the office.

"They took my watch," Hollister complained, massaging the empty space on his wrist. "What time is it?"

"They got more than your watch," Parker warned, closing the door of the office. "They got your ass. You were supposed to call me, you son-of-a-bitch."

Hollister wasn't sure if Parker was angry or frightened. "A hell of a lot of good it would do to have us both in jail. What time is it?" he asked a second time. He was uncomfortable and disoriented and beginning to worry. A cop in prison, especially a Mexican prison was a nightmarish thought. Hollister quickly pushed it from his mind.

"I called the lieutenant last night. He was so pissed he could hardly talk. He said he had to turn it over to Internal Affairs. Shit, by now the chief-of-police knows."

"Who gives a shit?" Hollister said, sitting down on a soft couch. "The Frenchman's dead." He wished he had a toothbrush.

Parker looked at Hollister's bandaged hand. It was brown with dried blood. "He died hard?"

"Three shots," Hollister answered. "One for the two patrol cops and one for Torres."

"I hope the snail-biting sonofabitch is in hell."

Hollister didn't answer. He wasn't certain there was a heaven or hell, and then the thought that he might already be there prompted a smile.

"Something funny?" Parker questioned.

"Naw, just glad it's over."

"You wanna come down to Texas with me? Sell a few of Daddy's cars, chase good looking women."

Hollister tried to see beyond being a cop. He couldn't. "Maybe," he said to appease Parker.

"I got a call in to the Protective League. Figure they'll help get you outta here."

"Maybe," Hollister agreed, but he didn't really think they would. "You still gonna walk away?"

"Fuckin' A," Parker answered. "Ain't nothing to stay for."

"Suppose not," Hollister mused.

A rap sounded on the office door. It opened to reveal Jim Forrester. He was dressed in dark slacks, a white suit jacket and shoes. He carried a Panama hat. "Hello, Hollister," he smiled.

"Who the hell are you?" Parker challenged.

"A friend," Forrester said, taking Parker by the arm. "The Sergeant and I need a moment alone."

"Not before I get a fuckin' answer."

"It's okay, Parker," Hollister answered.

"I'm beginning to feel like a whore in a convent," Parker complained as he stepped out. Forrester closed the door behind him.

"You're a long way from your office in Spain," Hollister said.

"Home is where the heart is," Forrester smiled.

"What brings you to Mexico, looking like Indiana Jones?" Hollister questioned.

"When in Rome," Forrester tossed his hat to a

nearby desktop. He pulled a small twisted dark cigar from an inside pocket and lit it with several heavy puffs. "Seems every time I see you, Hollister, you're in some foreign country up to your career in a world of shit."

"I got it, the LAPD sent you here to cheer me up," Hollister said sarcastically.

"I can understand their concern. One of their officers involved in a homicide on foreign soil."

"Guess what they can do with their concern?" Hollister suggested.

"The situation may not be as bad as you think," Forrester cautioned. "So, don't be so quick to flush your career."

Hollister looked to Forrester. "I'm listening."

Forrester sat on the edge of a desk. "Certain people of influence in government had an acute interest in the Frenchman. The fact you and Parker played a significant role in locating him, and in what now appears to be a justifiable shooting death, leaves them grateful. Therefore, I've been asked to intervene on your behalf with the Mexican authorities as well as with the LAPD. That's been done. There will be no reprisals from the LA.PD. The Mexican authorities have agreed to drop the weapons charges against you and Parker, if you agree to leave the country immediately."

"You're the one that located the Frenchman and got the information to Parker, aren't you?" Hollister suggested.

Forrester granted a smile. "You may say that, but I certainly never could. Now about leaving the country?"

"You wanna drive us to the airport?" Hollister questioned.

The Aero Mexico jet climbed steeply after lifting off the runway in Ensenada. The G force pull felt familiar as Hollister sat strapped in a window seat, looking out at the sleek wing. The sensation took him back to the missions over Iraq. He had left there feeling empty and uncertain. The victory he was hungry for, the hoped-for confrontation with the enemy, the release he sought, never came. The Iraq war hadn't ended, it just stopped. Investigating the murder of Shannon Roberts had been much the same. Perhaps, he allowed, as the painful realization settled in his mind, killing didn't solve problems, it just created them. Avenging the death of three cops and bringing down the man that killed Shannon Roberts. That's how it would be told. The brutal reality was, and Hollister silently accepted it as the truth, he had killed the man that killed his marriage. Assad had never met Kim Hollister, but he stole her just the same. He was the catalyst. His lawless act had ended much more than Shannon Roberts' life. The price of killing a man's dream was high.

The skies over Iraq had proven no deadlier than the streets of Hollywood. Bill Slack, his backseat radar man was dead in an eject, and Max had his foot blown off. There would be more wars, he accepted, settling in his seat as the jet reached altitude. There would be another Shannon Roberts. Hell. It was Hollywood.

"You're being quiet?" Parker questioned with a look at Hollister. He was strapped in the seat beside him.

"I've killed two men in the past eight days," Hollister answered, as if it were a confession.

Parker nodded agreement. "True. Both of them were armed wanted felons. In Texas we call that justice."

Hollister returned his attention to a layer of clouds the plane climbed through. "Justice, huh?"

Parker studied Hollister a moment before he spoke again. "Got an uncle down in Bastrop. My dad's brother. He's an evangelist. He once told me God deals in justice like we do, but God does it a little bit different. He deals in naked justice. No shooting review boards, no second guessing, no critiques and never a hung jury. Just plain old naked justice. I figure you got God on your side this time, Sarge."

Three hundred and eight miles north near the center of the glass towering maze of high-rises in crowded downtown Los Angeles, nine individuals sat around a polished conference table on the fourth floor of Police Headquarters. Chief-of-Police Moore sat the head of the table. The Chief's Executive Assistant, Karen King, a police lieutenant, although not in uniform, sat to the chief's right, along with Assistant Chief Delgado. On the left were Deputy Chief Searcy, Commander Thornton of Media Relations, Commander Harris of Hollywood Detectives and Commander Taylor of Internal Affairs. At the far end of the table sat Wayne Carson, the City Attorney for the City of Los Angeles. Carson's female deputy sat at his side.

"Here's the challenge," the chief said, tossing a folded morning copy of the Los Angeles Times onto the table. "The headline reads, "LAPD detective shoots and kills the murderer of Superstar Shannon Roberts in Mexico."

Silence answered the chief. All had heard of the shooting. All of L.A.'s media, primetime cable news channels and social media, all were alive with the news and it was fast spreading to the world.

"I understand our two cops in Mexico were there without official authorization. Correct?" the chief said, with a sober look at Commander Harris.

"Correct, sir," Harris answered. "No authorization."

"So, a rogue cop goes to Ensenada, shoots and kills a suspect and we learn about it from the State Department?"

"We should fire both of them today," the deputy chief suggested.

"If we do that," the Commander of Media Relations warned, "we're going to look stupid. These two men did what the world hoped for. Shannon Roberts' killer shot to death. Hell, they're being portrayed as heroes."

"Nevertheless, they carried firearms into a foreign country without notice or authorization and then shot and killed a man," the Commander of Internal Affairs warned. "That cannon be allowed to go unpunished."

"Gentlemen," the deputy City Attorney offered, "if I may, what I'm hearing seems to be a collection of bruised egos. I'm not a cop. I'm an attorney paid to protect the city. These two men did nothing to place our city in a position of liability. From what I understand you've got a collection of police policy violations. I suggest you tread lightly or chance looking like bitter bureaucrats."

It was quiet for a moment as attention returned to the sober chief. "I agree," Chief Moore said. "I don't want to be a bitter bureaucrat. Thornton, what can you do with this?" He was looking at the Commander of Media Relations.

"We could say these men were following a hunch. Time was critical. They didn't go down there to kill this man, but violence erupted during his arrest. Shots were fired. The Mexicans investigated it thoroughly. Case closed."

The chief slapped the tabletop. "I like it. Clean it up and put it out." He pushed from his chair. "Harris what are the names of these two?"

The commander pushed to his feet. "Sergeant Hollister and Detective Parker."

"What time's their plane land?"

"Three forty."

The chief looked to his assistant. "Let's get some people out there to meet them. Make it a real homecoming. Bring them downtown. Hell, we'll hold our own damned press conference."

Hollister and Parker were shocked when they walked out of the jetway at LAX to find a collection of uniformed cops and detectives from Hollywood station as well as a deputy chief, several commanders, and the press. The familiar faces were all cheering and applauding. Cameras flashed.

The press followed as the two men were escorted through customs and then outside to a waiting caravan of police cars. Hollister and Parker were hustled into a polished black SUV. "Damn," Parker commented in awe. "Looks like the chief's ride."

"It is," the driver answered as they pulled from the curb.

The caravan was making its way downtown when

Hollister's cellphone chirped. He pulled it from a pocket and looked at the screen. The call origin flashed "Kim". Hollister punched the answer key. "Kim?" he questioned apprehensively.

"Lee, can we talk? I...I made a mistake."

ABOUT THE AUTHOR

Novelist & Screenwriter, Dallas Barnes has written nearly two hundred hours of primetime television drama, as well as seven bestselling novels. His writings have won nominations for EMMY'S, in both primetime and daytime, as well as the famed EDGAR ALAN POE AWARD, the IMAGE AWARD and the HUMANITAS PRIZE.

Along with writing, Dallas Barnes is an executive level hybrid hospitality security professional with a unique blend of management, Law Enforcement and guest services skills. with over a decade of experience in investigations in demanding hospitality and gaming venues linked to a performance in risk management, safety, compliance, and loss prevention.